SKYWAY TO HELL
by
Jerrie Alexander

Jackie Pressley, my daughter. You're the best work I've ever done.

Dedication

Alexa
    Missing you isn't the problem...
    It's knowing you're never coming back that's killing me.

Acknowledgments

I would be remiss if I didn't acknowledge the following people. Their support, advice, and enthusiasm were invaluable.

To my editor, Eve Arroyo, I appreciate your honesty, keen eye, and gentle guidance.

Tara Mandarano, whose proofreading goes beyond what's expected. You're amazing.

To Kym Roberts, who always takes time to listen to my ideas and complaints. Thank you for your advice and patience!

Julie, the Formatting Fairy from heaven, you are so gracious and helpful. You handled all my changes with grace and patience.

My Beta readers, thank you, doesn't sound strong enough. You totally rock. I'm so lucky to have your support and honesty. You are truly dear friends. You stuck with me through the years of darkness and believed in me. I love and appreciate each of you.

I've been blessed with the best readers on the planet. Your support and encouragement keep me motivated and positive as I work though these stories. I hope you enjoy this book as much as I loved writing it.

Thanks to my daughter, Jackie Pressley. You will always be my greatest gift to humankind.

Any mistakes are my own!

Prologue

Angel Honeywell gritted her teeth and pushed her bruised and battered body upright. She swung her feet to the floor and stood, knowing no one was ever coming to save her. Even tonight, when she'd tried to stay silent and out of sight, he'd come for her. He always came for her.

Tonight, he'd gone too far.

This evening's poker game had ended with Angel's stepfather losing money he didn't have—again. As had become his habit, Jack offered her body as payment to his opponents.

She'd become his currency of choice shortly after her alcoholic mother, tired of the many beatings she'd endured, had walked out, leaving her nine-year-old daughter in his care.

A child he'd wanted to abuse even before the marriage.

The house reeked of sweat, beer, and cigarette smoke but was finally quiet. Angel dragged the filthy sheet off her bed and wrapped it around her naked body, partially hiding the scratches, bites, bruises, and semen the men had left on her fourteen-year-old bare skin.

She'd waited until she thought Jack had passed out before tiptoeing into the kitchen and retrieving a butcher knife. Her entire body trembled as if she'd been struck by an electrical current. She walked down the hall to the doorway of his bedroom and stared at his fat, naked body. All the suffering and anger that had built up inside her boiled over.

His eyes had flashed wide as she'd carefully, and with all her strength, plunged the blade into his heart. He'd stilled after the second stab, but she didn't stop. When she was satisfied he'd never hurt her again, there were seven wounds—one for each man who'd raped her this night.

As she stared into his lifeless eyes, it hadn't been remorse she'd felt. A strange peace of mind had washed over her. Angel gritted her teeth, wrapped her hand around his soft dick, and cut it off. His jaw was slack, and his mouth hung open, so she'd tucked it between his lips.

She wiped her bloody hands on the sheet she wore and pushed her tangled hair off her face.

Walking toward the front door, she noticed five cards on the table in front of Jack's chair. It was, she had no doubt, his losing hand. She stopped and turned over his cards.

She picked up the queen of diamonds and ran. Ran until she reached the busy highway, where she dropped the knife in the ditch before she stumbled into traffic. She sank to her knees, hoping to die.

Because only death could stop the pain.

Chapter 1

Fifteen Years Later...

A hand gripped her foot and startled her awake. Memories of being jerked out of bed and dragged to the living room to be shared by her stepfather's drunken friends sent terror racing through her veins. Even as she reminded herself it was just a dream, her throat closed, refusing her need to pull air into her lungs.

She fumbled with the switch on her bedside lamp until, finally, the room filled with light, proving she was alone.

Even though that bastard was dead, he wouldn't leave her in peace.

Closing her eyes, she willed her heart to slow down. She kicked off the covers and sat on the edge of the bed. Her body was soaked in sweat, yet she shivered with a chill. Her heart pounded against her rib cage as she dropped her head into her hands.

Memories flooded her mind. Even though she was twenty-nine years old, the scenes that played were so vivid, she felt as if it had been just yesterday she'd fallen onto the freeway in hopes of dying.

Instead, she'd been picked up and rushed to the hospital. When questioned, she'd told the doctors and the police she didn't remember anything about the death of her stepfather, saying only that he'd had a poker game, and after it was over, someone had killed him. She'd gotten blood all over her while trying to wake him up.

That period of her life had been a new kind of hell. Doctors had poked around in her brain until they felt she was ready to be put into the welfare system. For the next four years, until she'd aged out of foster care, she'd been shuffled from family to family.

They'd referred to her as a troublemaker. It was the truth. Angel had fought like a tiger every time a male member of the household decided she was their play toy to fondle or fuck at will. It wasn't long until she'd be gathering her things in a trash bag and moving to the next family.

Luck had smiled on her when she'd been placed in Mama Kay's house. Mama had only fostered girls, which eliminated the groping and filthy innuendos she'd suffered at the previous two homes. Mama Kay made sure her girls were fed, clothed, and educated. She'd been a flight attendant until she retired, and spent the rest of her life making a difference in young women's lives.

It was Mama's brother, Nick, who'd kept the house well supplied with food and the house kids in decent clothing. Angel had no doubt he was a criminal, or maybe mafia. He always had money and made no secret that he carried a gun. He'd talked to Angel like she was smart. Like she knew it was her responsibility to take care of herself. He told her there were lots of ways for her to make real money, and he wasn't talking about selling her body.

He'd never asked if she'd killed her stepfather, but somehow, she knew he knew. While she was studying to be a flight attendant, he'd taught her how to fight, shoot, and use a knife. Then he'd introduced her to the man who'd help her fulfill her destiny.

Angel pushed her thoughts about the past out of her mind. She shook off the shroud of depression, stripped, tossed her T-shirt into the hamper, and walked into the bathroom. She turned on the tap in the shower, got in, and let the cold water slowly turn to warm.

She'd succeeded in holding her nightmares at bay for years until last year when her friend Alice's thirteen-year-old daughter had been violently beaten, raped, and then murdered.

All the old memories had come rushing back, eating away at her soul and sanity. In her mind, she'd suffered the pain and cruelty she'd endured, over again and again. Afraid to close her eyes at night for fear of reliving her childhood, she'd felt as if she was going mad.

Six months later, she'd been watching the morning news on television and saw the bastard who'd killed her friend's daughter walk out of court on a technicality. He'd paused and waved at the camera. Instantly, Angel had known how she'd finally end her nightmares and find peace.

****

The sound of ice cubes swirling around an otherwise empty glass accentuated the passenger's impatience. He'd finished his third drink in record time.

Alice, Angel's colleague and friend, turned her back on him and grumbled, "That jerk makes my skin crawl. He tried to run his hand up under my skirt."

A flash of adrenaline burst through Angel's veins. Her heart rate doubled. "He what?"

"Twice. The bastard asked if we girls wore sexy thongs or granny panties."

Angel's nerve endings sizzled. "I'll go this time."

"I'm not going to argue."

As she approached the man, his gaze dropped to her feet and traveled no higher up than her breasts. She didn't flinch. Ignoring his behavior, she gave him a chance to redeem himself.

"Would you like another drink?"

"That's not all I'd like." He shifted in his seat, lowered his arm, and ran his fingers across the back of her knee. "A man like me has a big appetite."

She smiled down at him. "And how does a man like you satisfy his appetite?"

"With a tasty meal." His hand slid up to her thigh. "Guess what I want to eat?"

Her gut clenched with revulsion, but she spoke softly so he alone could hear her words. "You're in the mood for a special kind of pleasure tonight, aren't you?"

"Always." His gaze lifted to her face, and his lips pulled into a chilling smile. "My God, you are beautiful."

She placed her hand on his knee and squeezed. "Do you have a place in mind?"

"How about the Grand Fiesta? Is that fancy enough for you?"

She drew her eyebrows together as she pretended to consider his offer. "Excellent choice. Mister..."

"Vardon."

"Leave an envelope at the desk with your keycard and room number inside."

His hand inched farther up her leg. "I'll tell them an angel will be picking up the envelope."

Memories of dark rooms, filthy hands, and sweaty bodies flashed through her mind. Pushing them to the far recesses of her memory, she smiled down at him.

"You do that."

Chapter 2

Dalton Murphy walked down the hall to the boss's office. Nate Wolfe, standing in front of his desk, waved him inside and nodded toward a chair.

"I just got off the phone with one of your FBI contacts. Carl White is the special agent in charge at the San Antonio office now."

Dalton's interest was piqued. He sat, leaned forward, and then rested his elbows on his thighs. "I'm guessing he has a job for us."

"He does. Vincent Vardon was murdered in Monterrey, Mexico. Carl wants you to assist on the case."

"Vardon being dead is good news." Dalton leaned back and crossed his arms over his chest. "I hope he spent his last few minutes in agony. Fucker should've died a long time ago."

Nate, who never missed even the slightest reaction in people, backed up and perched on the edge of his massive walnut desk. "Is there a problem?"

"Not if he's dining with the devil now." Dalton huffed out a breath. "Vardon sold weapons to anyone who'd pay cash and buy in quantity. I arrested that bastard a few years back. Had built a damn good case." Dalton's chest constricted. "Airtight until both my witness and a damn good federal agent were murdered when the supposed safehouse they were in exploded and blew them off the face of the earth."

"I can see how you might be glad he's dead." Nate pushed a folder across the desk. "This case is going to get national coverage if or when the facts are leaked to the press. It's the third murder where a queen of diamonds playing card was found on the body. White said you were the king of serial killer convictions."

Dalton ignored the bad pun. Instead, he glanced over the limited information in the folder. "I'll see what I can do."

"There's an agent already there. You'll meet at the FBI office in Monterrey."

Dalton stood. "I'll fly out today."

Nate walked him into the hallway. "If you need us, we're here for you."

"Thanks."

Dalton returned to his office and booked the trip. He liked knowing who he was working with, so he called Carl and got the scoop. When he hung up, Marcus Ricci and his dog, Diablo, were watching through the glass wall. Dalton waved them inside.

Marcus, one of the original Lost and Found Inc. agents, took a seat while Diablo dropped next to his feet and then rested a paw on top of Marcus's boot. "What are you and Nate cooking up?"

Dalton brought Marcus up to speed. "I'm leaving for Mexico in a couple of hours."

"While you're there, take a minute to enjoy yourself."

Dalton bit back a smirk. "This is work."

Marcus shook his head and stood. Diablo moved to his side. "We're here if you need us."

Dalton nodded his head. "So I've heard."

****

Ashley Hunter sat at a desk in the Monterrey FBI suboffice and studied the picture on her laptop screen. She'd hoped to gain some insight into the man who'd been praised by her boss in San Antonio as the best agent ever to leave the agency for private practice. Her confusion came quickly. Why had the information on some of the cases he'd worked on been redacted? They were all high-profile ones that required someone with higher clearance to access.

His photo was the typical black-and-white FBI shot where you're told to look at the camera and not blink. She saw a rugged, masculine, and take-no-prisoners face. His eyes looked as if they held dark secrets. Secrets that had also been redacted. Even with no hint of a smile, his mouth appeared to be soft and kissable.

"So why did you walk away?" she mumbled to herself.

"You could always just ask me."

The male voice coming from behind her had a cold raspy edge to it, and yet it was still sensual. It sent chills rushing over her skin. Ashley rolled her chair back and then turned to find Dalton Murphy leaning against a column. He pushed off and walked toward her. His movements were languid and fluid, predatory like a big cat who'd spotted his dinner and had no doubt he'd make the kill. His gaze locked with hers and his lips dipped into what she interpreted as a scowl.

If he was trying to frighten her, he'd failed.

"Ashley Hunter." She smiled and extended her hand, which was swallowed in his firm grip. "I wasn't expecting you quite so soon."

"Obviously." Dalton released her and looked over her shoulder at her laptop screen. "Any gaps I can fill in for you?"

"You can't blame me for being curious about the legendary Dalton Murphy." Ignoring his question, she sat and pointed to the chair next to the desk she'd been temporarily assigned. "All the good stuff has been redacted. You worked some high-profile cases." She paused. "Is that why Carl wanted you on this one?"

Dalton remained standing. "What have you learned about the victim?"

He was ignoring her question. Maybe he was a tad intimidating. Hell, his size would jumble anybody's nerves.

"I know the body has been identified as Vincent Vardon. He's an American citizen who's been under investigation more than once."

Her gaze followed Dalton as he lowered himself to the chair, his thigh muscles straining against the seams of his black jeans. The sleeves on his navy-blue button-down shirt had been rolled up, revealing tan skin and muscular forearms. She wanted to ask about the missing pieces of information in his file, but her curiosity was squashed by the irritation flashing behind his eyes.

He opened his mouth and then closed it. For a few long seconds, he studied her face as if planning his words carefully. "Have you verified a playing card was found with Vardon's body, and if so, was it the queen of diamonds?"

"I just arrived this morning, and the local detective assigned to this case hasn't returned my calls. Other than the victim's name, I know what airline he was on, the flight number, and the name of the hotel where he died."

"He wasn't a victim." Dalton's expression remained unchanged. "He deserved to die."

"You don't play well with others, do you?" Not expecting an answer, Ashley handed Dalton the limited information that she'd managed to pull together.

"I don't play. Period."

She tried to breathe through her frustration while he read over the paperwork.

Handing back the documents, her temporary partner cocked his head to the side. "You checked with the hotel manager?"

"Of course." Did Dalton think she was an idiot? "He refused to confirm or deny anything for me." Damn, she'd sounded like she was making excuses, but it was the truth. "Then he referred me to the police."

"Any news on the autopsy?"

She shook her head. Dalton's short sentences didn't give her any encouragement that he was going to be agreeable to anything she'd done or would do.

"We need those results."

"I agree." Ashley suppressed the urge to say *duh*. "Did you take this case because of your history with Vardon or to catch a serial killer?"

The dark stubble on Dalton's face didn't hide the tiny cleft in his chin, nor did it conceal the twitch in his jaw. It was as if he was deciding what or how much to tell her.

"His death might heal a scab I've been picking at for three years."

She rolled her eyes at his vague answer. "Are you referring to Vardon's acquittal?"

"Do you ever give up?"

"No."

"I guessed as much." He shook his head. "I know somebody who might help. If he's still with the force, I can ask." Dalton pulled his cell from his pocket, scrolled through his contacts, and then tapped a number. He put the call on speaker and held it between them.

"Núñez." The voice on the line sounded warm.

"I'll be damned. I wasn't sure you'd still be alive." Dalton's tone had warmed to match it, and a hint of a smile lifted the corners of his mouth.

Núñez was the name she'd been given to contact. The name of the man who hadn't called back. She bit back the urge to say something about it.

Did Dalton have enough pull to have her removed from the case? She couldn't let that happen. Bringing this killer to justice would prove she could handle anything that came her way.

"I'm more surprised that you are, old friend. How can I help the FBI?" The change in the man's tone of voice was immediate—and decidedly friendly.

"I'm no longer with the agency, but I am here in Monterrey."

"If you're buying, meet me at El Choro's Steak House at eight."

"Sounds good." The nerves in Dalton's jaw started twitching again. "I need your help getting information about Vincent Vardon's murder."

"The FBI sent somebody."

Ashley leaned closer to the cell phone. "That was me. The autopsy was scheduled for yesterday. Can you get the results for us?"

"Dalton? This person's voice is much more pleasing than yours."

"Sorry," Dalton said. "I should have introduced you."

"Special Agent Ashley Hunter," she identified herself.

"Detective Rodrigo Núñez. I apologize for not getting back to you, Señorita Hunter. For you, I'll see what I can do." If a person could flirt with words, this man was, and she liked him sight unseen.

"It's Ashley, and I appreciate your help."

"No problem. A word of caution, Ashley. Be wary of your current partner. He has a way with the ladies."

"Shut up, Rod." Dalton's tone of voice was relaxed with the detective. "The faster we get answers, the quicker we get out of your hair."

"Meet me at the morgue in two hours."

"Thank you," she said.

"Don't thank me yet." Núñez ended the call.

Dalton stood and glanced at his watch. "Let's stop somewhere to eat and then get me checked in at the hotel on the way to the morgue." His forehead wrinkled as his dark chocolate-brown eyes raked across her face. His gaze seemed to map every inch.

"You're staring." She swiped her hand across her mouth. Had she left remnants of the blueberry muffin she'd eaten earlier behind? Or dribbled coffee on her blouse?

"You're very astute." His brows pulled together. "Ashley Hunter. Ash Hunter." He held his hands in front of him as if weighing the names. "Is it possible you're related to a Houston detective?"

She smiled, relaxing under his scrutiny. "You know my brother?"

Dalton nodded. One corner of his mouth curved upward. It wasn't exactly a smile, but it was enough to set her heart pounding. "I've only met him once, but we've spoken over the phone a couple of times." He gestured toward the door. "You ready?"

"Ready as you are." She slipped her cell into her pocket and headed out of the building.

Chapter 3

Dalton followed Ashley across the parking lot. She moved like a woman who knew exactly where she was headed and why she was going there. Her blonde hair, the color of wheat just before harvest, which had been pulled back in a low ponytail, glistened under the sun's rays. High cheekbones and piercing blue eyes complimented her creamy skin. None of those things had caught his attention as much as her mouth. Her lips, lush and plump, had sent a surge of heat through his system, kicking his imagination into gear with all the uses he could find for them.

The typical FBI khaki slacks, white blouse, and navy blazer helped camouflage her figure, but it didn't keep him from noticing the curve of her ass and the way her hips swayed when she walked.

His physical reaction to her was immediate and uncharacteristic. And he didn't like it one damn bit. Dalton shook the X-rated thoughts from his mind and glanced around at his surroundings.

This part of Monterrey reflected a recovering economy, with modern buildings and streets that had been well maintained. The crime rate was probably lower in this area as opposed to other parts of town. Too bad life had gotten better for some but not for all.

The wheels of change turned slowly, but with cops like Rod Núñez on the job, progress would happen.

"I'm parked right here." Dalton stopped at the back of his rental. "I'll drive."

"I'll navigate. Where are you staying?" she asked as they both got in the car.

"At the Grand Fiesta."

"That's where Vardon was registered." She slipped off her jacket. "But you knew that."

He nodded. "It's hot as hell, and you're in the field. Why aren't you dressed comfortably?" The second he got into the car, Dalton turned the air to the max.

She placed her coat in the back and slid into her seat. "My boss thinks it gives us an air of authority."

"But that pompous ass isn't here, is he?"

"Is there anything else you'd like me to change while we're working together?"

He grinned, liking her sharp comebacks. "Nothing yet."

"Turn right at the next stop sign. There's a locally owned restaurant in the middle of the block. Your file said you're living in Texas, so I think you'll like the food."

Dalton made the turn as directed. He parked beside the small café, got out, and waited for Ashley. Strips of paint had peeled off the sign so badly he couldn't decipher the name of the restaurant.

She opened the door and held it for him. "Is this place acceptable?"

"Of course." He nodded as he walked past her. "Thank you, ma'am. The best food usually comes from local cooks."

Once inside, they followed the instructions on a sign hanging from the cash register and seated themselves. The colorful walls, decorations, and strong aromas drifting from the kitchen reminded him of a long time ago when he'd been in the country with Rod.

The waitress brought their menus to the table, and Ashley chatted with her. He was impressed by how fluent she was in Spanish. They ordered lunch and drinks, but Dalton also asked for chips or tortillas and salsa to eat before their lunch was served.

"*Gracias*," Ashley said when she sampled Dalton's predinner snack. She picked up a tortilla and pointed it at him. "We work side by side gathering and sharing information?"

The lack of trust flashing in her eyes didn't escape him. "That's customary."

"Good."

Dalton scooped up a large helping of salsa and popped it into his mouth. "So, what's your take on the murders?"

"They were personal. To get this aggressive, the killer had to be seriously pissed off."

Dalton filled his mouth with the loaded chip. "That's pretty much the case with all murders. What makes this killer different?"

"Rumor has it Vardon's penis was cut off and stuffed in his mouth just like the other two men."

Dalton's surprise at her comment and the blinding heat of the peppers hit his taste buds at the same time. No way was he admitting the salsa had burned off the top layer of his tongue. He swallowed a cough and casually lifted his water glass to his lips and drank.

"Water just intensifies the burn."

He took a second sip. The woman either had a great sense of humor or was pure evil. Judging by the sparkle in her eyes and the smile on her face, he could guess which. She was enjoying his pain.

"That little tidbit wasn't in the notes I read. Was the mutilation pre or postmortem?"

She lifted one shoulder. "Pre."

Their food arrived, and both of them fell silent. Dalton concentrated on his beef enchiladas, rice, and refried beans, while Ashley ate her chicken fajitas.

When they were finished eating, the waitress returned with the check and laid it on the table. Ashley thanked her in Spanish. The two women chatted about the meal and how good it tasted.

When the waitress asked Ashley if they were a couple, he almost dropped his wallet. She vehemently denied it, insisting they were merely colleagues.

Dalton gave the waitress his widest smile, dropped cash on the check, and then said to both women, "*Ella podría hacer peor.*"

The waitress laughed. "*Sí.* She could do a lot worse."

He then followed a silent Ashley to his rental, slid behind the wheel, and turned to face her. "Where to?"

She buckled her seat belt. "Take a left at the next light."

"You've been here before?"

"No. First time in Mexico. Why?"

"You seem to know your way around."

"I like to have a mental picture of where I'm going before I plug anything into the car's computer. I'm a fan of Google maps."

He nodded his understanding. "Anal is good."

She coughed, and pink rushed up her cheeks. "You could have told me you spoke Spanish."

Interesting that she blushed. He wasn't being sexual. "It's in my file."

"I didn't get that far."

"How'd you know about the salsa?"

"One of the women in the office told me about it."

"You could have warned me," he commented.

"That was for staring at my ass in the parking lot."

"You don't know what I was looking at."

"I could *feel* you."

"Then it was worth the burn," he said, without cracking a smile.

Dalton drove to his hotel, checked in, and returned to his rental, where Ashley waited. He was glad he'd left the car running. The air conditioning kept her from sitting in the heat. "Sorry it took so long. There was a couple ahead of me."

"According to the directions, take a right at the end of the drive and a left at the second red light. The morgue is about five miles from there."

Dalton followed her instructions and soon turned into the parking lot of a long white stucco structure with *Servicio Medico Forense* painted on the front. Six light blue vans in badly need of a paint job were parked in front of the building. He drove into a slot one row behind them and killed the engine.

"We're early," Ashley said.

"So we are." He had no doubt she was going to continue to grill him, so he braced for it. "You have more questions?"

"You said you'd only met Ashton once?"

"Yeah, but I've never heard him called that."

"Ashton Hilton Hunter."

"The name doesn't go with his reputation."

"Which is?"

"That he's a cold-blooded bastard."

She shrugged. "Especially when he's pissed."

"That description fits a lot of people."

"I have no doubt." Before he could respond, she asked for more information. "Tell me about this Lost and Found company you left the FBI to work for."

"It's a great company. It was started by my boss, Nate Wolfe, and three of his old college buddies. After they got discharged from the military, they came together to help when Nate's ex-girlfriend, now his wife, was kidnapped and sold to a sadistic bastard. Lost and Found has grown at a phenomenal pace. The ultramodern compound outside of Dallas would make Quantico jealous."

"I doubt that."

"You haven't been there. Trust me."

"That's not so easy for me to do."

He sent an approving look her way. "That attitude might keep you alive."

Then Rod Núñez drove into the parking lot, putting an end to her questions. He exited his car and shook his head.

Dalton nodded as Rod entered the building.

"How long have you known him?"

Dalton narrowed his eyes at her. "You are full of questions."

"Always."

He figured she'd just keep asking, so he decided to humor her. "We went to the same college for four years. When he graduated, he moved here to help his grandparents. He decided to stay and join the police force."

Rod stepped out of the building and motioned for them to join him. Dalton got out but waited while Ashley slipped on that damn jacket. "Have you ever been inside a morgue?"

"No. Don't worry about me, I'll be fine."

"You're sure?" Dalton caught her wrist in his hand. Her muscles tensed under his touch, so he released her.

"I'm sure."

He stared at his fingers as she walked away. If she'd felt the sparks that had jumped between them, she hadn't blinked an eye.

Ashley extended her hand. Rod's grip was firm. His smile was as warm as his dark eyes. "I appreciate your assistance."

"No problem. We may be in reverse situations someday."

"Just call." She liked him immediately. It didn't feel like she was talking with a stranger.

"Let's get this done before somebody bitches that you Americanos are interfering." Rod chuckled softly. "Which, my friends, is *exactly* what you are doing."

With no more than a couple of whispered words to a guard at the door, Rod escorted them into the building.

Dalton entered last. "That was easy."

"My badge comes in handy sometimes. We're to wait here."

****

Ashley was assaulted with cool, damp air tainted with the aroma of blood, strong chemicals, and something she didn't recognize. Was this how death smelled? Her stomach roiled, but she wasn't about to mention it.

The Mexican food she'd enjoyed earlier now churned in her stomach.

The detective studied her face. "This shouldn't take too long."

"I'm fine." She tried not to breathe too deeply, but it was no use. She could almost feel her skin and clothes absorb the stench.

Rod moved to stand next to her. "It's acceptable not to be fine." His tone was compassionate and sincere. "Nobody is immune to the morgue."

A short man with a thick head of dark hair wearing black horn-rimmed glasses stepped into the hallway. "Almost no one."

Detective Núñez spoke quietly with the man. Neither Ashley nor Dalton mentioned they could understand Rod explaining their visit.

"Wait here." The director snapped the words out in perfect English, turned, and strode down the hall and out of sight.

"He's not happy," Ashley said.

"No, he's not," the detective said. "The coroner feels that because Vardon is an American, he's getting special treatment."

"By getting murdered?" Ashley asked.

"*Señorita*, this morgue holds many murder victims." Detective Núñez sounded impatient. "The people here work long hours, so each of the dead can share their story."

"You're right, of course. I apologize."

Doctor Molina returned carrying a file and an envelope. His steps were heavy for such a small man. The responsibility for this morgue had to be enormous, and the dark circles under his eyes made him look weary. He handed the items to Núñez.

"*Gracias*," Rod said. "*Apreciamos su ayuda.*"

The coroner spoke English to the detective. "A toxicology screen confirmed the deceased was given Rohypnol before being mutilated. I counted seven stab wounds, and his penis had been removed and found in his mouth." His words were flat and matter-of-fact as if this was an everyday occurrence. "A queen of diamonds playing card was in his hand."

"We'd like that card sent to Quantico." Ashley tried to speak firmly, but friendly.

"It, along with my final report, will be sent to the local police department. Where it goes from there is up to them."

"I'll see to it," Núñez said.

"Was Vardon alive when the cutting started?" Dalton asked.

"The drug would have rendered him helpless, but his heart was still beating."

"Any thoughts on the blade?"

"The entry wounds indicate a knife no wider than half an inch. Very sharp, and there were no signs of tearing. Were any of you acquainted with Mr. Vardon?"

Dalton stepped forward. "I was."

"Are you willing to make a visual identification for the record?"

"Love to." Dalton glanced at her and winked. He was pleased Vardon was dead.

"If you'll excuse us." Molina turned and walked toward the double doors.

"We'll wait out front." Detective Núñez took Ashley's elbow and guided her out the door. "Fresh air will help."

She turned her face upward and let the warmth of the hot sun sink into her skin, breathing in and out, trying in vain to expel the morgue smell from her memory. "It was stupid of me to say I was ready."

"If it's any consolation, we all hate going in there. It's not a place of happiness."

"I understand."

The detective's eyes stayed on her. "How long have you known Dalton?"

"A few hours."

Rod nodded his understanding. "You can learn a lot from him."

"Really?" Her desire to know more about Dalton pushed her to ask, "He's that good?"

The detective nodded his head. "His accomplishments are known here, as well as in the States. Watch and learn."

"Any advice?"

"Never lose your humanity."

She'd been asking for insight on Dalton, but before she could reword her question, he stepped out of the building. He walked as if he feared nothing. He moved with an easy gate and appeared to be the definition of confidence. Using her height of five six, she estimated him to be at least six two. His chiseled cheekbones, unsmiling lips, thick wavy hair the color of the midnight sky, and the barely-there scruff on his face held her attention. Other than a perpetual frown and a few barely noticeable lines at the outside corners of his eyes, his face gave no hint of his age.

He was masculine with just a hint of pretty.

She closed her eyes and wished she wasn't so curious about why he was so distant. He liked Rod. But her? Not so much.

Strong hands gripped her forearms. "Ashley? You looked a little pale inside."

"I was a bit shaky, but it passed." Her skin heated at Dalton's touch, so she stepped out of his grasp. His eyebrows lifted, as if questioning her reaction, but he didn't comment.

"This is where I leave you," Rod said. "You'll keep my name out of your reports?"

"Absolutely," Dalton said.

Ashley held back on confirming Dalton's promise. She offered her hand to the detective. "I appreciate your help."

Núñez surprised her by pulling her in for a hug. "My pleasure." He repeated the process with Dalton.

Ashley waited until Rod was out of hearing range before she challenged Dalton. "You just made a promise for me that I may not be able to keep. Carl is expecting updates."

"Intervening on our behalf could end Rod's career. He or his superior will send a report and the autopsy information to Carl. When you and I gather intel, we'll talk about what we share and who we share it with."

A welcome gust of wind stirred the air. The breeze swept a lock of Dalton's hair onto his forehead. He raked it back with a rough hand as if pissed it hadn't stayed in place.

"If you're not comfortable with the way I work—"

"Oh, no," she interrupted, shaking her head, "you're not getting rid of me." She opened the passenger door to his rental, got in, and buckled up.

Dalton slid behind the wheel, slamming his door so hard the car shook.

"Where the hell did that come from? As I was saying, you'll just have to get used to me." His growl made the hair on the back of her neck vibrate. "Know this: there are some sources we will protect, and Rod is one of them."

She'd opened her mouth to argue, but then Rod drove up next to them. He handed Dalton a folder through the car window and called out, "See you for steaks! Come with, Ashley."

Dalton started the engine and then drove out of the parking lot. "What got you interested in law enforcement?" He still held the folder. "Your dad? Mom?"

"My mother is dead." She snapped her mouth closed.

He reached over and set the air conditioner control to sixty-five degrees. "I'm sorry. What happened?"

"A drunk driver going the wrong way on the freeway killed her."

"That stinks." His tone had softened in sympathy.

"Her death was your motivation?"

"Helping people and proving myself capable has always been my goal."

Dalton nodded, handing the file to her. "Tell me what Rod gave us."

She opened the manila folder and found a picture of the body. Refusing to show any emotion, she'd prove her strength to him. Earn his respect.

"Vardon's body is stretched out on a bed with his arms and legs splayed spread eagle. The blood from his chest and groin is spread across the white sheets."

"Don't concentrate on the carnage. Study every inch of what you see. You might pick up something everyone else missed."

"Rod told me not to lose my humanity."

"That's good advice. If you ever forget that the victim was somebody's son or daughter, husband or wife, hang up your spurs."

"Even Vardon?"

"Even that fucker." Dalton ground out the words as he stopped the car for a red light. "Read me the coroner's preliminary report."

Ashley removed the document and put the folder aside. "The cause of death was an excessive amount of blood loss."

"Go ahead, I'm listening." This time when he glanced at her, his eyes held a hint of interest.

"There are no visible signs of a struggle." She took a deep breath and continued. "His penis was removed evenly. The blade was very sharp. His testicles were intact. He was stabbed in the chest seven times. That's all, unless you want to know the contents of his stomach."

"I do." A car turned right in front of them, and Dalton swerved to avoid hitting it. He mumbled something under his breath.

"Vardon's stomach held chicken, garlic potatoes, and green beans. Plus, a large amount of alcohol, and the Rohypnol."

Dalton drummed his fingers on the steering wheel. "We need the report on the other two murders."

"If they're not on my laptop yet, I'll follow up." She continued. "Vardon's personal items consisted of one change of clothes, a wedding ring, a room keycard, eight hundred and forty-three dollars in American currency, and 12,060 pesos, plus various credit cards."

Ashley glanced up and realized they'd returned to his hotel.

Dalton parked and turned to her. "You're joining us for dinner, right?"

"No. I'd like to get my rental and go back to my hotel."

"Sorry." His back stiffened. "I know better than to assume. Come up while I change clothes, then I'll run you to your car."

"Come up?" Her heart raced like a winning Indy 500 driver. No way was she going to his room. Glancing over at him, she said, "I'll wait in the bar."

"You're smart not to go to my room with me. I might ravage you or something." He got out, slammed the car door, and waited for her.

His tone was sarcastic, raspy, and harsh. Yet, for a split second, she saw something flash in his eyes. Had she bruised his ego? Hurt his feelings? That thought was ridiculous. He had no feelings. Especially toward her.

Huge glass doors sensed their approach and silently slid open. Cool, lightly scented air greeted them. Ashley entered first, walking straight to the bar.

She took a deep breath, noticing how the atmosphere almost seemed to smell of money. There was no hint of Mexican heritage here. The design was expensive European. A mural of the Eiffel Tower, complete with people walking past, decorated one wall. Carpet the color of coffee heavy with cream was thick and plush and cushioned her feet with each step.

A growl from behind her slowed her steps, but she tried to ignore it. She felt his presence. That her body sensed his nearness was unnerving as hell.

She slid onto a corner stool.

The bartender smiled. Tall and gorgeous, she wore black shorts with a matching low-cut satin vest. The woman's gaze went straight to Dalton. "What can I get you?"

"Put the charges for whatever the lady orders on room 1414. The last name is Murphy." He turned and walked away before Ashley could protest.

"Don't you dare." She leveled the woman with a glare. "I'll have a Corona with lime."

"You got it."

When the bartender returned, Ashley pushed cash across the bar. "He's not paying for my drink."

"Lover's quarrel? Make him grovel."

"Oh, no. We're not together."

"Really? Could have fooled me."

Ashley nursed her beer until she spotted him reentering the bar. She stood and walked to meet him. Wearing a dove-gray T-shirt that looked as if it might burst at the seams any second and faded blue jeans, he drew more than one hungry glance from the few women there. He stopped, swept the room with his gaze, and smiled while he waited for her to join him.

He knew he was gorgeous. He knew women and some men had turned their heads for a second look. Did he also know his dark eyes, steamy and full of trouble, caused a stir low in her belly? The spark of sexual energy made her uncomfortable for several reasons. Most importantly, he was off-limits and not interested.

She brushed past him and walked out to the car. "That didn't take long."

When they got there, he unlocked her door and held it open. "Did you really not feel safe going inside my hotel room with me?"

Ashley rolled her eyes. "If you're suggesting I'm afraid of you, you're dead wrong."

He blew out a breath, shook his head, and got in the driver's side. "I'm guessing you don't want me to pick you up in the morning."

"No, thank you."

Chapter 4

The next morning, Dalton parked next to Ashley's rental and walked the short distance to the building. He wasted no time getting inside, out of the heat and humidity.

He removed a flash drive from his pocket, leaned over her, and placed it on the desk in front of her. The scent of lemons or grapefruits or some fruit assaulted his senses. Did she have to smell so damn good?

"What's this?"

"A gift from Rod."

"When did he give it to you?"

"Last night during dinner. He was disappointed you weren't with me. I think he'd rather you have joined him than me."

A smile brightened her already beautiful face. Damn her and her tempting lips. Dalton quickly looked away. It would be beneficial to them both if he paid zero attention to her mouth. By both, he meant her and his dick.

Ashley plugged the flash drive into her laptop. "You ready to watch?"

"I'll find a couple of coffees first. How do you take yours?"

"Black." She pointed toward a hallway without taking her eyes off the screen. "Take a right."

He walked to a small break room where he found a Keurig that provided him with two fresh cups of coffee in a flash.

Ashley had added a chair next to her when he returned. Their thighs touched when he sat, causing a shiver to run up her spine.

"Are you cold?"

"No, I'm fine." Pink crept up her neck. "Ready?"

"Yes, ma'am."

She cut her gaze toward him. Her lips curved into a smile then vanished when she blew a breath across her cup. "Thanks for the coffee. You do have a few manners."

"I use them when it's appropriate."

She pointed to the screen and clicked the mouse pad. "Pay attention."

He lifted an eyebrow. "I was."

Fast forwarding the video, they sipped their coffee and observed each person who checked into the hotel and closely studied each woman who stopped at the front desk. Out of all the people who checked in, only one picked up an envelope. She'd kept her head down the entire time. The recording seemed endless, and Ashley fast-forwarded it until Dalton leaned across her and hit stop.

"That's Vardon." He had recognized the bastard immediately. As he'd reached over, she'd leaned forward, accidentally brushing her breast against his forearm.

Ashley jerked back as if burned. He ignored her reaction, allowing her to pretend it hadn't happened. It had been an accident. If he ever deliberately touched her like that, she'd know it.

Shortly after she restarted the recording, Vardon stepped off the elevator. He walked to his room, entered, and closed the door behind him. Dalton leaned back and sipped his coffee. "Now we wait."

She reached behind her head and pulled off the rubber band currently holding her hair in check. She sighed and rubbed her scalp, causing wild waves to cascade across her shoulders. Dalton had to look away. His dick had a mind of its own, and those golden locks had disturbed its peace.

"Sorry, I needed that."

"Not a problem. Back when I had to wear a suit, I couldn't wait to take it off. I'd strip the minute I walked in the door. Got me in trouble if I didn't hang them up right away."

Her head whipped around his direction. "You're married?"

"Not anymore." He was stunned that he'd shared any part of his past with her. He never talked about Gayle with anyone. He had to direct this conversation back to the case. "What do you think the queen of diamonds card means?"

"I wish I knew. Is she taunting us? Sending a warning? Three men have died because she's angry." Ashley grabbed her cell and tapped away for a few seconds. "Here's what the internet says about the tarot card queen of diamonds. She's a jealous, wicked woman who can manipulate men because they easily fall for her. But ultimately, she's the enemy."

"So, you think it's a woman?"

"Yes, I do. Think about it. That she sliced off that particular appendage tells me something happened to her to make her hate men."

"Particular appendage?" Dalton couldn't resist teasing her. "That's a delicate way of putting it."

"Really, Dad?" She bumped his shoulder with hers. "His dick. Those actions describe a woman who is majorly pissed off. I also think she's damn proud of her work."

"Well said, kid," Dalton laughed.

"I'll be damned." She smiled, flashing snow-white teeth. "You do have a sense of humor."

"Don't count on it."

"How old are you?" she asked, pinning him with her gaze.

"Isn't that question a little pushy for our first date?" Shit. He was flirting with her. He'd never fucked around on a job before, and wasn't going to start. "Concentrate on the computer screen."

Her cheeks flushed. "I'm glad you're here."

A warm rush of blood slid through his veins and heated his skin. He recognized

the feeling and reminded himself it was for high school boys and not him.

They watched the unchanging video feed as it continued to fast-forward. At the twenty-five-minute mark, room service delivered an ice bucket, a bottle of champagne, and two glasses to Vardon's room. The door swung open, giving them a second look at the man wearing a robe.

"He had no idea he'd be dead before morning."

"Bastard should've been dead a long time ago. He didn't give a shit who or how many were killed with the weapons he brokered. He was a murderer by proxy."

Thirty minutes after room service delivered the champagne to Vardon's room, a woman stepped off the elevator. She kept her head lowered, as if counting the squares on the carpet beneath her feet. Her long platinum hair fell forward and covered her face.

"Look up." Ashley leaned closer to the screen. Her tone was soft, as if she were afraid of being heard. "That's the woman from the front desk, and she knows she's on camera."

"Yes, she does."

The woman wasn't wearing any jewelry that might help identify her. A skintight dress hugged every curve. She tapped on Vardon's door and quickly disappeared inside.

Ashley stopped the video and faced Dalton. "Her purse looked more like an overnight bag."

"The screen says nine p.m. and the time of death was between ten and midnight. We'll see how long killing and butchering him takes."

"Does watching this, knowing what was happening, freak you out a little bit?"

Dalton shook his head. "I don't freak out over something I have no control over. You'll need to master that ability."

"Sage advice." She hit fast-forward again, stopping when Vardon's door opened. "Here we go."

It looked like a male stepped out of the room. Wearing low-riding jeans, climbing boots, and a sweatshirt with the hood pulled up over a ball cap, the person's face and hair were hidden from view.

"That's her," Ashley said.

"Yeah, there were only two people in that room."

A backpack was slung over her right shoulder. Again, keeping her head down, she walked down the hall and boarded the elevator.

"Fuck me. She's smart. Pulled it off without a hitch." Dalton scrubbed his hands over his eyes. "She won't be easy to catch."

"Where do we go from here? Do we search his house?"

"His home office for sure, which, lucky for us, is in Dallas. Let's see if we can get a flight out in the morning."

"Good idea." Both took out their cells and talked through times and seats. Within minutes, their tickets were booked.

"I need to tell the agent in charge I won't be back tomorrow and thank him for the use of a workstation."

Dalton rolled his chair back, stretched his legs out in front of him, and waited until she returned. Then he followed her to the parking lot and onto the highway, where they drove to their separate hotels.

Truth be told, Ashley stirred something inside him that had been long buried. Except for an occasional one-night stand, no woman had piqued his interest in a quite a while. His rule of not being in a lover's bed when the sun came up was sacred. Would he break that rule for Ashley? She was a mixture of smart, serious, and sensuous. He'd bet his paycheck she had no idea she had that kind of power over the opposite sex.

****

Ashley closed the door to her hotel room and sighed. She was ready for some quiet time to go over the events of the day. She kicked off her shoes, dropped her purse on the desk, and stretched out on the bed. The splashes of bright shades of orange, red, and blue, plus the picture of vaqueros on the wall, were great examples of Mexican heritage. Maybe someday, she'd come back for fun instead of work.

Instead of death and playing cards, Dalton filled her thoughts. Something about him intrigued her. It had been a while since romantic thoughts of any kind had plagued her. Now wasn't the time to have butterfly-wing fluttering inside her stomach. Her eyelids felt heavy as she nestled into the soft bedspread.

She woke sometime later with a stiff neck. Blinking a couple of times, she rolled over and checked the clock. Falling asleep hadn't been the plan for last night, and now at four in the morning, she was hungry and wide awake.

After she'd showered and packed, she dressed in skinny jeans, ankle boots, and a lightweight blue striped blouse. Makeup was a swipe of mascara and lip gloss.

Sitting at the desk, she opened her laptop, reading and answering emails until it was time to check out. She'd learned yesterday that traffic could be hectic, so she headed to the airport and car rental return lot early.

She'd considered her ability to analyze a person's personality to be good, but Dalton was a complete mystery. There were signs of suffering behind his eyes. Something had happened in his past he couldn't or wouldn't face. Right under the surface, she sensed a wave of anger that made him dangerous, at least to an enemy.

She'd teased him about his age, but he couldn't be more than thirty-five, making him six years older than her. When he laughed, it rolled up from his chest, full and hearty, making him outright sexy. Sometimes, his deep chocolate eyes warmed and sparkled with interest, sending heat straight to her core, but that warmth could disappear in the blink of an eye.

Her cell sang out the sound of a freight train. It was the ringtone she'd assigned Carl White, her boss. She drove while he talked.

"Dalton was a good agent. The best," Carl stated. "We need him back, and you have the perfect opportunity to convince him to return."

Her heart dropped to her stomach. Had she been allowed to stay on the case just as bait? Carl's words hadn't been presented as a demand, but she'd heard the underlying meaning and didn't like it one damn bit.

"Carl." Panic rose in the back of her throat. "I have no idea how to change his mind. He's very professional and seems happy with his current job."

"Nonsense. Use your skills. Find out what makes him tick. He's a man, and his mind can be changed. Keep me informed." Then the line went dead, leaving her confused, disappointed, and mad as hell.

The conversation with Carl had come out of nowhere and stunned her. She returned the rental car, checked in for her flight, and then went through security as if walking in a fog.

How would he react when she failed to bring Dalton back into the fold?

Once at the gate, she sat and considered telling Dalton her new instructions.

He was easy to spot as he moved through the crowd and down the aisle toward her. Sunglasses hooked in the neck of his black button-down shirt with the sleeves rolled up. His faded jeans clung to his long muscular legs, while his long strides closed the distance between them quickly. He walked with purpose and strength.

Ashley wondered what his broad shoulders and muscular arms would look like without a shirt. How would they feel under her hands? Her body reacted to the thought by sending pulses of electricity south. She shifted in her chair, failing to find a comfortable spot.

A couple of women turned their heads, their gazes tracking him as he strode past them without noticing their stares. Dalton was striking and handsome, but with a don't-fuck-with-me expression. Ashley smiled as he approached. His lips remained still with no hint of a grin.

"Hey," he said. "Watch my bag for me?" He dropped it next to her feet and walked away without waiting for her response. A few minutes later, he returned with two cinnamon rolls and two coffees. He handed her one of each.

"Thank you." It was a thoughtful gesture and much appreciated. "I needed this."

"You bet." He sat and rested his right ankle on his left knee. "Have you learned anything new?"

She couldn't hold his gaze. Should she tell him about her conversation with Carl or pretend it never happened?

It surprised her when Dalton's finger and thumb caught her chin and turned her head to face him. "What's wrong?"

"Nothing." His dark eyes searched her face. What if he got angry and quit the case? "I'm just tired."

"Take a nap when we get on the plane."

"I will." She shifted the subject. "Carl sent the files on the other two murders."

Dalton was silent for a minute. "You didn't have them on your laptop?"

It was time to be honest, about at least part of her assignment. She hadn't exactly lied about this being her case, but she'd let him believe it.

"No. I wasn't assigned to do more than verify the presence of the playing card and to ensure it was sent to Quantico. My expertise and background are in finance and technology. I've been working on money laundering and bank and credit card fraud." She gave him her sincerest smile. "But because you're with me, I'm officially part of the investigation team."

He sipped his coffee, watching her over the rim of the cup with his smoldering eyes. The darkness was still there, but a sparkle had taken center stage. She didn't detect shock or surprise in his expression.

She punched him in the arm. "You knew."

His head moved in a slight nod.

"You had the choice of me staying or Carl sending a more experienced agent?" It was a guess, but her gut said she was on the right track.

Another nod.

He was so damn frustrating. "You can use your words."

He breathed an audible sigh. "How old are you?"

"Twenty-nine."

"Ah, that was a good age."

"Don't try to change the subject. Why did you do it? I want the truth."

He ran his hand over the scruff on his face. "I didn't want to work with a gung-ho diehard. Somebody who knew everything about everything. Or one who'd tell me how stupid I was to leave the agency."

All the air left her lungs. She couldn't tell him. "Thank you. I owe you."

"I'll think of a way you can pay me back." He grinned. It wasn't huge, but it was all she needed to send her ovaries into overload.

"How old are you?" The heat from her cheeks slid downward and took up residence in her lower belly. "It's only fair you tell me your age."

His eyes darkened. He could speak to her body with simply a look. It was sending tiny electrical shocks racing around just under her skin.

"Six years older than you."

Exactly as she'd guessed. "Thirty-five's not too old."

His lips spread into a smile that could melt icebergs. "Not too old for what?"

"For anything." She cleared her throat and quickly changed the subject. "Have you heard anything additional from Rod?"

"Nothing except that Vardon's body and death certificate will leave for Texas tomorrow."

"Once we're in the air, I'll log in and download those files."

"Good. I want to read the details of each kill. She's what you feds call a mission-oriented serial killer, and she's angry at a particular type of man."

"How was dinner last night?"

"Good steak and great company. Rod was disappointed you didn't join us, as I said."

"What was his take on Vardon's murder?"

"He agreed we're looking for a female. Mutilating genitals isn't all that uncommon in Mexico, but they usually take the whole package."

A woman sitting behind them huffed out an audible gasp. She openly stared at them.

"Sorry, ma'am," Dalton said as he stood. "We can board now." He picked up his duffel bag and Ashley's overnighter. They made their way onto the plane and Ashley slid in, taking the window seat. Dalton folded his long legs behind the seat in front of him.

She put her seat belt on, clicked the buckle in place, and then leaned back. "We freaked that woman out."

"Yeah. That was careless."

When the flight attendant began giving safety instructions, Ashley closed her eyes. Soon the plane was in the air, winging its way to Texas. Ashley's body seemed to sense his comforting presence next to her. It was almost like a warm caress on her face.

"Are you staring at me?" she asked without looking at him.

"I am."

She opened her eyes and turned to face him. "I'm surprised you told me the truth."

"Don't be. You asked. I answered."

"Always with the truth?"

"Don't ask me a question if you don't want the truth."

"What if you're working a case?"

"Of course there are times information and opinions are withheld. But in real life, don't ask me if you don't want the truth."

"The truth as you see it."

"Right again." Dalton's eyebrows dipped into a frown. "Are you trying to start an argument with me?"

"Not at all." Maybe she was. Maybe if she didn't like him, her attraction to him would go away. "Sorry. I didn't sleep well last night."

He leaned his elbow on the armrest that separated her hip from his. "What's upset you?"

He smelled like the air after a good rain—and a green forest. It drifted off him and straight to her nose. She resisted the urge to inhale deeply. "Nothing. Everything," she admitted.

"Why don't you pull up the files on your laptop and let me study them while you rest?"

Ashley set up her laptop and handed it to Dalton. "That belongs to the FBI, so don't look up anything pornographic."

His chest shook with a silent laugh. "You do remember I used to have one of these?"

"Just reminding you." She winked then, stifling a yawn, and quickly put her hand over her mouth. "You'll wake me before we land?"

"Of course. I would never abandon a beautiful woman asleep on a plane."

"You didn't tell me why you were staring."

"You're right. I didn't." His eyes seemed to warm, and the corners of his mouth lifted slightly. And there it was, that small change in his expression transformed him from stoic to stunning.

Ashley turned her head toward the window. She dozed off feeling as if she'd accomplished something, but wasn't quite sure what.

Chapter 5

"I'll get it myself!" shouted a passenger.

Angel Honeywell hurried to help her coworker. "What's the problem?"

"This bitch refused to get me a whiskey!" he yelled, standing up and stepping into the aisle.

"Sir, we're preparing for takeoff," Angel said, almost backing away from the smell of alcohol wafting off the man. "Please take your seat and buckle your seat belt."

He shoved her out of the way. She stumbled backward into an immovable object.

"The lady said sit down," a deep voice said from behind her. She turned and looked up at the man. He stepped around her, his gaze locking on the troublemaker. "He's going to do as you asked. Unless you want me to sit him down."

Angel swallowed. The man helping her was tall with broad shoulders, and biceps the size of a lumberjack's. His gaze, fixed on the passenger, was dark and unforgiving. He gathered the front of the drunk's shirt in his hand and pushed him off the aisle, away from her and her coworker.

Then he looked over his shoulder toward her. "Or would you prefer he leave the plane?"

"If he promises not to cause any more trouble, he can stay."

The drunk, his eyes wide with fear, wasn't so brave now. He sunk into his seat and fastened his safety belt. "Fine. But only because I have to get to Dallas."

"One word out of him and I'll tape him to the seat, starting at his forehead." The man glared at the passenger. "Got it?"

The drunk nodded.

"Out loud. We can't hear your head rattle."

"Yes. I won't move or speak."

The big man turned to her. "Ready when you are."

Angel was speechless as she followed her hero back to his seat. Inviting him out for a drink was on the tip of her tongue when the woman in the seat next to him placed her hand on his arm and asked what had happened.

Angel went about her duties, but she couldn't keep her eyes from drifting back to the man of the hour. She opened her iPad and searched the passenger information. His name was Dalton Murphy, a frequent flier, and preferred first class. While he watched his seatmate sleep, Angel watched him. Maybe next time he'd be alone.

****

Dalton closed Ashley's laptop, put his tray up, and fastened his seat belt before the flight attendant issued the instructions. Ashley had slept through the short flight to the Dallas Fort Worth International Airport while he'd read and reread the murder files.

He'd also studied the sleeping beauty beside him. Smart and gorgeous was a troublesome combination where he was concerned. He couldn't remember the last time his body had reacted so strongly to a woman. He didn't believe she'd be interested in one night of raw sex, either. But after this case was over, he might find out.

She woke when the landing gear groaned and descended. "That was fast." She smoothed her hair into place. "Did I drool?"

"Nobody noticed except me."

She swiped her hand across her mouth. "I don't drool."

"Maybe. Maybe not."

She took her laptop from him and returned it to its case. The plane taxied and then stopped at the gate. He stood, letting her get up and stretch her legs.

Neither spoke as they deplaned and rode the shuttle to the offsite parking lot, where they walked to his truck. He opened the passenger door and waited until she had settled in before walking to the driver's side. By the time he'd slid behind the wheel of his pickup, Ashley was busy getting caught up on her phone messages.

"The search warrant for Vardon's property came through." She rolled her shoulders, as if stiff from the short plane ride. "If you see a coffee shop, I'll buy."

Stopping at the first opportunity, Dalton ordered at the drive-through. He paid, passed Ashley her cup, and then drove back onto the highway.

"Thank you." She held the cup under her nose and breathed in deeply. "What did you learn from the files?"

"Other than Vardon, we're looking at a high school soccer coach and a mechanic who lived in different parts of the country. Their lives couldn't have been more different, yet their deaths were the same."

"I'll bet you miss working for the bureau." Her tone of voice was laced with curiosity.

Dalton grunted. "That's a bet I'll cover." He took a drink of his coffee and then placed the cup in the holder.

"You wouldn't go back under any circumstances?"

"Nope."

"You might change your mind."

He could feel her eyes on him, but kept his gaze on the road ahead. "Not happening."

"What are we betting?"

He let her question sit for a few heartbeats. "I'll let you know when I win." He almost laughed as she sputtered in response.

"And so will I." The bravado in her voice didn't ring true.

"Let's pay Mrs. Vardon an unexpected visit. I'm guessing she won't care whether we have a warrant or not."

"Why wouldn't she care?"

"She hated him." Dalton drove through the exclusive neighborhood of West Hill Manor. The homes were palatial, spread out over well-manicured lawns, high fences, and behind locked gates. To him, they looked cold, distant, and unwelcoming. He pulled up to a speaker, rolled the window down, and pushed the call button.

"Vardon residence." The female monotone voice faded on a gust of Texas wind.

"Dalton Murphy to see Mrs. Vardon."

"The family is not receiving visitors."

Dalton leaned out the window closer to the speaker. "She'll see me. Tell her I'm here."

"Wait, please."

"You were here when you investigated Vardon the first time?" Ashley asked.

"Yeah, I interviewed Mrs. Vardon. The place was searched from top to bottom. They missed something. I fucking know it."

The ornate metal gates opened slowly. Dalton drove up the tree-lined drive and parked in front of the gray brick home built to resemble an old-world castle, complete with turrets at the two front corners.

"This place cost a lot."

"Paid for with blood money."

They walked up the steps together. She reached to push the doorbell, but before her finger reached the ornate pearl button, the massive double doors swung open. A diminutive woman with slate-gray hair and tired blue eyes greeted them with a stare that oozed contempt.

"Follow me." The woman then spun on her heels and walked away. The rubber soles on her shoes didn't make a sound on the white marble floor. They stopped outside a room with enough books to fill a city library. She waved them inside, told them to wait, stepped back, and closed the door behind them.

"Not very welcoming." Ashley rolled her eyes as she crossed to walnut bookshelves and ran her fingers across the horde of leather-bound tomes.

Dalton walked over to the oversized desk and thumbed through a stack of cards. "Condolences," he read one out loud. "Two are from state judges."

One of the double doors opened and Sylvia Vardon, dressed to the nines, entered the room. She ignored Ashley and kept her attention on Dalton. She'd flirted with him the last time he'd been there, but today she seemed more reserved.

"Mrs. Vardon, this is Special Agent Ashley Hunter. Ashley was instrumental in getting your husband's death certificate and body released."

"Thank you. The insurance company refuses to process the claim without a death certificate. Did you bring it?"

"No. That's not why we're here," Dalton said. "Agent Hunter and I are investigating his murder."

"Really?" Her eyes grew wide. "Why do you care?"

"I don't. The FBI does."

"He didn't even have the decency to die without embarrassing me. It's all over the news that he was mutilated."

"I assure you the leak didn't come from us."

"I know. The coroner in Mexico was interviewed this morning."

Ashley crossed the room to the widow. "I'm very sorry for your loss. Answering questions at a time like this must be difficult, but I know you want whoever murdered your husband brought to justice."

"I'd shake their hand, actually. He was a horrible man." Mrs. Vardon sat on the couch and waved them to the love seat across from her. "Wife one got smart and bailed before he beat her to death."

Ashley leaned closer to the widow. "Your husband abused you?"

Mrs. Vardon shrugged her shoulders. "Not until after I signed the prenup and married the bastard."

"I'm sorry you went through that. Do you mind answering a few questions?" she asked, interjecting a sympathetic tone into her voice.

"The first time I voiced my opinion at a dinner we'd attended, he waited until we got home and gave me a black eye."

Dalton let Mrs. Vardon vent for a few minutes. When she appeared to relax, he spoke up. "We have a warrant, but I'd rather have your permission to search his office."

"Be my guest." Her response came quickly, surprising him. "I'm selling this dump, so take what you want."

"Thank you. We're hoping to find something that will help solve a couple of other murders, too."

"Annie!" Mrs. Vardon called out.

The door opened and the older woman walked inside. "Yes, ma'am?"

"I'll be out of the house for a few hours. Bring some of those moving boxes for these two. Anything they don't take out of Vincent's office, throw in the trash."

"Yes, ma'am." She escorted them into the study led them down the hall, then opened a door. "I'll be right back."

Dalton entered the room, glancing around at the expensive desk, executive chair, and small couch. "It looks different than it did the last time I was here."

"Maybe he got careless, thinking he could get away with anything." Ashley pulled the closet door open. She lifted the lid off a couple of storage boxes. "These are full of files."

Dalton carried a computer, printer, and laptop to his pickup, and put them in the back seat to keep them safe. He returned inside to a stack of empty boxes which he and Ashley filled as they emptied drawers. They didn't stop to analyze anything. Instead, he loaded everything into the bed of his truck.

He returned to the house after taking out the last box. Ashley was waiting at the door with a smug grin spread from one ear to the other.

"You found something?"

"I sat down to wait on you and noticed the slight shade difference in the paint colors." She walked to the closet. "Look closely, right under this shelf. It's patched."

It took him a second to spot the perfect square that had been cut out, patched, and then repainted with a slightly darker beige than the rest of the closet. "Very good."

He smiled and a pink flush rushed to her cheeks. Then he pulled a box cutter out of the desk drawer to use on the Sheetrock. Once he pulled it away, a small safe about sixteen inches wide and high waited for them. "We may find all our answers right there."

He slid his fingers into the space and pulled out the small metal box. "We have a guy at the compound who will make this baby open up and spill its secrets."

Ashley rolled her shoulders. It was the second time she'd done it today. Maybe it was tension. "Where else should we look?"

"We're finished here." Dalton put the lightweight safe on the corner of the desk, turned her around, and started kneading her neck. He found a couple of knots and used his thumbs to rub them out. "You're tired and tense."

"I can't believe we found a safe. That's the first sign of progress we've had."

"*You* found it." He moved his hands and massaged her shoulders. When she rested her head back against his chest with a sigh, his breath caught in his chest. Damn. Every drop of blood in his body rushed south.

She stepped away, shaking her head, as if startled she'd leaned into him. "Sorry. You almost made me forget where we are."

He lifted his brows and smiled. "Almost?"

She hurried out of the house. In a couple of long strides, he was walking next to her.

"There's a room for you at the Lost and Found compound. Nate's wife loves visitors. You'll like her." Dalton tried to make casual conversation, but it wasn't working. His dick had taken notice of how good her body felt leaning against his.

****

Angel quietly closed the door behind her and looked around Kyle Beltrane's empty office. She'd received two voicemails and several texts since she'd returned from Mexico. They didn't talk business on the phone, so she'd decided to check in with him. It was, apparently, time for one of his lectures.

Kyle had no taste. His office looked sterile. Its soft gray walls and color-coordinated carpet were complemented by splashes of calming blue vases and clear glass lamps placed on dark walnut tables that screamed money.

Boring.

The expensive decor was fitting considering Kyle was housed on the fifteenth floor of the Callowell Professional Building, two floors beneath the corporate offices of the largest weapons manufacturer in the United States, Jones and Ward Inc. He used the phone sitting on the corner of his desk to ensure no legislative measures were passed that would impede the manufacturing and sale of all types of firearms, including the automatic weapons that were so popular. The bulk of Kyle's time was spent on gun lobbying for J&W.

Occasionally, he represented people who were willing to pay for an individual's death. She had no idea who'd contacted him when her services were needed.

The door to the executive washroom opened and Kyle entered the room, smoothing the front of his two-hundred-dollar shirt.

"Angel." He was determined to give off the air of being an important man, but he came across as a dick. With his short salt-and-pepper hair, hazel eyes, and well-practiced smile, he reminded her of a mannequin.

"Sorry for barging in, but no one was in the outer office, and your door was open."

He glared at her while he crossed the room. Then he reached out and caught her by the arm.

She jerked away, hurrying to sit in one of the buttery soft chairs across from his desk. The bastard knew she didn't like to be touched. Period. "One of these days you're going to put your hand on me and die for it."

"I don't think so. You need me."

She scoffed. "Why did I need to come to Boston?"

"Why?" he asked through gritted teeth. "You know why. It was a simple job. Vardon was supposed to die, but you went off the fucking rails. You've turned his death into the biggest story the networks have had in a long time."

"You know how careful I am. There's no way to trace it back to me." She freelanced for Kyle. That was the extent of their relationship.

"Careful? You left a fucking playing card on his body." He grabbed a pen and rolled it back and forth between his fingers.

She lifted her shoulder and shrugged. Kyle didn't deserve an explanation. The nasty prick was going to die anyway. "So what? There were no specific instructions. He's dead." Kyle didn't need to know Vardon was a sleazebag. "How do you know about the card?"

"I hope you wanted to be famous, because you succeeded. That playing card earned you national coverage, a nickname, and your very own team of investigators."

"Really?" She smiled. "What are they calling me?"

"The Queen of Diamonds Killer."

"I love it. Don't you think it's cool?"

"I think you're batshit crazy." He threw the pen across the room. It bounced off the coffee table and landed on the soft carpet.

"So I've been told." She liked leaving the card. It served as a reminder that all men were bastards. Exactly like her stepfather had been. "Vardon shouldn't have touched me."

The word *famous* circulated through her brain. The Queen of Diamonds would be her trademark. Like Apple, or the smile used by Amazon.

"This is a dangerous game you're playing." Kyle leaned across the wide expanse of his desk. "My clients don't like attention being brought to them. If they get pissed off, we won't get fired...we'll both be dead."

"Kyle," she said, standing and smiling at him, "they only know you. I'm an invisible resource to them."

He jumped to his feet so quickly, his chair rolled backward and slammed against the wall. "Not without me you're not."

"Enough." She hated people who whined. "I want you to find out who's working the case. I need every single detail of their lives."

"You what?"

"I mean it. Email it to me." She had resources of her own, but this would keep him distracted. She paused at the door. "Oh, Kyle?"

"What?"

"You make enough money. Buy a decent suit."

Walking out of the building, she felt an odd sensation wash over her. Happy wasn't an emotion she felt often, but as the word famous circulated through her mind, she smiled and drove to the closest drugstore, then on to the airport.

She needed a new deck of cards.

Chapter 6

Ashley wasn't sure staying at the Lost and Found compound instead of a motel was a good idea. She was attracted to Dalton. A lot. The fact he ran hot and cold didn't make him any less fascinating. The man was sexy as hell.

The idea of having a dedicated space to work and resources close at hand while she and Dalton dug through the information on all three murders was convincing, however.

"I tend to not get hungry when I'm working," Dalton said as he maneuvered his truck into the stream of airport traffic and onto the freeway. "Speak up when you want to eat."

"I'm good." She'd been so engrossed in the case and unnerved by the call from Carl that food hadn't crossed her mind. "Are we close to the compound?"

"Another twenty miles or so."

She took in the scenery as the city faded into the background, giving way to open pastures dotted with livestock. When Dalton left the highway, he drove down a farm-to-market road that could barely claim to have two lanes before turning onto a paved street. They were banked by huge trees and thick undergrowth on both sides. It surprised her when the landscape suddenly changed. Suddenly, tall, lush green shrubs lined the street on both sides. Sounds from also the freeway quieted, making the area feel isolated from the outside world.

"There's a checkpoint ahead."

A small building sat in the middle of a road that widened and swept around both sides of the structure. A man dressed in dark jeans and an Army-green T-shirt stepped out onto their path. A holstered pistol was strapped to his right thigh.

Dalton stopped and rolled down his window.

"How was Mexico?" The guard's deep voice filled the pickup cab.

"Hotter than here if that's possible." Dalton tilted his chin in her direction. "Zander Caine, this is Ashley Hunter."

The big man leaned down and flashed a snowy white smile. "Welcome. You're both expected. I'm here if you need me."

47

"Thanks." Dalton eased his truck into motion. "That seems to be our motto."

"I love that you have each other's backs."

"Yeah. They mean it, too." He pointed ahead. "Just around that curve is the Lost and Found Inc. compound."

"Are all the men working here that hot?"

The pickup slowed. "You think I'm hot?" His grin was lethal.

"What?"

"I'm just repeating your words."

She pointed ahead. "Go."

Four huge buildings appeared in the middle of a lush green pasture. White brick was highlighted by metal and glass; the largest was two stories, while the rest were single levels. Sidewalks winding between beautifully landscaped flower beds and patches of well-groomed grass connected them. "I wouldn't dare guess at the square footage. It's amazing."

"Nate is constantly expanding. He's been very successful. There's a bunkhouse with a gym and pool, a few guest rooms, a firing range, even a fenced-in area for dogs."

"Dogs?"

"Just one. Diablo. Marcus Ricci, one of the founders of Lost and Found, smuggled Diablo into the country from Colombia a couple of years back. He'd been trained to kill, but you wouldn't know that now. Just don't speak Spanish around him."

Her thoughts of a killer dog vanished when the door to the main building opened and a man and woman walked out, stopping at the curb. Ashley could feel her shoulders tighten. "Why am I nervous to meet these people?"

"Don't be. You'll like this group. Trust me."

"That's twice you've said that to me."

"Then it's about time you put a little faith in me." Dalton glanced at her, winked, and then parked directly in front of the couple.

Ashley opened her door and got out. A stunning brunette and another gorgeous man walked toward her, underscoring her earlier comment to Dalton.

"You must be Ashley," the woman said. "I'm Kay Wolfe, and this is my husband, Nate."

Ashley shook their hands. "I've heard good things about you both."

Nate and Dalton did the chest bump handshake thing.

Then Nate laughed. "Good things from this guy? Then you should probably believe them."

"You'll stay with us while you're in town?" Kay asked.

"If I'm not imposing."

"We have plenty of room." Nate smiled down at her. "Your brother is a good friend of mine. How is Ash?"

"The last time we spoke, he said the department was in an upheaval. Ash isn't the type to get involved with politics, and Houston has a new mayor and chief of police."

Nate pulled the door open and stepped back. "Maybe now's a good time to talk to him about coming to work with us."

"I don't know," Ashley said. "He loves Houston."

"Ash living in Houston wouldn't be an issue. We have an agent who lives in Colombia."

"Lunch is almost here," Kay said, changing the subject. "Come inside. Let me show you around."

Ashley smiled. "I'd like that."

"I'll tell you about 'Wolfe's pack' while we walk."

Nate patted Kay's back. "Dalton and I will unload the pickup while you ladies are busy."

Ashley followed Kay down a hall with see-through glass walls and then up the stairs to the living quarters. The soft beige walls accented by an occasional splash of green and yellow were a big contrast to the offices downstairs, which were filled with dark wooden desks and brown leather chairs.

A high-pitched squeal suddenly came from behind Ashley, causing her to spin around.

"Mama." The cutest baby ever, wearing pull-up jeans and a T-shirt shirt decorated with cowboys and horses, staggered into the room. He lost his balance, plopped down on his bottom, rolled over onto his tummy, and pushed himself upright. His gait was unsteady, but the grin on his face was priceless.

"Sorry." A woman had followed the child into the room. "He heard your voice."

"It's not a problem." Kay scooped the boy into her arms. "Kevin, you're supposed to be asleep."

His head shook from side to side. "No seep."

His mother kissed the top of his head. "Yes, seep."

Ashley cupped a bare foot in her hand. "He's beautiful."

"He won't be if he doesn't take his nap." Kay handed the boy to the woman. "Liz, this is Ashley Hunter. She'll be with us for a while."

"Pleasure." Liz then retreated to a room and closed the door.

"Dalton said your home was here on the compound. He didn't tell me how lovely it is."

"Thank you. We like having the all-in-one compound. Besides, it's safer," Kay said as she walked Ashley through the rest of the house.

"I understand you're the reason the company was founded."

"I wouldn't be alive if it wasn't for Wolfe's pack." Kay smiled as if a memory flashed through her mind. "I went to college with Nate, Marcus, Jake, and Ty. They were part of the starting football team and became close friends. The coach gave them the nickname. We all went our separate ways after graduation, with me coming home and each of the guys joining different branches of the military.

"I didn't know Nate had retired from the SEALS and had come home. I was so busy working for child protective services and was knee-deep in investigating a human trafficking ring here in Dallas. He reached out to me, but I'd been taken and sold to a sick bastard.

"He contacted Marcus and Ty, and the three of them found me before it was too late. But if it hadn't been for Dalton smoothing over a few bumps with the FBI..." Kay said, shaking her head. "Let's just say my guys stretched more than a few laws locating me."

"Dalton came on later?" Ashley couldn't help but ask about him.

"Yes. He's been with us a couple of years, but Nate had been trying to get him to join us for a long time. There's no one Nate trusts more than Dalton." She grinned. "Except me."

"Dalton's not very talkative about his past."

"I've noticed. I'm sure he has a life away from here. I just don't know what it is. Nate probably does, but would never share. Let's go downstairs. I hope you like barbecue. Judging by the aroma wafting up the stairs, Marcus is back with the food."

Kay's friendly demeanor put Ashley at ease. They walked past a conference room where Dalton and Nate were opening the boxes from Vardon's office. Kay called to them as she and Ashley made their way to a break room area where barbecue beef, beans, and potato salad had been spread across a large table.

A broad-shouldered man with his back to them was taking paper plates from the cabinet. He turned to face them.

"Marcus, this is Ashley Hunter."

"Welcome." The dog at his feet stood. Marcus made a sign with his hand to the dog. "Diablo, say hello to the lady." The animal lifted a paw.

"May I pet him?"

"Sure. Shake his hand."

Ashley crossed the room, bent down, and took the dog's paw in her hand. Dark eyes stared up at her as if looking into her soul. His black and brown fur with a splash of white on his chest shined brightly. She scratched behind his ear, and he leaned his head into her hand.

"He's magnificent."

"And a good judge of character." Marcus waved a hand toward the food. "Nice to meet you."

"You too," Ashley said, taking a seat at the table.

Marcus sat across from her. "So, you're partnering with Dalton on the case."

"I am." She accepted a plate filled to the edge with food. "That smells so good."

Two men walked in just as she put a fork full of beef in her mouth.

"I love it when we have company."

A blond male built like a linebacker was followed by a second man whose gaze slowly scanned the area.

Kay introduced her to Tank Jorgenson and Reed Ballatori. Ashley shook her head. Two more members of the team with movie-star looks. "Six of our operatives are out on assignments."

"Welcome." Marcus pulled a chair over next to her. "You should always sit next to me. Tank's appearance is deceiving," he said with a wink. "He looks like a sweet country boy, but don't let him fool you. No, ma'am, he's not sweet or a boy, and only the word country fits."

Marcus laughed. "On the other hand, Reed's time in special ops has left him jaded, but damn, he can be silent, invisible, and deadly when it's needed. His stint in the military earned him the nickname Ghost."

The one called Tank scowled. "You two stop that. You'll scare off our guest." He lifted his hand, and with two fingers, tipped an imaginary hat. "Ma'am, just ask my mama, she'll tell you I'm a sweet boy and her favorite son."

"She probably says that to all five of you brats." Reed's laughter filled the room, and the group joined him. Ashley didn't know anything about him except he could easily have been an Italian model. "If you and Dalton need help, I'm your man."

****

Dalton leaned back in the chair. He sat across the desk from Nate. "I hear you've already found a piece of property outside of Houston and plan to start building soon."

"Yes, Kay and I have been talking about expanding for some time. We'd like you to take charge of the new facility. If you're interested in a buy-in, so are we. If not, we want you to be the manager."

Dalton's brain was firing on all cylinders. Excitement, pride, and gratitude were just a few of the emotions racing through his body. There was only one logical response to Nate's statement. "I want to buy into the company."

"Good." Nate pushed a folder across the desk.

Dalton picked it up, read it for about five minutes, and pushed it back. "That's a fair price. I'll make a call and have a cashier's check delivered tomorrow."

Nate nodded. A laugh rolled from his chest. "No haggling? No having an attorney take a look? No questions? Just, I'll have a check delivered tomorrow?"

"This is the opportunity of a lifetime. And I have the money to buy in and help the company grow."

"When everything's ready to sign, I'll let you know. We'll do it right here in my office. It won't take long. I can't tell you how pleased I am to call you partner."

"Same here." This had come out of the blue. Dalton couldn't remember the last time he'd smiled so much.

"Even though you're working a case, I'll be feeding you information, the location, drawings, hell, everything. This is your baby, and I want your input every step of the way."

Dalton reached across the desk and shook Nate's hand. "It will be a successful partnership."

"I have no doubt." Nate stood. "Well, partner, let's join the team. Oh, I haven't made the announcement yet. Let's wait until we decide who will go to Houston with you and we have the chance to talk with them."

"Marcus supports this? I understand Tyrone won't come back, but doesn't Marcus deserve a shot at being a partner?"

"He's one hundred percent behind you coming in as part owner. He's not interested in relocating or having more responsibilities. His wife's animal rescue has grown into a nationwide charity. It's important to both Marcus and Chris. Ty is also still part of the organization. He's on an assignment right now, but he's not moving from Bogotá, Columbia. Ana's political career is important to both of them."

Dalton stood and shook hands with Nate. "Let's eat. Something smells good."

Nate joined him and they walked down the hall, letting the aroma of barbecue lead them.

"Did you leave enough for us?" Nate asked as they entered the break room.

Reed swallowed and wiped his mouth with a napkin. "You need to get your plates fixed before Tank goes for a second helping."

Dalton laughed with the group and sat next to Marcus, reaching down to scratch behind Diablo's ears.

Kay started piling food onto two plates. "I was just about to come after you two."

"Baby, you know when it's barbecue, I'll be here." Nate took the chair next to his wife. Glancing around the table, he asked, "Where's the little prince?"

"His name is Iain." Kay frowned at her husband. "And he had something to finish before joining us."

"Wait until you see him." Nate winked at Ashley.

Damn. A chill raced up Dalton's spine when she smiled. The need to explore her body grew by the minute, but that didn't mean he'd want to do it forever. He always kept his relations with women to one night and one night only.

He shoved those thoughts away and replayed his conversation with Nate. The words owner and partner swirled through his mind like a slideshow.

"Dalton? Where'd you go?" Ashley asked, snapping him back to the moment.

"Just thinking about the case," he lied as a hand clamped down on his shoulder.

He looked up at the red-haired, blue-eyed, freckled-face young man whose gaze scanned the room. "You ladies and gents were going to eat without me?"

Tank emptied his glass of iced tea. "Looks to me like we've already started. You wouldn't have come out of your office had the smell of barbecue not lured you."

"Aye. Tis probably true."

"Ashley Hunter, this is Iain McMaster," Dalton said. "Or the prince, as Nate calls him."

Iain's mouth spread into a toothy grin. "I'm thrilled at the nickname, but I don't see a resemblance to the prince." He shrugged. "Although, I wouldn't mind being that rich."

Ashley's hand met his across the table. "It's nice to meet you, Iain."

He sat tall in his chair and beamed. "Same here, for sure."

"So, you're the brains behind all this brawn?" she asked.

"Right you are. These NEDs needed a forensics expert badly. Lucky for them, I was ready to get away from Silicon Valley."

"NEDs?"

"Non-educated delinquents," Iain explained. "If it wasn't for me, these blokes would still be walking around in the wilderness."

"That's true," Kay said.

Dalton liked Iain, who, when he was excited, used Scottish words nobody in the company understood. He was twenty-two years in age, eighteen in appearance, and fifty in smarts. Hiring the young prince look-alike had been a smart decision.

Kay passed the kid a plate of food. "Iain has also brought a little humor to the team. Something we badly needed."

"You have family in Scotland?" Ashley asked.

"Aye, I'm the first to leave the motherland. Ma and Da still live in Glencoe. Evie, my baby sister, is attending The Glasgow School of Art. Sings like a bird, she does. My brother, Tobin, daft as the winter is cold, has been trying to get professional baseball rolling for the past two years."

"I thought Scotland was all about soccer. Sorry, it's football," Ashley quickly added. "Right?"

"Ya see?" Iain's hands were moving as fast as his tongue. "Even the lass kens it. Baseball is never going to be the sport of kings. Scotsmen play golf or football."

"So says the little prince," Nate said, laughing along with everybody.

The room turned quiet as they concentrated on their food. Except for an occasional request for a dish to be passed down the table, all you could hear was the ticking clock on the wall.

"That was delicious." Ashley stood and began collecting empty plates. "Thank you."

"You and Dalton have work to do." Kay took the dishes from her. "Guests never help clean up on their first night. Now go."

"If you have time, we have a chore for you and a couple for Iain," Dalton said to Kay.

"No worries," Iain said around a mouthful of food.

"How can I be of assistance?" Kay was always ready to help. She'd worked with the team until Kevin was born. She'd told them that being a mom was the most rewarding job she'd ever had.

Dalton could've argued that point, but didn't. His mother hadn't considered it an important or rewarding job.

"Ashley and I have a couple of pictures that need to be downloaded and printed so we can get a better look."

"How large?"

"Until they begin to get blurry."

"You got it."

"I'll bring you the flash drive."

"What about me?" Iain asked.

"Vardon's personal computer, laptop, and a small safe." Dalton pushed his chair back from the table. "We need to know everything that's in or on them."

"Plus his contacts from his cell as soon as we get our hands on it," Ashley said. "We need to know who he's been in touch with. I'll send you pictures of the queen of diamonds card left on the victim. It looks like it's from a garden-variety pack, but it would be a big help if it was a special order."

"I'm on it."

"Wait." Tank's hands went into a time-out sign. "Your killer leaves a calling card?"

"After stabbing them and then removing their penis." Ashley delivered the news without flinching.

"Holy shit," Reed said. "Seriously, if you need help, I'm in."

"Me too." Tank quickly threw his name in the hat.

"Thanks. I'll remember that." Dalton turned to Ashley. "You ready to get to work?"

"Absolutely." She stood, hung the strap to her bag over her shoulder, and followed him to the small conference room.

The work area had a large rectangular table, soft upholstered chairs, and a whiteboard that ran the length of the narrow end of the room. A cabinet stocked with pens, pads, and paper would keep them supplied. The brightness of the overhead lights could be adjusted to their need. Dalton grabbed a handful of office supplies and spread them out on the table.

"It's back to you and me, kid." He opened a couple of the boxes he and Nate had carried inside and then handed Ashley stacks of folders. He took a handful for himself and sat next to her.

It was on the tip of his tongue to tell her about Nate's offer, but he didn't. They needed to wrap this case up quickly.

Ashley located Vardon's bank records and income tax forms and lined them up next to her laptop. "His finances are where I'll be most helpful. If there's anything hidden, I'll find it."

"Good, because I'm counting on your expertise with numbers paying off."

They settled into a quiet routine, working for hours. Occasionally, he got close enough to her that the scent of her hair interrupted his train of thought. Despite how distracting she was, he liked working shoulder to shoulder with her.

He reached for a pen at the same time she did. His hand landed on top of hers, and neither moved for a second. A sizzling sensation shot straight to his chest, then ricocheted straight to his groin.

She slowly moved away from him. "I think I found something."

"Tell me."

"Not yet. I have to verify."

Dalton pushed his curiosity to the back of his mind and concentrated on Vardon's calendars, checking his appointments and travel, and finally got lost in the number of trips he'd made after his trial. "The son of a bitch made quite a few trips to Mexico."

"And he used a separate credit card for those trips than the ones used for business or household expenses." Ashley stood, grabbed a marker, and started writing dollar amounts and dates on the whiteboard.

Dalton stopped what he was doing, stood behind her, and tried to make sense of what she was putting on the board.

At last, she turned and exhaled deeply. The overhead lights bounced off her eyes, highlighting the circle of cinnamon around her irises. "This is interesting."

Dalton's gaze followed the movement of the marker in her hand. "What did you find?"

"I found an account in Vardon's name in a Grand Cayman bank. The balance is six million dollars. That's a lot of cash hidden from taxes."

He tapped his finger on the board. "That will be important to a couple of government agencies." She was so close and so tempting. "Almost important enough to kiss you for it."

"Almost?" She lifted up on her toes, cupped his face in her hands, and then kissed him. "Like that?"

Her soft lips and the smell of her skin washed over him. She'd opened the door and he was damn sure going to walk through it. He caught her by the waist and pulled her to him, crushing her breasts against his chest.

"You're never going to believe what I found!" Iain said, bursting into the room. Then he skidded to a stop. Color flooded his cheeks.

Ashley jumped back as if a bolt of electricity had blasted through her.

"What?" Dalton growled. He suppressed the urge to choke the kid.

"Receipts in the safe that include the purchase of a Maxim 9mm, travel expenses, and bank records, plus instructions on how to build a gun with a 3D printer. He also had contacts on the dark web."

"And?" Dalton spoke through gritted teeth. "What did you find on the dark web?"

"Are you kidding me? It took me this long just to find his entry point. There are layers and layers left to break through before I can tell you exactly what he was doing."

"Well? Go do it." Impatience dripped from Dalton's tone.

Iain rolled his eyes. "I'm going."

"Good." Dalton followed him to the door, closed it, and flipped the lock. He wasn't missing this chance. "Where were we?"

Her lips curved up in a grin. "You do remember this room has a glass wall?"

"I do." He turned off the lights, leaving nothing but the glow from the hall to guide his steps. Without hesitation, he closed the space between them, stopping less than an arm's distance from her. Ashley's lips slightly parted and her breath came in short gasps. Her eyes reflected a combination of desire and uncertainty.

Dalton tugged her, making her take the final steps to close the gap between them. When her breasts brushed his chest, his fingers cupped her head, holding her in place. His lips covered hers, firm and dominating. His teeth nipped her bottom lip, and she opened her mouth for him. His tongue dipped inside, mating with hers. He lifted his head for a moment, his gaze holding hers as he gave her a chance to back away.

God, she was even more beautiful when her eyes were full of passion.

She melted against him, grabbed his shirt in her hands, and guided his lips back to hers. His tongue delved inside her mouth again, tasting and exploring. The need to possess her, to make her moan with pleasure, permeated every cell in his body. Dalton dropped his hand lower, cupping her ass and lifting her against his erection.

Ashley's soft body pressed against his, and a low moan filled the room. Who had made the sound? Hell, he didn't know if it had been him or her, but it snapped him back to reality.

He'd lost his mind.

Dalton pulled her hands away and stepped back, leaving them both gasping for air. She looked up at him with hooded eyes. Her lips were swollen and damp.

He wanted to carry her to his room and spend the night checking to see if she tasted as good as he thought she would. Fuck. He couldn't let that happen. The risk of ruining their work relationship and screwing up her career was too risky. Hers was just now about to blossom, and he couldn't risk being the reason she failed.

She held his gaze, never flinching. The desire in her eyes was almost too much for him to ignore. His dick was pushing painfully against the zipper in his jeans.

He moved another step back from her. "I'm sorry. We'll pretend this never happened."

"And why would we do that?" The tip of her tongue brushed across her bottom lip as if searching for the taste of him.

His dick protested loudly, pressing even harder against his zipper. Damn it, he wanted to park her sweet ass on the edge of the table and take her right then and there. But he wasn't a horny kid anymore.

"The last thing you need to do is get involved with me."

She tilted her head. "What the hell kind of answer is that?" The arousal in her eyes faded to confusion. Seconds later, anger flared as if flames were licking the back of her pupils. "Answer me."

"Because I'll fuck you senseless tonight, and by morning, I will have forgotten about it. But you won't. You'll get out of bed tomorrow so sore you'll remember it with every step."

She stared at him for half a second before she laughed. The sound rolling out of her wasn't a chuckle. Oh, hell no. It was one of those head-thrown-back belly laughs. And damn, that made him want her even more.

"There's nothing about fucking me that you'd forget by morning." She lifted both eyebrows. "That is, if you survived the night."

He was almost struck dumb. "You're probably right."

"I am. But you're right, the last thing I need in my life is complications."

Dalton saw disappointment flash and quickly fade from her eyes. Ashley was a beautiful woman, but she was also smart as hell, and had good old-fashioned common sense. She knew starting something between them was a bad idea.

Holding his lust for her at bay was going to be a true test of his determination. "It's late, and we both need some shut-eye. We'll start fresh in the morning." Dalton tried to sound calm and collected. He failed miserably. "I'll show you to your room."

He grabbed both their bags and led her through the labyrinth of hallways past the doors to the gym and the firing range before they reached the residential area. "Fresh towels, soap, and the like are in your bathroom. The outside exit is next to your room. The sidewalk will take you to the front office or allow you to walk around and see the compound better."

She pointed back down the hall. "That's the inside way back to the conference room?"

"Right past my room." He opened his mouth to say good night. Too late. She'd closed her door. "Sleep tight, little girl," he said to no one.

There'd be no sleeping for him, so he changed clothes and hit the gym. An hour later, sweat poured from his body. The chemistry between them still boiled through his veins. In the morning, they'd go back to work, and he'd keep his distance. Ashley was the type of woman who'd want a long-term romance, but there was no room in his life for more than one night.

He'd been down that road before and had no intention of taking a second trip.

Chapter 7

Ashley dropped her bag on the chair next to the bed and went straight to the bathroom. She was tired, angry, and more than a little hurt. She'd offered herself up for pleasure and he'd turned her down.

She stripped, turned on the shower, and then stepped inside. Soon the knots in her muscles relaxed, but lust still thrummed through her body. The memory of Dalton's mouth on hers and the heat rolling off his body made her knees weak. His touch burned hotter on her skin than the water sluicing over her body. She sighed and considered the magic he could've made with his tongue. Damn him. He'd wanted her. The memory of his impressive erection pressing against her had been permanently imprinted on her brain.

She got out and wrapped herself in one of the large fluffy towels while dozens of thoughts whirled around in her mind.

The dark mahogany headboard, dresser, and chest stood out against pale gray walls, muted light shades, and slate curtains. The decor was designed to inspire rest for the Lost and Found team—or guests. Sleeping tonight might be hard to accomplish. The urge to slip down the hall and into Dalton's bed kept leaping to the forefront of her thoughts.

The case, the chance to learn from him, and the request to convince him to return to the FBI were never far from her thoughts. He struck her as a man who didn't change his mind easily. Should she have confessed she'd picked up an additional assignment?

Naked, she slid between the cool sheets, her nipples pebbling as the soft cotton slid across her breasts. She turned off the light, hoping the darkness would pull her into a deep sleep.

Ashley didn't know what time she dozed off, but when she woke, daylight streamed through a gap in the curtains. A quick look at the clock had her rolling out of bed with a groan.

She was dying for caffeine, so her trip to the bathroom was a quick one. She hadn't even stopped to apply mascara. She made her way down the hall while pulling her hair back into a high ponytail and then twisting it into a messy bun.

Dalton's door was open, so she took a glance at the empty room. Not that she was hoping to catch him stretched across the sheets asleep, with his fine naked ass showing.

No. Not at all.

She stopped at the conference room, where he sat reading a document. "Morning." She waited until he lifted his head. "Want me to bring you a coffee?"

"No, thanks." His gaze lifted from the document in front of him. The corners of his mouth raised into a smile. "Get a good night's rest?"

"I slept like a rock," she lied, refusing to allow his grin to affect her. She shook off the urge to tell him not to read too much into their kiss. She wasn't the clingy type, and she damn sure wasn't in the market for a husband.

With each step down the hall, her mood lightened. The laughter coming from the break room was contagious. She followed the aroma of coffee wafting out to greet her.

Two of the men who'd been introduced to her yesterday were leaning against the counter watching the television.

"Good morning." Ashley paused in the doorway to ensure she wasn't interrupting.

"Morning." The gorgeous dark-haired man turned in her direction. Reed was stunning, but he didn't stir the deep rumbling in her stomach like Dalton.

"You ready for a cup?" he asked, waving her into the room. "We're watching a car thief trying to outrun the Dallas police department."

"Yes, please." She joined the two men. "It's Reed Ballatori and Tank Jorgenson, right?"

"Yes, ma'am." Tank pulled out an empty chair at the table before sitting in the one next to it. "Have a seat."

Reed slid a cup into the slot on the coffee pot and lifted two pods for her to inspect. "Regular or unleaded?"

"Regular and black." She turned toward Tank. "I really should get to work."

"Oh, come on. We can't let Dalton monopolize all your time," Reed said with a wide smile. "Tell us about yourself."

Ashley accepted the cup he offered and then she joined Tank. Reed's dark wavy hair and almost-black eyes made it hard not to stare at him.

"Go." He leaned back against the counter.

"There's not much to tell. I'm a natural-born Texan, and lucky to live and work out of the FBI office in San Antonio."

"Family?" Reed prompted.

"I grew up in a law enforcement family in Houston. My dad semi-retired by taking a job as sheriff of a small town outside of the city, and my brother is a detective in the city. My mother died when I was twelve, so my big brother practically raised me. I was recruited by the FBI and went straight to Quantico after graduating from college."

"I'll bet they're proud of you." Tank beamed, as if impressed.

"My brother has always been very supportive," she continued, without mentioning her father. They hadn't agreed on much since she'd announced her plan to major in criminal justice and minor in political science. He didn't believe she'd make a decent law enforcement officer of any kind, going so far as to say she was stupid to think she could survive Quantico. "Do either of you know Ash Hunter?"

"I've heard of him. Nate has worked with him in the past." Tank then glanced at Reed.

Reed shook his head. "No."

"He and Nate go way back," Tank said.

Reed studied her for a second. "Your dad hated the idea of you being a fed. Still does."

"What? Are you a mind reader?" she said with a chuckle.

"Not mind. Your body language speaks volumes."

"He doesn't hate the FBI. He hated having a daughter." That was more than Ashley usually shared about him, and she wasn't sure why she had.

"Really?" Tank's elevated tone of surprise made her smile. "That's his loss."

"I guess." She'd tried, but had never quite shaken the sting of her father's disapproval.

Reed turned his head toward the door. "Are you coming in or just observing?"

Ashley turned to find Dalton leaning against the doorframe. His gaze was unreadable, and the grim line of his mouth showed nothing. Had he forgotten the kiss? She hadn't, and wouldn't for a long time. Her hormones had never roared to life that fast.

"Join us," Tank said.

"No thanks. I have work to do." Dalton grabbed a bottle of water from the fridge and disappeared back the way he came.

"Would you look at that?" Tank broke into a grin that spread from ear to ear. "Dalton's jealous."

"No, he's not." Ashley laughed at the idea. "He's impatient."

Tank's eyes sparkled with humor. "I think you've gotten under Dalton's skin. Take him out and teach him how to have some fun."

Reed stood. "Dalton's a good guy. He just doesn't talk about his past or personal life. If we're smart, we'll leave it alone." He offered her a hand to help her stand. "Go easy on him."

"I have no idea what you're talking about." She left the break room carrying her coffee and shaking her head at the ridiculous idea Dalton gave a damn about her. The only thing they had in common was a killer they needed to catch.

Dalton pushed a manila envelope across the table as she entered the room he was working in. "Kay dropped off the enlarged pictures. No help there. Still can't see her face. Iain was in a few minutes ago. Vardon has been on the dark web asking about the viability of mass printing 3D weapons. The government stopped the downloading of the blueprints, but about fifteen hundred were downloaded before they did. Vardon was trying to find one of those people who could manufacture them in large numbers, and wanted to make lots of money."

Ashley slid onto a chair. "He was going to mass-produce them even though they hadn't been proven to function properly? Holy shit."

Dalton lifted his right eyebrow. "Exactly."

"I need to call this in right away." She paused. "Unless you've spoken with Carl this morning."

"Now why the hell would I have done that to you? Who found Vardon's stash in the Cayman's? You did." If Dalton's eyes had been cold a few minutes ago, now they were iced over. "Your case. Your phone call."

"Thank you." The words stuck in her throat. She'd insulted him, and now she felt guilty.

"If it was my case, I would contact the ATF. I'd do it first, include that in the briefing, and keep Carl out of the decision-making loop." Dalton pushed a new flash drive in front of her. "Vardon's contacts on the dark web."

Ashley's heart pounded against her rib cage. "This is a great piece of intel. Where'd you find it?"

"Iain. Or Penkill. That's his username."

"I'll make sure he gets credit for his work."

"No. The fewer people who know he was digging around on the dark web, the better."

She thought about that for a minute. Somebody, probably her boss, would request the source of this information. "Another source I'm supposed to keep a secret?"

"Yes." Dalton stood and walked around the conference table. He turned and his dark eyes lowered to meet hers. Then he released an audible sigh. His expression seemed to be weighing the pros and cons of explaining his requirement.

"Normally, I'd refuse to discuss Iain's private business with anyone, but I have to trust you not to repeat me. He risked a lot by getting on the dark web again. When he started his first job, he fell in with a group of technology geeks that were almost as brilliant as him. Eventually, they turned hacking into a game to prove who was the best. No company's vital information was released to the public or corrupted, but as each of their skills increased, the targets got larger and more difficult. When Iain hacked the ATF, all hell broke loose."

Ashley's heart raced. Iain had made a huge mistake. "Were charges filed?"

"No, and the kid is damn lucky. An old client of Nate's called and asked him to help Iain. Which is why he works here." Dalton folded his arms across his chest. "Enough said. Let's move on."

She picked up her cell and scrolled, searching through the phone numbers. "I'm contacting the local ATF office as you suggested, and then I'll call it in."

He shrugged. "Iain didn't find anything else about the two men on the dark web."

The ensuing conversation lasted maybe ten minutes, and Ashley was assured an agent would be in touch. She was nervous when she called her boss. She sighed with relief when she set her cell on the table. "You were right. He's happy with what we uncovered, and the ATF will take the lead on the weapons issue."

"He should be."

Had she detected a note of disappointment in his voice? "Do you wish you were working the weapons case instead of the Queen of Diamonds killer?"

Dalton's gaze rose from his laptop. His fingers drummed a rhythm on the table. "No, and we've spent too much time on what Vardon was doing. I've allowed my hate to sidetrack us. Let's concentrate on your homicides."

The word *your* sent chills racing down her arms. Ashley reached for her cell to put it away, but it slipped from her hand and slid under her chair.

"I've got it." Dalton leaned down, his head almost in her lap. Close enough she could have run her fingers through his black hair. Was it as soft as it looked?

He picked up her phone and handed it to her.

Her hand betrayed her by trembling when she accepted it.

His dark gaze caught hers as the corners of his mouth lifted. "Do I make you nervous?"

"No." She watched a sexy smile spread across his face. "Yes."

"Good." His gaze dropped to her mouth. "This drive can go to the ATF, but we need to keep a copy."

She patted her laptop. "I'll download it."

"Fine, call me old-school, but I want a copy I can hold in my hand." His gaze went back to his computer.

"Old-school, my ass," she muttered softly.

"I heard that."

"Has Iain found anything related to Vardon's death?"

"Nothing that helps. The playing card is an everyday brand that you can buy just about anywhere. No fingerprints." He pushed back his chair and stood. "Let's take a break. There's a café south of here. Good home cooking. My treat."

She couldn't hold back the smile. Was he warming up to her? Thank God he didn't know that kiss had almost incinerated her panties.

****

Angel slipped out of the Uber and onto the noontime crowded sidewalk. She'd been surprised to hear from Kyle, but apparently, this had to be done right away. She wasn't the least bit curious why Brenna Hawley had to die. This was business, pure and simple.

Watching the life slowly drain from the bastards who thought they could touch her or force their way between her legs? That gave her a high that lasted for days, but this type didn't usually cause a blip on her enjoyment radar.

Except Brenna, a senator's wife, would rate national news.

The target exited the building right on time and joined a group of strangers already waiting on the corner. They moved in mass when the light changed, crossing the street without looking at the person next to them.

Angel wore a nondescript beige jacket, matching linen skirt, silk blouse, and scarf, which she'd pulled over her brunette wig. Its purpose was twofold. Not only did it partially cover her face, but it also protected her against the hot sun. She blended in with the crowd and calmly walked across the street. Her three-thousand-dollar FENDI handbag that carried her pistol hung from her shoulder.

Once they stepped onto the curb, and at the precise moment the crowd dispersed in separate directions, she tapped the women's shoulder. "Excuse me. I believe a set of keys just fell from your pocket."

Brenna turned and glanced at the keys on the sidewalk. Confusion pulled her eyebrows together. "No. They're not mine."

Angel's hand was inside her purse, her fingers curved around the butt of her Maxim 9mm. Her instructions were to throw the gun in the lake, but after trying it out at the firing range, she was keeping it. She hated to destroy such a beautiful bag, but she pressed it against the woman's chest, and gently pulled the trigger. Between the chatter and big city noises, no one even blinked. She silently blessed the inventor of the weapon's built-in suppressor.

Then Angel smoothly turned the corner and walked two blocks to a dress boutique. A black lace teddy displayed in the window had caught her eye. Twenty minutes later, purchase in hand, she ordered an Uber to take her to the airport. She relaxed and enjoyed the scenery through the car's windows.

She covertly wiped down the weapon with her scarf, lifted the undergarment from the gift box, placed the gun with her sexy purchase, and wrapped it in the tissue paper.

The airport was situated on the outskirts of town, giving her a chance to go over the upcoming conversation she'd have with her new friend, George Dawl, who was meeting her at the airport. This was a huge risk, but if it worked, he'd prove invaluable.

The driver stopped at the terminal, and she exited while looking for the one person who'd promised to transport her package to his apartment.

George waited off to the side of one of the entry doors. "Hello, gorgeous." He smiled around a disgusting cigar that looked like he'd been chewing on it for days.

Using all her strength to appear happy to see him, she wrapped an arm around his shoulder and hugged him before handing him the sack. "I have something for you."

He studied the boutique's name and logo before peeking inside. "It's heavy."

"Don't you steal a look inside that box. If you do, I won't model it for you after you finish your run to Oklahoma City."

"I promise. Whatever you wear, I can't wait to take it off you."

She bit back a cringe. This had to work, because she wasn't giving up her pistol, regardless of Kyle's instructions. "I've got a plane to catch. See you soon."

She couldn't wait to get home. Kyle had hired someone to pull together the information she'd requested. It would be emailed to an encrypted mailbox. Soon she'd have pictures and backgrounds of the federal agent and private investigator.

Excitement bubbled inside her. Another new emotion she was unfamiliar with, and she liked it.

Chapter 8

Dalton carried two coffees into the conference. He slid one in front of Ashley. "Black, right?"

"Exactly." She lifted the cup to just under her nose and breathed deeply. "Thanks."

He sat across from her. "Thanks for lunch."

"As long as I can turn the cost in on my expense account, it's my pleasure." She grinned, folded the receipt, and slid it into her briefcase.

Dalton studied the background information of the first victim who'd had a playing card left on his body. He spoke out loud, but was really talking to himself. "Charles Brogan, a high school soccer coach in Minton, Minnesota, was responsible for twenty-four teenage boys. The morning after an away game in Fort Sails, he was found dead in his motel room with his dick cut off. How does that make sense?"

"Means he couldn't keep it in his pants." Ashley had risen and was standing behind him, reading the coroner's report over his shoulder. "The manager of the Winfred Motel found the body and called the police."

Dalton's chest tightened, making it hard for him to breathe. Christ, didn't she realize her hand was on his shoulder and her breasts were inches from his mouth? If he turned his head, he could bury his face between them.

No. Not going there.

"Seven stab wounds in his chest and a queen of diamonds card in his hand." Ashley's voice broke him out of his lusty haze.

Dalton changed screens and continued to read. "The soccer team was in Minneapolis for the state playoff games. Everyone interviewed, including the assistant coach, Donnie Purcel, said Brogan was a devoted family man with a wife and two kids. Purcel stated the coach occasionally disappeared after an away game. Smelled of alcohol the next morning."

Ashley leaned over his shoulder again. "Maybe Mrs. Brogan was sick of her husband's loose zipper and had him killed." She shook her head. "Sorry. Bad joke."

Dalton turned his head at the venom in her tone so he could see her eyes, and caught a flash of pain before she stepped back. Anger swelled in his chest at the bastard who'd hurt her. "You've dealt with infidelity in the past, haven't you?"

She rolled her shoulders. "Let's move on."

She'd completely shut him out. Dalton could've told her he knew all about infidelity, too, but now wasn't the time.

He continued to read out loud. "The second kill with the same pattern is Wayne Arber, a single forty-year-old motorcycle mechanic from Cabena, a suburb of Fresno, California." He paused. "We need to reinterview the victim's families. What did these men have in common that warranted their death?"

"Whatever it is, it must be horrendous." Her eyebrows pulled into a frown. "If I remember correctly, you're from California."

"I am. My dad still lives there."

"How long since you've seen him?"

He arched an eyebrow. "Too long. We need travel arranged."

She returned to her seat and picked up her cell. "I'll take care of it."

"Remember, I'm six-three and prefer first class, but before you do that, you need to make that flash drive for me."

Kay stuck her head inside the conference room, ending their discussion. "Are you expecting somebody from the ATF?"

"Already?" Dalton glanced at his watch. "Sorry, I should have told you he was coming."

She waved him off with a flick of her hand. "Clayton Wright is at the front gate and isn't happy about being made to wait while he's cleared."

Dalton heard a low groan from behind him. "Stall him for ten minutes."

"Done." Kay turned and headed back to the front office.

Ashley's face had flushed a bright red. Hate beamed from her eyes like hot lava spewing from a volcano.

"You two have a history?"

"Son of a bitch probably heard I was on this case and volunteered." Her hands clenched and unclenched.

Dalton put his hands on her arms, feeling her tense under his touch.

"If you can't deal with him, copy the flash drive and stay out of sight until he's gone. I'll take care of it."

She tilted her head back and glared up at him. "I might just do that."

"You afraid of this asshole?"

"No," she said through gritted teeth.

"Then stand tall and face him." Dalton put his hands on her waist, lifted her off the floor to eye level, and crushed his lips against hers. Her hands gripped his shoulders. Angry passion poured from her as their tongues battled for dominance.

He put her down and glanced at the text on his vibrating cell. "You have about five minutes to decide."

"Like I'm supposed to walk after that," she said, chuckling as she hurried to complete her task.

Dalton pushed the memory of the kiss from his mind and walked up front. He met Kay in the hall, with a man right behind her.

"Mr. Wright, this is Dalton Murphy." Kay beamed up at him. "Dalton is one of our best agents. He's working on a case with FBI Special Agent Ashley Hunter."

"You're consulting for the feds?" Wright asked with a scowl, ignoring Kay, who turned and walked away.

The hair on the back of Dalton's neck rose. Disrespecting Kay put Wright immediately in the asshole column.

He turned and let the man follow him down the hall. Ashley stood in the doorway to the conference room. Damn, he was proud of her for not hiding from this arrogant jerk.

"Clayton," she said, turning and walking back to her chair.

"No introductions are needed, so let's get to it." Dalton was sure Ashley was right. Wright had come because of her.

"Let's." Wright walked to stand by her side. "Ashley and I are old friends, aren't we?"

"I would call us acquaintances." Her tone was cold and professional.

Dalton waved at a spot across the table from her. "Have a seat." Then he took the chair next to Ashley.

"You have information for me." It wasn't a question, sounding more like Wright thought he was too busy to waste his time on them.

"We do." Dalton shoved the flash drive across the table. "In the course of our current investigation, we ran across intel that homemade weapons are being manufactured and certain people are interested in buying in volume. You have everything we know about it in front of you."

Wright picked up the drive as if it were alien. "The instructions were removed from the web almost as quickly as they were leaked."

"Apparently, not fast enough. We figured you'd want this right away." Dalton could feel the tension in the air.

"Of course." Wright leaned back in his chair. "Exactly what investigation are you two working on?"

This prick's superior attitude, combined with the smirks he threw in Ashley's direction, grated on Dalton's nerves. His hands itched to take a crack at the jerk's nose. "The Queen of Diamonds murders."

Wright directed his gaze at Ashley and winked. "Looks like you caught a big one."

She placed her hand on Dalton's bicep and squeezed. "Yeah. I did." She smiled at him before turning back to Wright. "Oh," she laughed, "you meant the case."

Dalton almost choked holding back his laugh. "We don't have anything else for you," he said, thinking Wright would take the hint and leave.

"How did you become privy to this information? It takes a certain ability to ferret out this intel."

"I'm afraid I can't say," Ashley replied, speaking in cold, flat tones.

"Come on, even you know that's interfering with an investigation."

Dalton bit back a growl. He didn't give two fucks what Wright thought about him, but Ashley deserved to be treated with respect.

He leaned heavily on his next few words. "In the few minutes you've been here, you've managed to disrespect two women. You can either take what we have given you or not. It makes no difference to us."

Dalton pinned him with a stare and rested his arm on the back of Ashley's chair. Wright had a decision to make. He could either back down or walk out of there with nothing.

"Sorry, it's been a rough morning at work." Wright blew out a breath. "I shouldn't have brought my problems here with me."

"The usernames and contacts are on the drive," Ashley said, turning to face him. "Dalton, do you have anything to add?" She'd held her head up high, showing him yet another side of herself.

"Not a thing." Dalton stood. "Wright, I'll walk you out."

Wright tucked the flash drive into his shirt pocket and then pushed his chair back. "I appreciate this." He rose, keeping his gaze on Ashley. "May I have a minute?"

"No. There's nothing we need to talk about." Her expression showed no interest, anger, or regret.

Wright's jaw muscles twitched. "Suit yourself." He stopped in the doorway and looked back.

"Goodbye, Clayton." The cold tone of her voice dropped the degrees in the room a few points.

Dalton ushered their guest out the front door. Kay was smiling at him when he turned around. The gleam in her eyes piqued his curiosity. He walked to her desk and propped a hip on the corner. "Ashley and I are going to interview the victim's families. I'll keep in touch."

"Fieldwork?" Kay waggled her eyebrows up and down.

He tried not to react but couldn't hide his smile. "What? You're about to burst. Say it."

"I like Ashley." Kay's grin spread across her face. "And so do *you*."

"You're right. I like her professionally."

"And more." Her hands went up in a "whatever" move. "I'm just saying."

Dalton leaned down close to her ear. "Put your bridal magazines away."

"Good luck, and be careful."

"Yes, Mom," he said over his shoulder.

"Want me to handle reservations?" she called out to him.

"No thanks. We got this."

Ashley wasn't in the conference room when he returned, but she'd left her personal information for the trip. He booked their airline tickets, car, and hotels. Finished, he texted the information to Kay and Ashley.

He kept extra clothes at the compound, but Ashley lived in San Antonio, so she'd have to decide how to handle the situation. He stood to go pack, stopping when she entered the conference room.

The tan slacks and white blouse she wore looked like she'd just picked them up at the dry cleaners.

"You look fresh and crisp."

"This is my extra change of clothes. I saw a mall on the drive here. I can pick up a few things there."

"We have plenty of time. I'll throw together a bag and meet you in Nate's office when you're ready."

Dalton made his way up front after he'd put his suitcase together. Keeping extra clothes at the compound had paid off more than once. He stopped by Nate's office to bring him up to speed. He could hear Ashley's voice up front talking to Kay.

"Ashley and I are headed out. We're going to interview the families of the first two murder victims. I'll keep Kay updated, so you'll know what I'm up to."

Nate nodded. "You want Tank or Reed to go with you?"

"I don't see a need yet. One or both would be assets in the Houston office. I also like what I've seen of Zander."

Nate lifted an eyebrow. "Already thinking ahead. I like that."

"Absolutely."

"You ever work with a female partner?"

"A couple of times, but on minor cases. Ashley's input on this case should be helpful considering we're looking for a seriously angry woman."

"Ashley is also a beautiful woman." Nate leaned back in his chair, a shit-eating grin on his face.

"She is that."

"You know federal agents carry handcuffs?"

Dalton laughed. "I do."

"Maybe she'll let you handcuff her."

Chapter 9

Ashley fastened her seat belt while Dalton programmed in the address for their first stop. He drove away from the Saint Paul International Airport in an SUV large enough to hold ten people, and she had to tease him about his selection. "You own a pickup and rented a Nissan Rogue. If I was a psychologist, I might try to analyze your need to drive large vehicles."

He huffed out what might have been a laugh and glanced at her. "If you're insinuating I'm compensating for the size of my dick by driving large automobiles, full disclosure, I also own a Harley Davidson Fat Boy."

"Wow. That's a big one." Crap, that was the last thing she should have said.

"So I've been told. If you're a good girl, I'll give you a ride someday." Even though he faced away from her, his grin was broad enough for her to see he was enjoying torturing her.

"I walked right into that."

"Not yet."

"Stop it." She laughed hard while trying not to blush at his comment. "You have to admit this SUV could hold ten people."

"Seven, if you want to be accurate. But enough about me. Tell me everything we know about the first victim and what you read between the lines."

"Yes, sir." She retrieved her laptop and turned it on. "We know Brogan was a fifty-two-year-old coach for the boys' soccer team. He was also married with two kids. Both are under fourteen years old. He and the team were on a road trip when he was found in his motel room stabbed and mutilated. The playing card was in his hand. That's nothing more than we already know."

"Never hurts to hear the details again. Tell me your thoughts."

"I think it would be pretty damn stupid to bring a woman to his motel room with an entire soccer team nearby."

"He took advantage of being away from his wife. What else?"

"We should dig deeper into his financials. Bank and credit card records to see where he spent his money. The earlier interviews didn't indicate he'd had a lot of unexplained expenditures."

"And?"

"I think he fooled around at the expense of the school system."

"Good." He glanced at her and smiled. "You take care of that information. Iain stays busy with the agents working for Lost and Found, and he's already looking into Vardon for us. We won't use him unless it's necessary."

"I'll put in a request for his financials to our tech guys." She texted her ask along with a follow-up that she'd send her notes from the interview with the two victims when they were complete. "Done."

"How'd you get mixed up with Wright?"

Ashley turned in her seat. "That's an abrupt change in topics."

"I'm aware."

"You're going to give me a case of whiplash. We both worked a money laundering case at one of the smaller casinos in Las Vegas." She was quiet for a minute while she decided whether she truly wanted to tell Dalton everything. "I went in as a waitress and Clayton came on a couple of months later as a bartender."

"You were still a rookie!"

"I was. What was supposed to be a few months turned into fourteen. I was a nervous wreck until my handler told me Clayton was coming and I could trust him. It was my first case, and having him around made me feel safer. One thing led to another, and we became a couple."

"Whoever sent you into a situation like that for your first time was an idiot." Dalton lifted his foot off the gas pedal and the SUV slowed. "They sent a green kid into a fucking casino full of criminals? You could've been killed."

"They saw something in me. They believed I could get the job done, and I did. We uncovered the cartel who'd forced the owner into that situation."

"So, you and Wright were together when the assignment ended."

"For a few months. Then I learned he'd been sleeping with any woman within a ten-mile radius of the office who'd spread her legs for him. I ended our relationship. It wasn't long before he transferred to the ATF."

"He's still interested in you."

"His pride was injured. He said I was too stupid to know a good thing when it was standing right in front of me." She held up her index finger to stop any comments. "His words, not mine."

They rode without speaking for a while. She fidgeted with the radio dial, trying to find a music station, but finally gave up.

Dalton broke the silence. "You volunteered for the assignment to prove yourself."

She studied his profile. "That op was my chance to prove I'm smart, capable, and competent. It earned me more important cases, but in the world of finance."

He glanced in her direction. "You're capable of doing anything you set your mind to."

His praise put a smile on her face. "Thank you."

"Just calling it like I see it. You hungry?"

Her stomach growled. Her hand went to her abdomen as if to calm it, and she laughed off her embarrassment. A truck stop was up ahead with a café attached to it. "I must be."

"You up to giving this one a try?"

"Sure." She was ready to change the subject, and food would do that.

****

Ashley swiped the napkin across her mouth, surprised she'd eaten most of her BLT and fries. She leaned back and watched Dalton while he finished his meatloaf, mashed potatoes, and green beans. He'd eaten every bite, plus a couple of biscuits with butter. Then he moved his plate to the side and set hers on top of his.

His eyebrows pulled together. "You eat like a bird."

"Sorry, Dad. You have to admit you're bigger than I am and need more calories to keep you going."

"Dad?" he said with a sinister smile. "I'm betting your father didn't spank you when you were a kid."

"My father was too busy to punish me. Too busy being important. Too busy to give a damn about a daughter." The words came out fast and harsh, and she regretted saying anything. "Sorry. I've already said enough about my family."

Dalton didn't respond. He picked up the check and carried it to the counter to pay while she walked outside. She tilted her head back and let the breeze caress her cheeks. A few minutes later, he walked around and opened the door for her.

"Thanks." She mentally kicked herself for the comment about her dad. She'd started to sound like the bitchiest person on the planet.

Dalton rounded the SUV, got in, and buckled his seat belt. When they were back on the highway, he still hadn't commented on her outburst.

"Why don't you call ahead and let the Brogan family know when to expect us? Then call the principal's office and alert him we're coming, too. I don't want to skip anyone who dealt with the coach."

After she'd done as he asked, she decided to apologize. "I'm sorry I come across as bitter. My dad gave me and Ash a good life. Neither of us wanted for anything."

"You wanted intangible things. I'm glad you had Ash."

"Yeah. He's always been my hero." Memories of Ash showing up at school activities, practicing volleyball with her when she knew he didn't care for the sport, and teaching her to drive all flashed through her mind. "He's a great brother. Nobody messed with his little sister. None of his buddies would dare date me. Not with Ash watching every move they made. He stood sentry over me right up to the day he left for college. I worried that closeness wouldn't be there after he returned."

She paused, remembering the night the two of them went to dinner for the first time in years. "But it was like he'd never been away. We just fell back into the routine of big brother and little sister."

"I understand he's been invited more than once to join the Lost and Found team. We're opening an office in the Houston area. I just bought in as a partner, and the new compound will be mine to run. I'll probably talk to Ash. See if he's interested."

"That's incredible. How are you so calm? I would be pinging off the walls."

"It's just on paper for now. There's too much to be done before I celebrate."

"Wow. Just wow. I'll bet you're calm in a crisis."

"How does Ash feel about you being a fed?"

"I think he's proud of me." She turned in her seat to face Dalton. "Your interrogation skills must come in handy."

He met her gaze with a mock confused expression. "I have no idea what you mean."

"Bull. With just a few questions, you know more about me than most people do. Tell me about your family." He'd made it plain that he didn't talk about himself the first time they'd met. She hoped now that she'd been so honest and forthcoming with him, he might open up with her.

He didn't respond. Instead, he took an exit and drove into a residential area. It was a nice neighborhood. The houses weren't brand new, but they were well kept with beautifully cared for lawns. He turned right at the next street, entering a dead-end street.

"The last house on the left," she said, reaching for the small case that held her laptop and a few personal items.

She pulled down the visor and looked in the mirror, smoothing a few loose strands of hair with her hands. She usually wore a little makeup, but what she'd put on this morning was long gone. She sighed, grabbed some lip gloss out of her case, and swiped it across her lips. Nothing to do about it now.

"You look beautiful." Dalton's words not only surprised her, they sent a sizzle of heat to her lower stomach.

She fought the heat rising in her neck. "I do not."

His eyes narrowed. "If I say you look beautiful, you do." She opened her mouth, but he cut her off. "Don't argue with me."

She didn't get the chance to challenge him because he parked in the driveway of an older ranch-style home. The yard was mowed, and a basketball hoop hung from the top of the garage. He got out and walked around to her side. Then he pulled open the door and stepped back.

They weren't dressed like they were on official business. He wore black jeans and a tan pullover. Ashley had to admit the casual approach might make the victim's family more comfortable. She was glad she'd bought a couple of pairs of jeans and some colorful blouses at the department store they'd stopped at on their way to the airport.

Mrs. Lauren Brogan opened the door before Dalton could knock. She ushered them inside a homey living room with a brown leather couch and chair slanted toward a massive television screen. She held a small black poodle in her arms that was barking with a fierceness belying its size.

Dalton let Ashley make the introductions and identify herself as a federal agent.

Mrs. Brogan waved her hand indicating they should sit on the sofa. "Please have a seat."

The dog wiggled free, ran across the carpet, and jumped up on Dalton's legs. He reached down, scooped him up, and the little rascal settled down in his lap.

"Zeus is a man's dog for sure. He's just recently stopped grieving that Charles hasn't come home."

Ashley slid to the edge of the couch. "I'm sure you're tired of answering questions, but we need as much information as we can gather. Will you tell us about your husband?"

"He wasn't the man I thought he was, but he didn't deserve to be mutilated. Our children don't want to go to school. There's nothing left to do except move. But where to?" She grabbed a tissue and blotted her eyes. "I heard on the news it's happened again."

"That's correct. That's why Dalton and I were recently added to the case." Ashley emphasized the woman's husband hadn't been forgotten. Then she leaned toward her. "We're sorry for your loss, and I promise we won't get into the details of his death. It would just be helpful if you could tell us a little more about your husband."

Mrs. Brogan blew her nose and reached for another tissue. Ashley noticed the underlying anger in the woman's eyes.

"I've already told the police everything I can think of. What do you want to know?"

"No one knew him more intimately than you." Dalton's tone was soothing and warm. "What about your husband's likes and dislikes? Was he happy with his coaching position? Did he travel other than for work? Nothing is too trivial. Whatever pops into your head, we'd like to hear it."

"Do you mind if I record our conversation?" Ashley asked. "It helps us to not miss the smallest detail."

"Not at all." The widow pulled another tissue from the box and started pulling it apart.

For the next hour, Ashley and Dalton listened to the story of a happy couple and their family. Ashley sensed there was more, but Mrs. Brogan didn't seem to want to share.

"Were you and Mr. Brogan having problems?" Ashley asked.

"Not as far as I knew." She bit the words out as if they were bitter. "But apparently, I didn't know him at all. Not if he had another woman in his room."

"I apologize for this line of questioning, but it's important. I'm sure it's painful to talk about him."

The widow dropped the shredded tissue onto the table.

"This is a small town, and rumors have been flying that Charles was unfaithful. I never picked up any signals that he was sleeping around. Maybe you should speak with his assistant coach. He spent more time with my husband than I did. Between practice, home, and away games, if anyone knew him, it's Donnie Purcel."

She stood and retrieved a scratch pad from a drawer in the end table, quickly writing something down. Taking her seat back on the couch, she handed it to Ashley.

"That's his telephone number. This time of day he's probably at practice."

Dalton and Ashley both stood. "We can't thank you enough."

"I hope you find the bastard." Mrs. Brogan stood. "If you'll excuse me, I have to pick up my kids."

Chapter 10

"There's nothing like being dismissed." Dalton plugged in the address to the school, read the directions, and drove back onto the highway. "Mrs. Brogan has a lot of healing to do."

Ashley slid her computer onto her lap. "I didn't intend to upset her."

"You have nothing to apologize for. Your interview skills are excellent."

"I noticed you didn't say much."

"There wasn't any need. You gained her confidence a lot faster than I would have."

"Thank you."

He glanced at her in time to see a smile spread across her face. She had no idea the effect she had on him. He had to keep reminding himself she was off-limits. But thoughts of showing her how amazing she was kept running through his mind. He shifted in his seat. Getting hard just thinking about having sex with her wasn't a good idea. "You were sensitive to her."

"I understand why she's bitter. She thinks that assistant coach knows more."

"She's probably right. I'll bet he does."

Ashley pulled out her cell. A minute later, she started to read aloud. "Roosevelt High's soccer team is rated one of the highest in the state."

He listened closely while he drove into the school parking lot. Dalton liked the sound of her voice. It warmed his blood.

When he parked, she lifted her head. "Wow. This is a big campus for a town this size."

"It looks fairly new." He got out, and before he reached the front of the SUV, she was on the ground walking to meet him. He lifted an eyebrow.

She looked up at him and batted her eyes. "See? I'm a big girl."

"I open your door out of respect, not because I think you're incapable of doing it yourself."

Her grin vanished. "It was a joke. I was teasing you. Get it?"

"Got it." Feeling like a complete ass, he waved his hand toward the school entrance. "After you."

****

After thirty minutes of talking with the principal and hearing how badly the coach's murder had damaged the school's reputation, a young woman escorted them to the field house, where the assistant had taken over the team. The girl chatted nonstop the entire way, regaling Dalton and Ashley about all the high points of the school and why their son or daughter would love it there. Neither of them corrected her when she escorted them through the gym to an office with a half-glass door.

"Thank you." Dalton finally stopped the girl from talking. "We'll take it from here."

The man inside the office stood and walked to meet them. "Donnie Purcel." He shook Dalton's and Ashley's hands before waving them inside. "Please, come in and take a seat."

Purcel was tall, muscular, and much younger than the coach had been. His dark hair was cut short, and judging from the tight jersey he wore, he spent time in the weight room working on his upper body.

Dalton wasn't impressed that his gaze was glued to Ashley.

"The school is still reeling from Coach's death. The team's second place win at the state tournament has been all but ignored after the murder and the news he'd been cut up."

"He was well-liked?" Dalton asked, drawing Purcel's attention away from Ashley.

"The team loved him. They've taken his death pretty hard."

"You two got along?" Ashley asked.

"Absolutely. We were good friends. I learned a lot from him." Purcel shifted in his chair. "I've already shared everything I can think of with the other investigators."

Dalton spotted the twitch that had just appeared in Purcel's right eye. The son of a bitch was holding out on them. "You do know lying to a federal officer could lead to criminal penalties, right?" He continued, not waiting for a response. "We can't compel you to answer truthfully, but you could face serious repercussions."

"I didn't lie to anyone."

"If you withheld information that's important to this case, you could be in trouble." Ashley's tone was cold and harsh. "You worked with the coach every day. Traveled with him. You probably knew him better than his wife."

Dalton felt an inappropriate sizzle of heat rush through his veins. Damn it. They were at work. He shouldn't find this side of her hot as hell.

Purcell's head dropped into his hand for a long second, then he exhaled and leaned back in his chair. "Look, I know for a fact it would destroy Lauren to learn Coach screwed around every chance he got. At home, he was a model husband, but when we traveled, something happened to him. Whether the team won or lost, after the boys were tucked in for the night, Coach trolled the bars until he found a willing woman. They were just one-night stands and meant nothing to him. Please, you have to keep this from his family."

Dalton leaned forward and rested his hands on his knees. "I see no reason to talk with Mrs. Brogan again, but I can't promise anything. Tell us what you know about Coach's escapades. When did you realize what he was doing?"

"I've only been here at the school a couple of years, so I don't know when it started. It was my first year here, and on the third away game, I had to roust him out of bed. He smelled of alcohol. I finally asked him if he was having an affair with someone who followed the team. You know, maybe one of the single soccer moms." Purcel grabbed a water bottle that was on his desk and took a long drink. "He acted as if I'd offended him. He said it was exciting going to a local bar and picking up a new woman. Said those women liked it rough, and he gave it to them in spades."

Ashley leaned forward. "You're sure it was a different woman every time?"

"It was until the last time. He mentioned he'd met a woman who didn't put out, but he was going to see her again." His eyes widened. "Do you think it was her?"

Dalton could feel Ashley's eyes on him. "We don't speculate. Go on."

"I guess he got comfortable with me waking him up after a night on the town. More than once, the woman was still in his room. I tried to talk some sense into him, but he didn't listen. As long as it didn't affect his family, he didn't see how it was wrong."

Dalton and Ashley stood. "If you think of anything else, give us a call."

"Am I in trouble?" Purcel asked.

Ashley paused at the door. Looking over her shoulder, she shook her head. "No. You got lucky this time."

****

Dalton started the rental and drove away from the school. Ashley had handled herself like a pro even though Purcel had had a hard time keeping his gaze above her chest. Dalton had gritted his teeth and kept his mouth shut for only one reason. Her. He had no doubt she'd be busting his chops if he'd intervened on her behalf.

He jerked his foot off the gas when her hand fell on his knee. He glanced at her only to see her look away.

"Where were you? I asked a question, and you didn't hear me."

Should he tell her? Tell her he wanted to gouge out Purcel's eyeballs for looking at her like he wanted to strip her naked and take those tight nipples into his mouth? Tell her he'd noticed them too? More than once? Her breasts were perfect. Her plain blouse did nothing to hide the fact they were full and round. Just the right size to fit into his hands.

"You know he just gave us missing information. The women liked it rough, and this last woman didn't have sex with him the first time. If he'd tried to abuse her, why meet him again?"

"Good question." Dalton couldn't help but grin at Ashley's excitement. "We wanted to know what pissed her off enough to kill a guy. The lady didn't like it rough."

"You're way too calm."

"I'll get excited when she's in cuffs. Our flight isn't until tomorrow afternoon, and we can bump it back a day if we find something interesting at the crime scene motel."

Her fingers flew over the navigation screen, and in seconds, instructions for the Winfred Motel appeared. She was silent for a few miles and Dalton glanced at her to find her eyes closed. He wished he had the luxury of watching her sleep, but they'd both wind up in the ditch. With her head leaning against the glass, and the sunlight on her face, she was stunning.

He couldn't help glancing at her every few minutes. Her peaches-and-cream skin and natural pink lips seemed to beg for his touch. He couldn't remember the last time a woman had stirred more than fleeting lust in him. Something about Ashley pulled at him. Intrigued him. Made him want to peel back all the layers and find the sensuous woman she kept hidden under the drab clothes she wore. He ran his fingers through his hair. Wherever these thoughts were coming from, he needed to bury them. Deep.

"You're staring at me again." Her words were heavy and drowsy-sounding.

"You're mistaken. I can't stare at you and drive at the same time."

She chuckled. "When are you going to admit you're attracted to me?"

"You couldn't tell when I kissed you? Wasn't that admission enough?"

Jesus, she was going to be the death of him.

She sat up straighter. "That was quickly followed by a threat to have sex with me and then promptly forget about me."

"That's the way it is with me. No holds barred, and no lingering emotions."

She pulled her seat belt slack and twisted to face him. "Hmm. Why?"

"What? Don't try to psychoanalyze me."

"You truly believe that you can go through life having sex without ever getting emotionally involved? Sooner or later, you're going to tangle with a woman who makes you care."

"Not likely. It's hereditary. Members of my family fail miserably at long-term relationships, and I've seen it happen to friends too many times."

"Nate and Kay seem happy."

"That's a rare example."

"So, you've never been in love?"

He glanced at her. Her eyes were wide and full of curiosity. Normally, he'd be pissed at her for getting so personal, but she'd been open and honest about her past. To his surprise, it didn't irritate him that she wanted to know more about him.

He took a deep breath and decided he might as well get this over with. "I thought I was. I was on an assignment when I received the text informing me that my love for the FBI was greater than my affection for her. She wrapped her engagement ring in tissue paper and mailed it to me."

"What a bitch."

"I learn later that she'd been sleeping with an old buddy of mine for a year before she called it quits."

"That stinks."

He shrugged. "My mother divorced my dad and me when I was a kid. She quickly remarried, and they moved to Seattle."

"Did she stay in touch with you?"

"Some. She'd given dad full custody, but I visited a few times during the summer. After a couple of years, she had a new family and finally stopped inviting me."

"I'm sorry." Ashley reached across and squeezed his shoulder. "So, we have something in common besides the FBI. We both grew up without a mother."

"True. But mine chose to leave me." Dalton gritted his teeth at his cruel words. "Sorry. That was harsh."

"Same loss. Different reasons."

"You're relentless."

"So I've been told. I hope your dad was more interested in you than mine was in me."

"It was just the two of us, and he was a hands-on father." Dalton chuckled. "He still is."

"You're still close."

"Damn right." He drove through the streets of the small town to the motel. "Have you finished your inquisition?"

"I'm sorry. I just wanted to know you better."

"We've had that conversation."

"I wouldn't call that a conversation." She twisted around again, facing forward. Then she pulled her case onto her lap, opened it, and removed a picture of Brogan. "Maybe we'll learn more about the coach."

"He liked rough sex. I think he finally picked one who didn't."

Chapter 11

Angel looked around for any clues she might be leaving behind. Seeing none, she slid her Maxim 9mm into her purse and walked to the door.

George had disappointed her. He'd become greedy and demanding. She'd picked him up because she'd thought he might come in handy if she needed to get a weapon transported. He was just seedy enough not to ask too many questions. Her purpose tonight had been to end the friendship.

Dying had been his fault. Pushing her up against the door and grabbing her between the legs had sealed his fate. No man touched her. Not intimately. Not if he wanted to live.

He shouldn't have demanded goodbye sex. It earned him a bullet in the heart.

She sighed and dropped the queen of diamonds card, which landed on his chest. Her new fans needed to know she'd been here.

They would come, and she'd be here to watch him in action.

Satisfied, Angel quietly left George Dawl's apartment without so much as a look back.

****

Ashley glanced up at the bright green neon sign in front of the locally owned and operated Winfred Motel. With white siding and gray trim, the building and the grounds appeared to be well taken care of. The parking lot was clean and half full. From the number of pickups and the heavy equipment secured to the trailers they pulled, she guessed a road crew was staying.

Dalton pulled open the door for her to enter. "This shouldn't take long."

The interviews with the widow and assistant coach had taken longer than she'd expected. She was disappointed they hadn't learned anything helpful, and hoped this stop would be more productive.

"Welcome." The light in the older woman's eyes and the smile on her face looked sincere as she stood behind a counter.

"Thank you." Ashley flashed her ID while introducing Dalton and herself.

"I'm Carrie Wisdom. How can I help you?"

Ashley returned the woman's smile. "If I had to guess, I'd say you were here most of the time. Am I right?"

"You are. Jeff and I own this place. One or both of us are here most times." A slight frown pulled her eyebrows together. "How can I help you?"

"No doubt you don't want to rehash the Brogan murder, but we have a few more questions."

"It's a sad thing that a crime like that would bring us more business. I think some people who stayed here were just looky-loos." Mrs. Wisdom glanced over her shoulder at the open door behind her. "Jeff," she said in a commanding tone. "Get in here."

Dalton's eyebrows lifted, and Ashley did her best to ignore his look of surprise. Mrs. Wisdom had left no doubt who the boss was in the family.

"Yes, dear?" A chubby man with white hair and rosy cheeks appeared in the doorway. All he needed was a beard and he'd look like Santa.

"The FBI has more questions about Coach Brogan."

His lips narrowed and he frowned at Dalton. "We've already told the police everything we know. They cleared the room for use, and it's been completely redone."

Dalton waved him off. "We don't need to see the room. However, people occasionally remember things later."

Mr. Wisdom glanced at his wife and then motioned for Dalton and Ashley to follow him. "You better join me in the office."

He led them around the counter and into a small but cozy area. Once they were seated, Dalton started the conversation.

"Are you reluctant to discuss Mr. Brogan in front of your wife?"

Mr. Wisdom cleared his throat. "She just doesn't want to hear about it anymore."

"I understand," Dalton said. "How well did you know Mr. Brogan?"

"The coach and team have been staying with us for a few years. The boys are always well mannered, and we enjoy having them." Then he fell silent, staring at his hands as if they might help him know what to say next.

"We're trying to stop this woman from killing again," Ashley said.

"Every town has its seedy side, and we're no exception. A couple of years ago, Coach discovered the Back Forty. It's a bar that attracts a rough crowd.

It became his routine that after the boys were in their rooms for the night, he'd disappear. A couple of times, I saw him bring a woman back to his room. My wife says if I'd put a stop to it, the coach might still be alive."

Dalton shook his head. "You're not responsible for the coach's death. We'll need the location of the bar."

Mr. Wisdom nodded. He turned to his computer, looked up the address, and then wrote it on a piece of paper. He stood and handed it to Dalton. "If they give you any trouble, tell them Jeff sent you."

Ashley and Dalton thanked the couple for their help and then walked outside. She waited until they were in the car before she spoke. "We're going to the bar, right?"

"You bet." Dalton turned toward her in his seat and smiled. His dark eyes sparkled. She hated when he did that. It made thinking of him in a strictly business way very difficult. He had this particular expression that sent bolts of heat rolling south every time he did it. She closed her eyes and looked away, trying to push her thoughts away from him and back onto the case.

She took the address from him and entered it for directions. "We need to go. We'll be late getting to our motel as it is."

He straightened in his seat, buckled up, and started the car. He drove out of the parking lot and wove his way through the small but quaint town. A lot of old buildings had been restored. The homes looked freshly painted and had large front porches and manicured lawns. A few minutes later, their surroundings changed. Gone were the picturesque houses and businesses. What they saw now were rundown homes, dirt lawns, and a road that hadn't been maintained in years.

Dalton turned onto a gravel parking lot. "Damn, this side of town seems to have been forgotten. It's too bad."

The only indication they were at the right place was a small sign over the door. Two cars and three motorcycles were parked close to what looked like a house that had been converted into a bar.

Ashley unhooked her seat belt. "You're right about that."

"Sucks." Dalton parked and turned to her. "Ready?"

"As I'll ever be," she replied, chuckling. Then she pulled her blazer from the back seat and slid it on to cover the pistol on her hip.

"Stay close," he said.

She opened the door and stepped inside the darkness.

His arm slid around her waist. "Give it a second, and your eyes will adjust."

She caught herself leaning into him. Her body remembered how solid he was when he'd pulled her against him and kissed the hell out of her. She could recall his lips on hers as if it had just happened minutes ago. She took a deep breath. The smell of stale cigarettes and beer jerked her back to reality.

A barely discernible figure waved a hand from behind the bar.

"Just walk toward the sound of my voice."

"Will do."

Dalton snugged Ashley closer.

Her eyes adjusted quickly, and by the time they'd reached the counter, her vision was fine. She slid onto a stool, and Dalton stood next to her.

A fortysomething woman walked to their end of the bar. "What can I get you to drink?" Her red hair was shot with streaks of silver. Her black pullover revealed a little cleavage, but not too much.

"I'll have whatever's on tap," Dalton said.

"Make that two." Ashley smiled at the bartender, nodded at a man sitting on a stool a few feet away, and then glanced around the room.

The Back Forty was small inside. Three tables were pushed against the wall, with four chairs at each one. A light hung over a pool table, and two men were playing while a third man watched. All of them wore black leather cuts. Was a motorcycle club based nearby, or were they just passing through?

Dalton smiled at the bartender, and her face lit up as if she'd just won the lottery. He pulled a bill from his wallet and dropped twenty bucks on the bar.

Ashley took a long drink from the glass of beer in front of her. It was cold and slightly bitter, but felt good going down.

"I'm Nell. I own this place. You have questions written all over that handsome face of yours. Let's have 'em."

"We're looking into the death of a man named Charles Brogan. I understand he came for a beer occasionally."

"You talking about Coach?"

The man sitting at the bar stood and sauntered over to Ashley. He leaned on the bar and watched Dalton.

"Yes, ma'am." Dalton's back seemed to stiffen.

"Dan?" The woman's gaze was on the man who was now paying close attention to the conversation.

The stranger's gaze drifted to Ashley. "Coach was a friend. I'm interested in what you people know about his murder."

Ashley decided to be honest with Dan. "Very little. That's why we're here asking for help. Was he here the night he died? Was he alone? Jeff said we might find some answers if we came here. His wife would like to know why her husband was killed."

Dan's jaw dropped. "Coach was married?"

"Married with kids," Dalton said, his hand resting on her back.

Was he expecting trouble?

"Exactly why I never married again," Nell scoffed. "None of you sons of bitches can be trusted."

"You guys hear that? Coach had a family," Dan said loud enough that the men at the pool table turned in his direction.

One of the men hit the black pool ball and watched as it rolled across the green felt and into a corner pocket. "He was always on the hunt for a willing woman. After a few beers, he would've fucked Nell here if she'd let him."

"As if." Nell rolled her eyes. "The last time he was here he left with some woman, as usual."

"Yeah." Dan nodded. "Coach was expecting her. Said they'd met in an airport bar."

Ashley couldn't hold in her excitement. "Can you describe her?"

Dalton cleared his throat, pulling her attention to him. He smiled and took a drink of his beer. She did the same, hoping her rapid breathing slowed.

"They sat over there." Nell pointed at one of the tables. I never saw her before or again." Then she turned to the men at the pool table. "Boys, come here."

Both men put down their pool sticks and walked to the end of the bar. The older of the two scrubbed his hand over his gray beard and nodded at Dalton. The younger guy crowded between her and Dan.

Ashley whirled, twisted the guy's arm behind his back, and shoved his head down on the bar. He tried to push her away, so she rammed his arm farther up his back.

"Get off me," he grunted.

"So you can grab my ass again? I don't think so."

"It was an accident!" the idiot yelled.

"Try that again, and I'll break your arm." Ashley released her hold and stepped back. "Get away from me."

She glanced at Dalton. His eyes were cold as ice, but a slight smile tugged at his lips. He didn't look surprised she'd had a problem and taken care of it herself.

"Get over by your dad," Nell said with a wave of her hand.

The guy glared at Ashley but gave her a wide berth as he did as instructed.

The older pool player took a long pull of his beer. "From what I saw, she was a looker. Long silver-blonde hair and legs for miles. Medium height. Maybe five six. She didn't acknowledge or talk to anybody except Coach. They left soon after she got here."

"Anybody get her name?" Ashley asked again.

"Not me," Dan answered, looking at the two pool players. Both men shook their heads and remained silent. They were pissed she'd gotten the best of one of them.

Ashley's blood raced through her system. Excited that they'd uncovered previously unknown information, her body was alive with energy. She wanted to jump up and down.

"You have any more questions?" Dalton asked her.

"No. I think that covers it."

He bought everyone a round of beer before they said thank you and he escorted her out the door.

Ashley stopped in the middle of the parking lot. "I can't believe we just confirmed what we saw on the video. The hair color is the same as the woman we saw going into Vardon's room."

Dalton nodded. "At least we have a description of her."

His calm demeanor made Ashley crazy. Why wasn't he as hyped up as her? "Mexico, Minnesota, and California. She gets around."

"She does."

Ashley rubbed her hands together. "We have a call to make, and I can't wait."

"You have a call to make."

"We'll FaceTime." Her heart raced like a kid in a candy store. Didn't Dalton realize how important this was? Of course he did, but clues and killers were old news to him. "We both should talk to Carl."

"No." He walked closer, caught her chin between his thumb and forefinger, and lifted her head. His dark eyes sparkled under the overhead lights in the parking lot. "Your case. Your call."

His gaze dropped to her lips, then moved back up to her eyes. He released his grip on her chin, slid his hand to the nape of her neck, and pulled her body snugly against his chest. His thumb softly stroked her skin for a minute. She saw the struggle behind his eyes. She could tell he wanted to kiss her but wouldn't.

Damn him.

Well, she would. She cupped his cheeks, lifted up on her toes, and pulled his lips to hers. His body stiffened, making her think she'd made a mistake, but then his hands slid around her back, lifting her higher and pulling her closer. His lips were soft and commanding as he swept his tongue into her mouth, teasing hers and sending erotic images to her brain with each stroke.

His scent drifted through her senses, sending fire racing through her blood. Molten lava wasn't hotter. She melted into him, loving the power his touch had on her.

Then he abruptly pulled away from her. His hands moved to her shoulders. The air instantly cooled between them as he stepped back and looked down at her.

His eyes were full of lust as he slid his knuckles across her cheek. Ashley's heart was pounding so hard he had to know how he affected her. She pulled her wounded pride together.

He turned away, slowly walked to the passenger side of the car, and opened her door.

As soon as they were both settled in their seats, he started the engine and drove to the freeway. So many questions coursed through her. Had he been unaffected by the kiss? Why was he hell-bent on denying the attraction between them?

"Instead of driving on to Minneapolis, let's see if we can find a motel around here and call it a night. I'll take care of canceling our reservations after we check in."

"Fine with me. I am pretty tired." She used her cell to search motels on the way. "There's a brand name with great reviews about thirty miles up the road. Want me to call?"

"Sure. Do you need my credit card?"

"No, thanks. I have a company card."

She called ahead and reserved two rooms.

"You up for some fast food?"

"I'm starving. Anything sounds good."

The stretch of highway was pretty bare, and they stopped to grab a bite at the first place they saw. She had no idea how awkward sitting in the Chicken Shack and eating in silence could be. That kiss had turned into the elephant in the room. The one where both of them knew it was there, but neither would question how it had arrived.

Once they were finished and on the highway again, she leaned the seat back a notch and closed her eyes.

****

A hand on her knee woke her.

"We're here. Let's get checked in so you can get some quality sleep."

Dalton's hand remained on her, burning her skin through her pants. Neither of them moved. His grip tightened, so she opened her eyes and faced him.

He released her and unbuckled his seat belt. "Can we not be so awkward about that kiss? We were standing in the middle of a bar's parking lot, and I felt like we should move on. Given the chance, at least two of those men would've loved to join in."

She rolled her eyes. "Please."

"Dan couldn't keep his eyes on your face. He was too damn interested in checking out your breasts. And the young punk who had the nerve to touch you? I would have happily kicked his ass for you. Although, it *was* hot watching you take him down." Dalton got out, walked around to the trunk, and then grabbed both their bags.

Ashley didn't move. Couldn't. Had he been jealous? He'd probably deny it if she challenged him, but there was no doubt in her mind. Feeling better about what happened in the parking lot, she hopped out and hurried to catch up with him.

They checked in and rode the elevator up to their floor in silence. Assigned rooms next to each other, they paused and said goodnight. Dalton quickly disappeared behind his door.

Once inside the privacy of her own space, she kicked off her shoes, dropped onto the bed, and stretched out. Her nap had her wide awake. So, with no hope of sleep, she got up and went to take a shower. She stood under the warm water, hoping to wash away the tension of the day.

She tried to convince herself the kiss she and Dalton had shared in the parking lot was a simple celebration. A moment of excitement. So why did it feel like so much more?

The feel of his lips, the taste of his tongue, and his strong hand wrapped around her nape holding her to him were embedded in her memory. Her fingers brushed across her lips, hoping to bring back the sensation. Need coursed through her body, consuming her thoughts. Her breasts tightened. The same heat she'd felt earlier boiled in her lower belly.

She shouldn't be so attracted to him. Having sex with him would break the rule she'd held steadfast since Clayton. Hell, she'd learned her lesson the hard way.

These feelings weren't a good thing. So why couldn't she turn them off? She was on a runaway train going full speed ahead around a tight curve, about to derail.

She turned off the water, grabbed a towel, and quickly dried herself. Standing in front of the mirror, she dried her hair and then slipped on a tank top and boy shorts she'd bought in Dallas.

She dug her Kindle out of her suitcase, slipped on a pair of warm socks, and crawled into bed. Nothing in her library interested her. These were her favorite authors, yet all she could think about was that damn kiss.

"Enough," she said out loud. She grabbed her keycard and stormed out the door.

Chapter 12

Dalton checked his texts and messages for the third time. Finding nothing to keep his mind off the woman in the room next to his, he showered, slipped on a pair of warm-ups, and turned on the TV. He scrolled through the ESPN channels, found a baseball game, and kicked back on the couch.

Twenty minutes later, he couldn't have told anyone what inning it was or who was winning. What the hell was wrong with him? Sure, she'd kissed him, but he'd yanked her against him and tried to devour her. Then she'd slid her arms around him and held on as if she never wanted him to turn her loose.

He'd messed around and let her get under his skin. Initially, he'd worried about her getting too attached, and the last thing he wanted was to hurt her. But the more time he'd spent with her had convinced him she wasn't looking for forever.

Ashley was seriously invested in her career, and he respected her for it. He also wanted her in his bed. If she understood this was temporary, why couldn't they enjoy each other's bodies until the case was over?

Fuck it. He was done sporting a painful hard-on when she was in the next room. He swung his bare feet to the floor and headed for the door. She'd face him tonight and decide. If she wanted him, he needed to hear her say it out loud. Right fucking now.

His hand was on the door handle when somebody knocked. Not bothering to look through the peephole, he jerked the door open.

Shock froze him in place for a second. "Ashley."

"Oh." Her hand covered her heart. "You startled me."

"I was about to walk out the door."

Her gaze seemed to be frozen on his bare chest, which made his dick harder than it already was.

"Where were you going?" Her voice was so soft he almost couldn't hear her words.

He reached out, caught her arm, and pulled her inside. He slammed the door closed, pushed her back against it, and then crowded his body into hers. The shock in her eyes at being manhandled went straight to his groin. "Your room."

She recovered quickly as the surprise in her gaze morphed into lust. "Why were you coming to my room?"

"I'm tired of ignoring my attraction to you. I want you, OK? I said it out loud. I want you."

"Thank God."

His lips collided with hers. Hard and possessive, he let his kiss speak loudly and clearly. Their tongues clashed as they tasted each other. Rough. Demanding. He couldn't get enough. He ravaged the inside of her mouth with voracious hunger. Seeking and finding every sensual nook and cranny she hid, and then plundering it until the grip she had on his shoulders tightened. A flash of conscience flitted through his brain. The fear that someday he'd hurt her was pushed to the far recesses of his mind. He'd worry about right now and face the fallout later.

Her hands cupped his cheeks. He turned his head, kissing her palms. "I want to be inside you. I need to hear you call out my name." He slid his hands under her ass and lifted her off her feet. She locked her legs around his waist, pressing into his erection. With a whimper, her body softened against his, and she dropped her head into the crook of his neck. He stood very still, letting this moment sink in. "Before we go any further, tell me you want this, too."

She lifted her head and met his gaze. "I want you. I'll take everything you're willing to give."

Dalton thought about cautioning her not to start planning weddings or think about having babies, but her tongue swept inside his mouth, stopping him cold. The blood in his veins hummed as need blocked out everything but her warm body softly rubbing against his.

In a few long strides, he got to the bed. When his hands gripped her waist, she unlocked her legs and slid down his body.

"Get comfortable." His words were a growl.

She turned her back to him and crawled up the middle of the mattress. The sight of her gorgeous ass gave him all kinds of ideas. He could think of many ways he'd like to please her.

She glanced at him over her shoulder. "Do you want me to undress?"

"No. I'll do that myself." He climbed onto the foot of the bed, caught her hips, and flipped her onto her back. "Arms up."

His fingers grasped the hem of her tank top, pulled it off, and tossed it to the floor. His breath caught in his chest as her bare breasts were revealed. They were perfect. A little more than a handful, with rosy nipples that had hardened to tight peaks. He forgot his current job of undressing her. Instead, he cupped them in his hands, kneading the soft skin.

"Look what you've been hiding under that cotton blouse. They're perfect." A low moan rumbled from his chest as he lowered his head and licked one nipple and then the other. "Sweet. Just how I knew you would taste." He licked his lips. "I wonder..."

"What do you wonder?"

Her eyes had darkened, and her voice had a lusty quality.

"If the rest of you tastes as good as this does." He pulled her nipple into his mouth, rolled his tongue in circles, and then sucked deeply.

"Oh, God." She lifted her chest, offering herself to him. "You're killing me."

He chuckled. "I think that's my line." He moved to her other breast and showered it with the same tender touches. Then he sat back on his heels and admired her rigid nipples. "So beautiful. I could spend all night worshiping these masterpieces."

Her chest turned pink, and the color rushed up to her cheeks. Dalton wanted to see that again and again.

His breath caught as her hands lifted to his chest. Her fingertips trailed over his collarbone down to his pecs, slid around his ribcage, and back to his stomach. His muscles flexed as her nails dragged across his skin.

"I'm not the beautiful person on this bed. You are."

She lifted onto her elbow. A frown crossed her face and she put her index finger on a small scar. "You were shot? How? When?"

He pulled her finger from his chest and into his mouth, where he sucked on the tip. "You want to talk about work, or would you rather finish what we've just started?"

"Since you put it that way."

Her hands ran over his shoulders and down his arms while he ravaged her with his lips and tongue. The outside world faded away. Nothing existed except her luscious body and the pleasure he wanted to give her.

His fingers locked at the waistband of her shorts and slowly slid them and her panties over her hips to her ankles. He swallowed hard as he tossed them aside and stared at her almost-bare pussy. He settled between her thighs and ran his fingers over the softly trimmed line of hair at the top of her mound. "You are full of surprises."

She lifted one eyebrow. "You don't like it."

His hand cupped her sex. "I can't think of anything about you I don't like." He slid his hand up to rest on her pubic bone and teased the soft skin just below with his tongue.

She gasped, and he smiled against her flesh. "Feels good?"

"Oh, yes, but why aren't you naked, too?"

"Easily remedied." He slipped off the bed and dropped his warm-ups to the floor. He hadn't bothered putting on underwear, so his dick stood up strong and proud.

Her gaze dropped to his erection. He couldn't resist showing off a little, so he took himself in hand and stroked backed and forth.

"You're not only beautiful, but you're also enormous," she whispered.

He tried to keep his smirk in check. "I'll bet you say that to all the guys." He rejoined her on the bed, climbing back between her thighs, nudging her legs farther apart with his knees.

"Can you not accept a simple compliment?"

"That was a compliment?" He grinned. "I thought it was an observation."

Before she could speak, his lips descended on hers. The kiss started as a soft exploration of the inside of her mouth. His tongue stroked every inch, possessing her, slowly gaining momentum. Her taste was addictive, and he couldn't get enough.

Her hands roamed up and down his back. Her fingernails, while kept too short to score the skin, scraped lightly, sending his need to be inside her even higher. Her hips lifted and his cock fit perfectly between her inner lips. He slid back and forth in the wet heat. "So wet for me."

"Please."

Her whisper was soft, but not unheard. Dalton wasn't rushing this, even though his dick protested. He slowly worked his way down her body, licking, tasting, and kissing as many inches of skin as he could. She was soft, silky, and smelled so damn good. Her gentle moans grew louder as he slowly reached her sex.

This would not be a quick fuck. Ashley deserved so much more than that, and he intended to give it to her.

"Tell me what you want?"

"You. I want you on me, in me, all over me."

He lifted her legs over his shoulders and then slid a hand under her silky bottom, lifting and holding her up as if for a meal.

"Open your eyes. Watch me."

Desire filled her gaze as she did as he asked. She licked her lips, and it went straight to his groin. It took all his strength not to bury himself balls deep inside her. *Too soon*, he cautioned himself. He wanted to worship first.

"I wish you could see what I see. You're so damn beautiful." He lifted her hips higher as he lowered his head. His tongue stroked her delicate flesh, and then he licked her from back to front.

Her fingers grasped a handful of his hair. "Oh. My. God."

Dalton lavished her with his tongue. Her soft cries drove him on. He didn't stop. Couldn't. He'd thought the taste of her kiss was addictive, but nothing compared to the sweet moisture she produced for him.

He took her clit into his mouth and sucked. The deep-throated moaning coming from her grew louder and nourished his soul. Her body trembled when he flicked his tongue back and forth. He slid a finger inside her, pumping in and out a couple of times before adding a second. God, she was tight, wet, and felt like an oven set on broil.

"Yes, so good," she murmured.

When she tightened around him, he flatted his tongue and upped his pressure on her clit.

"Dalton...I'm...I'm coming."

He gripped her hips as she thrashed and whispered his name as if praying to a deity. He continued loving her with his mouth until she fell limp in his hands. Then he lowered her until she was flat on the bed.

Watching her come had been the most erotic thing he'd ever experienced. Would one night with her quench his thirst? Would a hundred? When his assignment ended, so would their relationship. Would he survive?

"You're unbelievable." He slowly kissed his way back up her body while fighting the need to bury himself deep inside her. He kissed a spot on her forehead and leaned back to look into her eyes. "You all right?"

"Never better."

"Good, because this night isn't anywhere near over." He rolled to his back, pulling her on top of him. "You comfortable with this?"

Sprawled across his body, she shifted, spread her legs, and nestled her pussy over his hard erection. "Yeah, I can think of a couple of things we should do before morning."

"I'll do my best to complete every one of them."

She rubbed back and forth on his erection. "Of that, I have no doubt."

"Come here." He caught her long hair and wrapped his hand around the soft locks.

She lowered her head, stopping a breath away from his mouth. She ran her tongue across his bottom lip. He nipped her gently with his teeth before tugging her the rest of the way and capturing her lips with his. The world faded as they crashed into each other, tasting, torturing, seducing. Both were gasping for air when they separated.

"There's a condom in my billfold."

"Where'd you leave it?"

"Bathroom counter." He started to rise.

"I'll get it." She jumped off the bed and took off in a run.

He rolled to his side and watched. His mouth watered at the sight of her gorgeous ass jiggling on the way, and her beautiful breasts bouncing as she returned.

She stopped by the bed, ripped open the package, and him handed the contents.

He rolled to his back, caught his erection in his hand, and held it for her. "Put it on me."

"You want me to do it?" The hesitancy in her voice made him sit up. She wasn't joking.

"Is that a problem?"

Pink rushed up from her chest to her face. "I've never done it before."

"Come here." He took her hand and placed the condom on the tip of his cock. "Leave a little space at the head and just roll it down." He watched her face as she followed his instructions. He noted the slight tremble in her hands. He wanted to know why this was a first for her, but that question could wait for later. His erection jerked and twitched at her soft touch. She really was going to be the death of him.

She looked at him with a proud smile spread over her face. "That wasn't too hard."

He gathered her against him, tilted her head to the perfect angle, and then devoured her mouth before rolling her over onto her back. "If it gets any harder, it might break."

"Anybody ever tell you that you're a show-off?"

"Not without having a smile on their face." He settled his body between her legs, leaned down, and nipped the tip of her nipple before licking it with his tongue.

Her back bowed, and a low moan rolled from deep in her chest. He moved back and forth between the soft mounds until she was squirming. His hands roamed over her body because he just couldn't touch her enough.

Then he reached down and lifted her legs over his hips. "This one may not last as long as I'd like, but I need to get inside you." He lined himself up at her entrance, easing just his head inside.

Her hips rose to meet his. "More."

"The lady wants more." He drove into her hard, all the way to the hilt, and then paused to let her body adjust to his size. He started moving with slow thrusts, sliding in and out, feeling her get wetter and more comfortable with his girth. His gaze dropped to where their bodies were joined and he watched as he entered and retreated, liking how their bodies blended. The sight was addictive, and if he wanted to last more than a few minutes, he needed to count backward or something.

Anything.

Her eyes were closed, but Dalton needed to see her passion, witness her in the throes of her climax. "Look at me. I need to see you come."

Her eyelids lifted, locking on his gaze. Her heels dug into his ass. "I won't look away again."

Their hips found the perfect rhythm, driving faster and harder, pushing each other toward the inevitable. Dalton shifted his weight to one arm and slid his hand between them. Seconds after he rubbed his fingers over her clit, he felt the first spasm.

"Come for me. Come right now."

His hips jackhammered again and again until she cried out his name. With her spasms tightening and releasing, he buried himself deep and ground his pubic bone against her clit until they both exploded into body-racking orgasms.

After, Dalton dropped down on one elbow for a second before rolling off and pulling her against him. He held her until she completely relaxed.

"That was amazing." She looked up at him through lowered lashes. "I've never had an orgasm that strong."

"Well, we'll see if we can best that one. The night's not over yet."

Chapter 13

Cradled in his arms, Ashley coasted through the clouds, allowing the tsunami of pleasure to subside. She wanted to relish the strongest, most intense orgasm she'd ever had. Dalton had showered her with attention, and she wanted to do the same for him.

"Hmm." She lifted her head from his chest and looked at him. "That was amazing."

"It certainly was. You're so beautiful when you come."

His dark-brown eyes had shifted to the color of hot dark chocolate. Or coffee so strong it's almost black. Or hot fudge without the ice cream. Her brain wasn't functioning well enough to decide.

His lush lips curved into an evil grin. "And we're nowhere near finished."

She reached for him, pulling his face closer. How greedy did that make her? She wanted more. She needed him inside her again, their bodies blended into one. "I like the sound of that."

She stiffened when she heard his cell buzzing on the nightstand.

"Not answering." He covered her mouth with his.

She leaned into him. His hand cupped the back of her neck, holding her to him. The kiss was demanding, controlling, and passionate. She dug her fingers into his hair and met his tongue with her own.

His cell quieted, but immediately buzzed again. "Fuck. It must be important," he muttered under his breath.

Tamping down her disappointment, she reached over, grabbed his cell, and handed it to him.

His eyebrows dipped into a frown. "It's Carl."

"Oh shit. My phone is in my room." She reached for her clothes, dressing as fast as she could.

Dalton said hello, and she paused at the door to listen.

"Yeah. Want me to go check on her?" He held up his hand to stop her. "Last time I saw her, she was headed into her room. Come to think of it, she mentioned getting a snack before bed. She's probably down the hall at the drink and candy machines."

She nodded and silently returned to her room. Grabbing her cell off the nightstand, she checked her messages. Sure enough, she'd missed Carl. She waited a few minutes and pressed call.

"Hi. I was going to wait until tomorrow to update you."

"That's fine. I'm emailing you what we have on two recent murders. At least one of them is related to your case. Ballistics matched the shell casings to the murder of Senator Haley's wife a couple of weeks ago and the recent death of a truck driver. The gun is the only solid connection, but a playing card was on his body."

"Was a card left on Mrs. Haley's body?"

"No, just the truck driver."

"OK, I'll let Dalton know."

"I just spoke with him."

Ashley filled Carl in on what they'd learned at the bar and then ended the call. She grabbed her laptop and went back to Dalton's room. She knocked, the door opened, and he pulled her inside just as he had earlier.

His lips crashed down on hers, smashing the small computer between them. He lifted his head, gifting her with one of his sensual smiles.

"Kay is changing our travel reservations to Houston. She'll email a new itinerary."

Then he took her laptop, set it on the coffee table, and walked her backward until her legs bumped against the mattress. "While we wait to hear from her, we have some unfinished business."

Ashley put her hand on his chest. "Wait."

He stilled. His eyebrows lifted in question.

She slid her hands from his broad shoulders down over his chiseled abs, stopping to linger on the V-shaped groove that ran from below his ribs and vanished under the warm-ups he'd slipped back on.

"I love your Adonis belt." She leaned closer, slowly sliding his pants down. His erection grew under her gaze. "Exercise much?"

"That V can come from a person's genes as much as exercise."

She rolled her eyes. "Must I remind you? Just accept my compliments gracefully." Ashley flicked a playful glance up at him before leaning forward and licking the tip of his penis.

"Thank you." He choked out the words.

She took him in her mouth, slowly sliding toward the base, and then back to the head a few times. Just as she started to get serious, he picked her up and tossed her on the bed. She squealed, laughing out loud as he made quick work of removing her clothes. He caught her ankles and pulled her to the edge, effectively silencing her.

He dropped to his knees, lifted her legs over his shoulders, and studied her like she was a banquet laid out for just him. Normally, she would have been embarrassed, but all she could think about was what he was about to do.

"Hmm. Where was I before we were interrupted?" His grin was pure lust and hunger. "Right. I remember."

His fingers spread open her outer lips and his tongue caressed her swollen, wet, skin. Each stroke circled her clit and pushed her closer and closer to an explosive climax.

Her fingers sunk into his thick hair and dug into his scalp while she lifted her hips to meet the onslaught of his mouth.

Two fingers slid inside her, and she begged, "Please. Please."

He lowered her hips to the mattress and then kissed his way up her body until he was braced on his arms looking down at her.

"What do you need, baby? Tell me and it's yours."

"You inside me," she said in a voice that truly didn't sound like herself. "I'm clean and on the pill. No condom. Just you and me."

"You have my word: I'm clean, too."

"Then make me come."

"My pleasure." He lifted her to the middle of the bed and kissed her again. This time they fought for dominance. Tongues dancing, circling, tasting, memorizing. She bit down on his bottom lip too hard, but he didn't flinch. Instead, a chuckle rolled from deep in his chest.

She felt him nudge her opening, and then his head slid inside her. He didn't stop until he was fully seated deep in her body. Her mouth dropped open in a silent sigh and her eyes locked on his. She'd never had sex without a condom, and the feeling of his flesh against hers was so intense. Personal. Delicious. Nothing good could come from wanting him the way she did, but for now, he was right where she wanted him to be.

Dalton swept the loose hair that had fallen off her face. He pumped his hips a couple of times. "You feel incredible. This must be what heaven feels like."

She lifted her hips and ground against him. "So good."

He slid his forearms under her knees and lifted. The effect spread her wider and allowed him to sink even deeper. His thrusts began in a slow rhythm, but she needed more.

"Harder. I promise I won't break."

He plunged in and out, harder and faster, touching places that had never been touched without a condom. Putting his weight on one arm, his free hand slid between them. Pulling up some of her juices, he coated her clit, and rubbed his fingers in circles.

Heat built low in her belly and rushed south. Nerve endings burst into raw sensations as he stroked, skin against skin, driving deep then retreating, over and over again. Pushing her higher and higher.

"Dalton." She murmured his name again and again. The explosion of nerves started quickly, spreading like wildfire from her center to her spine and every nerve, muscle, and tendon in her body. She spasmed around him, clenching and releasing.

"Fuck," he groaned, holding himself deep inside her as she climaxed. "You're pulsing and gripping me. I can't hold back."

His hands gripped her hips tightly and his body slammed against hers. A deep roar rolled through him as he pulsed inside her. His head dropped to her shoulder while he fought to catch his breath. She ran her hands up and down his damp back.

His arms wrapped around her, holding her tightly. The sweat covering their bodies went unnoticed. And for a few quiet, glorious minutes, they were the only two people on the planet. Slowly, he relaxed, rolled, and pulled her head onto his shoulder.

His lips touched her forehead in the gentlest of kisses, and his fingers brushed her hair off her face. "You are fantastic."

A pang of sadness slammed into her heart so hard it hurt. She'd miss him when this was over. That she was sure of.

She breathed out a big sigh. "So are you."

"I could become addicted to you," he whispered into her hair.

She understood, and agreed. "Do you think there's a twelve-step program for people like us?"

A chuckle vibrated from his chest. "I don't know, but I think we need more of each other before deciding whether we should seek help or not."

She smiled and ran her fingers through the dusting of dark hair on his chest. "I think you're right."

Ashley cringed when his cell buzzed again. There "more of each other" might be over.

Dalton swung his feet to the floor and sat up. His back was turned to her and the scar from an old bullet wound was definitely more noticeable than the one on his chest. She ran her fingers over his well-defined muscles and then placed her palm over the scar. She leaned up and touched her lips to it, kissing it tenderly.

He spun around, and his eyes had gone dark and angry. She hadn't realized his call had ended. The longing and passion that had been in his eyes had vanished. His distant gaze held her for a few heartbeats. Where had the scar taken his thoughts?

"Don't feel sorry for me. My friend's family only had pieces to bury after Vardon had the so-called safe house blown to hell and back. I got shot but was too far away from the blast to suffer their fate. We never learned how or who leaked that location."

"You didn't see pity in my eyes. I won't ask for details, but I'm not going to apologize for treating you with tenderness."

His expression relaxed, and the corners of his mouth lifted. "I think I like this tender side of you."

Before she could respond, he was on his back, and she was sitting on the hard surface of his abs.

"The call wasn't bad news?"

"Depends on who you ask. Our flight is not until tomorrow morning."

"No flights out tonight?"

His hands cupped her breasts, softly squeezing and massaging them. "Nope."

She lowered her chest, giving him access to her nipples. "I feel guilty but happy at the same time."

Ashley closed her eyes and reveled in his caresses, licks, and occasional nip. She rubbed her hips against him, trying to find relief.

She pulled her breasts away and scooted backward. The realization that she'd left a wet spot on his belly should have embarrassed her, but it didn't. She wiggled her way between his legs and took his cock in her hand. She stroked him up and down, relishing the sighs he made as she felt him getting harder.

"I didn't finish what I started." A drop of pre-cum surfaced. It was all the incentive she needed to take him in her mouth. His stomach muscles tensed when she slid up and down his shaft using a gentle suction.

"Your mouth is so damn hot and wet. Feels so good."

His hands tangled in her hair and his hips started to move.

She stilled, letting him work his way in and out of her mouth.

Letting him show her how he liked it.

Letting him take control.

But only for a minute. Then she took charge and slowly slid him to the back of her throat. She almost gagged, but that didn't stop her. The desire to please him pushed her on. She needed to show him without words how badly her body wanted his.

"Stop." His grip tightened on her hair. "I'm not coming in your mouth. Not tonight."

She released him. Her eyes held his as she moved over him. Her hand guided him to her entrance, and she slowly impaled herself. Once they were skin to skin, she stopped moving. She wanted to enjoy the sensation of how he filled her. His length touched places previously unexplored, and she paused to relish the sensations.

"You like being on top," he said with a grin and a hard pump of his hips.

"I do."

"Then ride me." His voice was deep and raspy. "Just know I'm holding on by a thread."

His hands gripped her hips, and together they set a frantic pace. It took only a few minutes until his fingers slid down to rub her clit, and she dropped her head back.

"Dalton," she whispered. "Dalton."

His grip tightened on her hips as he started lifting her up and down, faster and faster. "Look at me when you come."

She caught his gaze—and lost herself in a wave of ecstasy, crashing into the flood of feelings as her body clenched around his girth.

Suddenly, she was on her knees with her head down and ass up. He thrust deep inside her. His pace sped up so that all she could hear was the slapping of flesh together. This new angle had him hitting her clit with every stroke.

"I'm coming again. Dalton. Oh. My. God."

He growled. His body went rigid as he slammed deep inside her. Jets of semen filled her and set off a second orgasm.

He slid out of her and dropped beside her. His chest rose and fell rapidly, but his smile thrilled her. It was the look of sheer contentment.

"There will never be a cure." As he had earlier, he moved her tangled hair off her face and then kissed her forehead.

They rested in silence for a few minutes. "Shower with me?"

"Sure thing." His almost-smile sent chills up her spine.

****

Ashley woke to the aroma of coffee. She opened one eye and found Dalton standing next to the bed holding a cup.

"What time is it?" She straightened her legs and pushed her arms over her head to stretch, and discovered she was stiff and sore in places she didn't remember ever having been tender before. She smiled inwardly.

"Five thirty. We need to get moving."

She scooted to the side of the bed and sat up. The sheet fell off her shoulders and onto her lap. Dalton's gaze landed on her breasts. He shook his head, handed her the cup of coffee, and then walked to the window. He pulled the curtain back a little and looked outside.

"How long do I have?

"Fifteen minutes if I stop looking at you."

"Then keep your back turned," she chuckled. She dressed, hurried to her room, and quickly showered before slipping on clean clothes. There was nothing to do with her wet hair except pull it back into a knot at the nape of her neck. The barest of makeup, and she was ready to go.

This time when she knocked on Dalton's door she expected him to come out lugging his suitcase. Instead, he stepped back and motioned for her to enter. Once she was inside his room, he kicked the door shut, pulled her against his chest, and kissed her hard. His tongue slid across her surprised lips and then dove inside. She wrapped her hands around his neck and gave as good as she got.

When he pulled away, they were both breathing like they'd run a marathon.

His thumb caressed the line of her jaw. "Today it's back to business."

The tears that tried to fill her eyes were quickly batted away. "Yes. We have work to do."

They checked out, tossed their luggage in the trunk, and were soon on the freeway. Neither spoke for a while, and that was fine with her. She'd needed that time to get her head back in the game. She opened her laptop and pulled up the information Carl had emailed.

"Read it to me," Dalton said.

"George Dawl, a middle-aged truck driver, was shot and killed in his apartment. The body was found on Wednesday. He was naked on the bed, with one bullet to the brain. No mutilation to the body. He'd been arrested three times for disorderly conduct related to bar fights. No charges were ever filed. Two DUIs spread out over ten years. No family of record."

"His package was still intact?" Dalton shook his head. "What the hell kind of sense does that make?"

"None. Is this a copycat? If not, why did she leave the card?"

"Let's hope some nutcase hasn't started killing and trying to put the blame on her." Dalton pulled into a small restaurant's parking lot. "We have time for a quick breakfast."

As soon as they were seated, they ordered bacon, eggs, and toast for a quick turnaround. The place was almost empty that time of morning, so he put his cell between them and made a call.

"Iain's going to be pissed, but we need more information."

"I might as well move to the compound." Iain's brogue had blended with the American accent so well, most people couldn't tell where he was from. "I'm assuming this is important."

"It is. I need information on a George Dawl. We know he lived in Houston and was a middle-aged truck driver. And he's dead. Dig deep."

"He's the one Nate added to your playing card case."

"Yes. He had a card, but there was no mutilation. He was shot. It was on the news last night."

"I don't watch TV. I've better things to do with my time. I'll get back to ye."

More coffee and their breakfast arrived at the same time Dalton ended the call. "He sounded pissed, but he's used to being under pressure. We need information by the time we get off the plane."

"I'll text Ash we're coming, but there's no way I'm calling him this early."

They ate quickly and then got back on the freeway and rode in silence. When they entered the city limits and took the exit for the airport, Dalton lay his open hand, palm up, on her thigh.

"No regrets?"

She wove her fingers through his and squeezed. "None."

Chapter 14

The minute she'd taken his hand, Dalton knew they could work together without any problems. The attraction between them was powerful, palpable, and real. Not to mention fucking unnerving. They could and would control it.

In all his years as a federal officer, he'd never had a sexual relationship with a coworker or a victim. Sure, it happened between some agents, but to the best of his knowledge, not often. It created a weakness in the partnership. One that could get one or both of them killed. There was no need to mention it to Ashley. She knew.

Since leaving the motel, neither had mentioned the incredible sex they'd had. He was still surprised by his need to have her again. It was new to him, and it made him damned uncomfortable.

She'd been subdued in the airport. Once seated on the plane, she'd stuck in her air pods, leaned back, and closed her eyes. He'd peeked at her cell and saw she was reading a mystery novel.

He was finding it too easy to be distracted. Her scent. Her nearness. Everything about her was becoming too important to him.

****

Dalton had heard traffic in Houston was as congested as Dallas. It was confirmed during the drive from the airport to police department headquarters. Highway construction had two lanes blocked, slowing cars to a crawl.

He took the exit into the main part of the city and made his way to a parking garage a few blocks away from their destination, tucking the rental into an empty slot.

Ashley got out, stopping at the hood of the rental. Her hands smoothed down the front of her blouse and she hooked her ID on her waistband. She hadn't worn one in Mexico.

Dalton leaned against the hood and watched. "You look very professional."

"Big girl," she said without an ounce of humor as she started walking down the stairs.

"Woman," he corrected.

She shrugged. "Private joke."

"I can keep a secret."

"That's what my dad used to say while he was explaining what I could or couldn't do. 'There are certain things a female isn't built to do. Be a big girl and accept your shortcomings.' "

"Your dad's an asshole." Dalton's blood boiled at the insult, but he regretted saying anything about her father. He tried to lighten her mood. "You showed him though, didn't you?"

"Damn right I did."

They stopped in the crosswalk and waited for the light to change. He glanced down at her, picking up on the tight lines around her mouth. "You said your brother didn't agree with him."

"Not at all. He's always stood up for me. Says I can do anything I set my mind to."

"Then I'm glad I'll get a chance to know him better." They crossed the street, stopping in front of the huge police headquarters building. "Ready?"

"I need to talk to you before we go any farther."

"Sounds serious."

"There's something I should have already told you."

His gut clenched. "You're involved with someone?"

"No," she said quickly. "Carl couldn't have been clearer about why I was allowed to work this case. He told me to convince you to return to the FBI."

Dalton caught her by the arm and moved them against the side of a building. "I didn't like that bastard when I worked with him, and I like him a lot less now. He put you in a position where you can't win. Fuck him. When you solve this case, you'll be famous. This one will put your name at the top of the bureau's go-to list."

"You're not angry with me?"

He couldn't help but smile. "Do I think you had sex with me as an attempt to change my mind? No. You weren't faking when we had sex. You're too honest to even try." He stepped back out into the sunshine. "Let's go talk to your brother."

"Let's." Her face beamed with a wide smile as she pulled her cell out. "I'll text him we're here."

They climbed the steps and entered the outer area of the police department. The building was huge, and people in and out of uniform were moving through the security checkpoint.

As they fell into the line waiting to be cleared to enter the main part of the building. Dalton leaned down next to her ear. "You're a damn good FBI agent. I'll testify to it."

The line through security moved quickly, and just as Dalton retrieved his things from the plastic bowl, he saw a tall man coming straight to them. His long strides covered the tile floor quickly. He'd only met Ash once, but the resemblance between brother and sister was obvious. Both had wheat-colored hair and blue eyes with sharply honed features. Women probably loved the inch-long scar high on his cheekbone.

Dalton's prior contact with Ash had been brief, and a few years ago. He hadn't formed an opinion of the man, and Nate and the team had great things to say about Ashley's brother. But was he happy his sister was poking around in a murder in his jurisdiction?

Ashley cleared security first, and Dalton watched as the siblings made eye contact. A smile spread from ear to ear across Ash's face as she hurried to him, walking into his open arms.

Ash looked over his sister's head and nodded. "Good to see you again."

Dalton closed the distance between them and shook Ash's hand. "Thanks for seeing us."

"I knew somebody would be coming, but I had no idea it would be the two of you until I got Ashley's text. I've let my team know they're to cooperate with you or answer to me."

"You threatened them?" Ashley jabbed an elbow into her brother's ribs. "I can take care of myself."

Dalton laughed at Ash's feigned injury and pain.

"Let's go before you ruin my reputation," Ash chuckled.

"We're not going to see your new office? Does this mean you're coming with us to the crime scene?" Ashley asked as they followed him out of the building. She'd expected a sit-down meeting or at least a tour, but was excited at the possibility he was going to join them.

They stopped at the light on the corner, and he wrapped an arm around her shoulders.

"No. I have a couple of meetings this morning. An officer will meet you there to let you inside."

"Is this because of your promotion?" she asked.

"You were promoted?" Dalton extended his hand. "Congratulations."

Ashley beamed up at her brother. "He's the commissioner of homicide."

"That's one hell of an accomplishment." Dalton noticed Ash's grip was firm.

"At thirty-six, he's the youngest ever." Ashley's face glowed with pride. Dalton wondered how it would feel if she looked at him that way.

Ash took a deep breath. "It was a stupid move. I let my ego make the decision when the job was offered."

The pedestrian green came on and the three of them crossed the street. Dalton hadn't seen an ounce of excitement in Ash's face, or felt it in his handshake. It occurred to him that Ash might be interested in joining him at the new Houston Lost and Found agency after all. "You regret accepting it."

Ash stopped at a coffee shop. He opened the door and motioned for Dalton and Ashley to go inside. Once they were seated and had ordered a late breakfast, Dalton sat back and waited for the rest of the story.

"You're unhappy." Ashley hadn't missed the tone of voice her brother had used.

"I'm not an ass-in-the-chair-all-day-behind-a-desk sort of person. I joined the police force straight out of the military because I wanted to continue making a difference. Handing out assignments, going to briefings, and talking to the press isn't what I wanted to do."

The waitress delivered their drinks, and the three fell silent for a few minutes. Dalton knew very little about Ash. Their one exchange was when Nate and a couple of his men had a close encounter with the Houston PD while working on a case. It was well known that the Lost and Found team did whatever was necessary if someone's life was in danger. As a federal officer, Dalton had been able to step in and smooth things over.

Despite the comments made by Nate about Ash being a cold-hearted son of a bitch, Dalton thought he had an easy way about him. He smiled to himself. He could hear Nate's voice in his head. When the brother and sister slowed down enough for him to get a word in, he reminded Ash of a job offer.

"You always have a home with the Lost and Found team. Nate speaks highly of you."

Ash took a sip and then placed the cup back on the table. "He's mentioned it a couple of times. I don't mind the traveling, but I'm not interested in moving to Dallas."

Dalton seized the moment. "What if you didn't have to?"

"What do you mean?"

"Lost and Found is opening a new office here in Houston. I'll be moving here as a partner." Dalton held up his hand. "You'd be a major asset to the team. I don't need an answer right now, but I'd like you to consider joining me."

Ash's face was unreadable, but he nodded his head. "Believe me, I will."

They finished eating, with Ash and Ashley sharing stories of their childhood. Dalton sat back and enjoyed the interaction between the two. It was obvious they had a strong bond. After a while he excused himself, paid the bill, and stepped out onto the sidewalk. While high humidity bothered some people, it reminded him of home. He'd grown up on the California coast and knew all about moisture in the air. How long had it been since he'd called his dad?

"I'm going to head back," Ash said, his sister tucked under his arm. "You two have been cleared through my office." He smiled down at Ashley. "You need to stay in touch. Text me."

"You text me, too," she grinned back at him.

"I will. Anything we have or get on this case will be sent to you as well as me."

Dalton shook his hand. "It was good to see you again. Your sister has a great career ahead of her." He winked at Ashley. "Don't tell her I said so."

Ash nodded and then hugged her close. "Call me."

"Back at you."

He turned and headed back to his office, but then stopped and called over his shoulder. "Have you called Dad lately?"

"No," she answered, sharp and quick. "Have you?"

He laughed. "No."

****

Angel paced back and forth across the worn carpet. How long could she stay before somebody realized she'd broken into the empty apartment across the courtyard from where George used to live? To her, it was a risk worth taking.

The team of investigators assigned to her would come. They had to come. Why else would she have left the queen of diamonds card on George? She needed more than names and who they worked for. Who were her opponents? How would they play the game? Deal with their failure? Their case would prove to be unsolvable. Why? She was, if nothing else, meticulous. She never left evidence behind.

She'd spent hours in this empty apartment with nothing to sit on but the floor. She rose to her knees to take one last look through the narrow slit in the blinds before leaving. A smile spread across her face. A woman flashed a badge to the policeman outside George's door. She wore ugly khaki slacks and a plain white blouse. Her blond hair had been pulled off her face and rolled into an unattractive knot at the back of her head. The federal agent looked to be all business.

The man walking up the stairs sent her pulse racing. Dalton was tall, with broad shoulders and arms like tree trunks. His walk spoke of strength, dominance, and self-assurance. Wearing black jeans and a blue button-down with the sleeves rolled up, his muscular forearms were the second thing she'd noticed. His face, what she could see of it from her vantage point, was rugged, masculine, and wore a scowl.

Who was he, really? What was his relationship with the federal agent? Was he a good man? She hoped so, because she'd decided he could be president of the fan club. She chuckled to herself. Of course, she knew she was being silly.

Which meant she'd kill them both when she tired of the game.

Thirty minutes later, the man and woman walked out onto the landing, spoke with the officer, and then moved to the neighbor's door and knocked.

She tweaked the short spiky black hair of the wig she wore today. Skinny jeans torn at the knees, a Houston Texan football T-shirt, and ankle boots completed her disguise. She went to the kitchen counter, removed a playing card, and wrote a short note. She dropped it on the counter next to a sign-in log for prospective renters, opened the door, and fell in step with a young woman carrying a grocery bag on one hip and a toddler on her other.

"Hi," Angel said with a big smile. "What a beautiful baby. Here." She held out her open arms. "Let me carry that bag for you."

"Thank you, she's getting heavier every day," the young mother said, handing the sack over with a sigh. "Are you thinking about renting that apartment?"

"I was." She fell in step with the woman. "It's too small for my family."

"Too bad." The woman shifted the kid onto her left side, pulled out a key chain, and stopped to unlock a door. "We would've been neighbors."

Angel glanced over her shoulder and saw that the investigative team had gone inside George's neighbor's apartment. "Yeah. It's too bad."

She casually walked down the stairs to her rental, got in, and drove to the far side of the street. She parked and leaned back to wait.

Would they find her card and see the note? Maybe not, but she'd felt compelled to try and communicate with Dalton. He was the first man who'd stirred an ounce of lust in her. Her heart might break if he turned out to be like the rest of the men she'd met.

Her cell rang. Kyle always managed to call when she didn't want him to, but he wasn't someone she could ignore. She accepted his call.

"Do you have a job for me?"

"I do, and if the newscaster was right, it's timely. See if you can schedule a trip to London. The sooner the better. Your ass needs to be out of the country for a while."

"I'll see if I can find someone who'll cover or swap with me, and then get it approved." She didn't want to be away from Dalton for too long. "After this trip, I'm taking a few weeks off."

****

Dalton had parked in a visitor's slot at George Dawl's apartment building. The location was a twenty-minute drive from police headquarters, and by the time they'd arrived, Ashley had logged in and was opening the reports her brother and Iain had emailed.

She read the information out loud. "There's not much here. The coroner will send the card and bullet to Quantico for analysis. Detectives interviewed Dawl's neighbors. There's a description of the scene."

"No mention of a family?"

"None."

"Ready?" Dalton asked. He waited for her at the hood of the rental. "I like how you and your brother are close. As an only child, I missed that bond."

She stopped right in front of him and turned to face him. It was so quick that he had to grab her arms to keep from bumping into her. She smiled up at him as if he'd just given her a present.

"What's funny?"

"I'm slowly getting to know Dalton Murphy. I think he was probably a good kid."

"You don't need to know me."

The sparkle in her eyes that he'd been getting used to faded. Well, hell. He'd hurt her feelings.

"Thanks for the reminder." She whirled on her heel and walked—no, she stomped—to the apartment with a uniformed officer standing in front of the door.

He followed her inside, and together they made their way from room to room. The crime scene unit had already been there. No doubt anything interesting had been taken to the lab, but it didn't hurt to look around.

"I'm sorry I was rude. I don't share well." The tightness in his shoulders eased when a hint of a smile touched her lips. "Am I forgiven?"

The little minx tapped her lips with her index finger. "I'll think of a way you can make it up to me."

Instantly getting hard, he leaned down close to her ear and whispered, "Think all you want, little one, but I asked for forgiveness, not for a way to make it up to you."

Then he pulled out his cell. "I should have heard from Iain by now. I'll put it on speaker."

"Don't tell me you didna receive my email?" Iain said. "What else do ye need?"

"Hello to you, too," Dalton said with a chuckle. "I haven't had time to check my email. Text me next time."

Ashley leaned toward the phone. "Iain, thank you for the information. Will you email it and anything else you find to me? Unlike some people, I check my email regularly."

"I'll do that, lass."

"How are things going otherwise?" Dalton asked.

"Nate has had me up to my ears in research. Reed and Tank just returned from the French Riviera. Some rich guy's daughter ran off."

Dalton liked both men. They'd worked together a few Christmases ago, and he'd had the chance to get to know them. Both seemed to enjoy trying to get a rise out of him. He didn't mind letting them try and fail. "They got her home all in one piece?"

"That case was a piece of fluff. She wasn't missing. She'd gone on vacation to party with friends."

"Iain," Ashley said. "I just texted you my email and cell number."

"Got it. Let me know if ye need anything," he said with a syrupy tone.

"I'll let you know if we need anything else." Dalton scowled at the phone. Was the young pup flirting with her? He slid his index finger across his throat, letting her know to end the call.

She handed his cell back, pulled her laptop from its case, and started scrolling.

Chapter 15

Ashley breathed out a discouraged sigh when the most recent neighbor of George Dawl had the same information to offer as the other three. Nobody knew much about the deceased. He minded his own business, was quiet, and had no friends in the complex that they knew about.

She stopped at the door of the apartment across the walk from George's and knocked.

"That unit is empty," the manager said. "I showed it to a woman this morning, but haven't heard back from her."

"Then I think we're through here." Ashley started to turn away but stopped. "She?"

"Yeah. She."

"Describe her for us," Dalton said.

"Medium height. Spiky dark hair. Maybe thirty, with a pretty face."

Ashley looked at Dalton, and he nodded. His gut was telling him the same thing. "We'd like to take a look, if you don't mind." He walked to the door and waited. His face was taut. He looked serious enough, the manager knew not to argue.

A moment later the door was opened, and Dalton followed Ashley inside.

"Wait here," she instructed the manager.

They were met by the aroma of industrial cleaner and fresh paint. The beige carpet was soft under her shoes as she entered the living area. Dalton broke off and walked through the bedrooms. Ashley turned and spotted something on the breakfast bar.

"Dalton!" she called.

His footsteps landed heavily as he cut the distance between them to nothing in a few long strides. Peering over her shoulder, he read the words on the playing card. "Looks like your hunch paid off."

The queen of diamonds card addressed him by name.

Congratulations, Dalton.
You've been selected to be president of my fan club.

Ashley stepped back. "What the hell?"

Dalton bolted out the door. She didn't ask why. He was sweeping the area for any signs of the killer. Before she joined him, she called Ash and updated him on their find. He'd have the crime scene unit on-site as soon as possible.

She thanked the manager and let him know the apartment wouldn't be available for lease for a few days. She scanned the area before going up the steps to the next level, hoping Dalton had gone the other direction. Finding no one, she walked to the parking lot and waited.

That the killer knew Dalton's name was unnerving as hell. Only a few people knew he'd been added to the investigation.

"Damn it," he said from behind her. "I saw nothing."

"Me either." She reached out and wrapped her fingers around his bicep. "How the hell does she know your name?"

"I don't know. If the news somehow got ahold of it, Nate would have called."

"Let's get out of here." Her nerves were in turmoil. Dalton didn't act as if it had upset him that the killer had communicated with him, but it had to concern him.

His hand rested on her back. "I have the name of the woman who called about the empty apartment. Iain can take a look, but I can't imagine she used her real one."

Ashley nodded her agreement. She was tired and hungry, but didn't want to stop just yet. "We can still speak with Dawl's coworkers."

****

By the time she and Dalton called it a day, they'd spent hours speaking with various people who had contact with Dawl regularly. He was apparently an ordinary guy with few debts and fewer friends. He'd stopped for a drink with a couple of coworkers occasionally and had mentioned a new woman in his life. Nobody knew her name, but one guy remembered George referring to her as an angel. "Blonde" and "hot" were all they had provided in the way of description.

"What did he do to piss her off?" Ashley wondered out loud.

A large hand landed on her knee. Her skin heated. Dalton's touch, no matter how innocent, sent her hormones into overdrive. She placed her palm over his knuckles and wrapped her fingers around him to keep him from pulling away.

"Long day." His grip tightened. "Let's get checked in to our motel. We both need a meal and a shower. This has been a bust."

"That's not true. We learned she has a crush on you. A big one, if she's brave enough to leave you a note."

"You're not jealous, are you?"

"Of a woman who will cut your dick off if you make her mad? I don't think so."

Dalton wove his way through downtown Houston and parked under the porte cochere of the Marriott Marquis hotel.

Before she could comment, her door was opened, and a hand extended to aid her exit from the car.

A valet smiled down at her.

"Thank you," she muttered, while waiting to admonish Dalton. "This is too extravagant."

"No, it's not." A waiting young man took their suitcases. "My treat."

"You're incorrigible." She relaxed as Dalton's arm slipped around her waist and escorted her inside. "A Holiday Inn would have been fine."

"We're working tonight, and I see no reason not to be comfortable."

When he beamed down at her with those dark eyes, she had no willpower to argue. While he checked in, she walked through the lobby, admiring the dark wood paneling, leather-covered furniture, marble countertops, and flooring. The air was cool, and the aura of rich comfort surrounded her.

A shiver of electricity ghosted across her skin. She felt him standing close to her. How she knew he'd walked up behind her was a mystery.

"Ready?"

She turned and smiled up at him. "You're spoiling me."

His laughter rolled from his chest. "You should be spoiled."

The elevator ride was blazing fast, and soon the doors to the fortieth floor swished open. Dalton swiped the keycard, pushed the door open, and stepped back for her to enter.

Behind her, she heard the door click shut and the deadbolt slam home. Her heartbeat sped up. He'd reserved a suite instead of two rooms. The living area came with a conference table, plus the couch, chairs, and large screen TV. Double doors to a separate room revealed a king-size bed. Her entire body shivered to see both of their bags sitting in front of the closet.

She turned to face him. He was leaning back against the locked door. The heat in his eyes made her knees weak. "Our bags made it before we did."

"I see that." One corner of his mouth lifted. "You noticed the one bed?"

She willed words to come out of her mouth, but her brain hadn't given her the go-ahead, so she simply nodded.

His eyes were filled with lust as he took a step toward her. "If you prefer, I'll take the couch."

"You do, and I'll smother you in your sleep." She crossed the distance between them as fast as she could, grasped his shoulders, and jumped, wrapping her legs around his hips. His large hands clutched her bottom and pressed her against the large bulge in his jeans. She arched her body and rubbed against him. Then she covered his mouth with hers.

His tongue invaded. Owned. Controlled. Hard, but soft. Demanding her complete surrender. Which she gladly gave. She'd never been kissed like this. A low groan from him had her pulling back and peppering his face with kisses.

"Bed." His word came out as a low growl. His hands gripped her ass, and his long legs made quick work of the distance needed to travel. He set her feet on the floor, pulled her blouse out of her slacks, and quickly unbuttoned it. His gaze lowered. Leaning down, he nuzzled the valley between her breasts. "I've waited all day to do this."

His tenderness tugged at her heart. "I thought maybe you'd had enough of me." She shrugged her shoulders, and her shirt hit the carpet.

Suddenly, their hands were everywhere. Hers tried to get him undressed, while he removed her bra and pushed her slacks to the floor.

"Bullshit." He scowled. "You couldn't have believed that."

"You didn't have second thoughts? No guilty conscience?"

"No. None."

"I'm glad."

"Unless we hear compelling news, this day is over. Even federal agents take time off."

"Yes, we do, and I've waited all day to have your hands on me." She kicked off her shoes, removed her socks, and reached for her panties.

Dalton's hand stopped her. "I'll do that."

"Then I'll be naked, and you won't. Hardly seems fair."

His hand cupped the nape of her neck, tilting her head slightly before his lips took command of hers. His tongue demanded entrance, drove inside, and touched every available space. He stole her breath from her lungs, leaving her gasping when he released her.

"The woman wants me naked." He unzipped his jeans, and with great efficiency, stripped the clothes off his gorgeous body. A huge smile broke across his face.

It occurred to her that he was smiling now more than he had when they first met, but her thought abandoned her when he dropped to his knees and peeled off her panties.

He leaned in and kissed her mound before sliding his tongue through her outer lips.

"You taste so damn good."

Ashley's knees almost buckled, so she clutched his shoulders. Somebody groaned. Was it her? It didn't sound like her.

He stood, scooping her into his arms as he rose, then placed her in the middle of the mattress. With one knee on the bed, he paused and let his gaze travel over her body. His fingers slid across her forehead, down her jawline to her chin. From there he blazed a trail across the planes and valley of her skin, convincing her spontaneous combustion was in her immediate future.

She shivered when his travels took him through her wetness. He took his time, almost as if worshiping her. Her chest tightened. It was as if he wanted to map out every inch of her body. Ashley almost felt as if he was worshiping her. Her chest tightened.

Was he stashing the memory away to call up after they'd gone their separate ways?

Pain tore through her heart at the thought of never seeing him, but she willed those thoughts away. Instead of worrying about tomorrow, she took the opportunity to watch him. She loved how the muscles in his broad shoulders moved. How his arms flexed. And the way his ripped abs tightened as he moved.

His gaze lifted to meet hers. He caught her knees in his hands, using them to spread her legs wide before he knelt between her thighs.

"You are so damn beautiful."

"Funny. I was thinking the same thing about you."

"Real men aren't beautiful. But if you have to compliment me, I prefer handsome, hunky, or better yet, manly."

She loved how his eyes sparkled when he teased her. "Manly? You certainly are that."

Ashley dropped her heels to the mattress, bent her knees, and pushed herself to sitting.

His eyebrows lifted. "Going somewhere?"

"I am." She shifted her position and then wrapped her fingers around his erection. He was so hard, and yet, velvety soft. Before he could agree or disagree, she leaned forward and licked the drop of pre-cum that was just about to run down over the silky skin.

His hands caught her hair, pulling her so she had to look up at him. Lust radiated from his dark eyes. "You don't have to do that."

She looked up at him. "You want me to. Right?"

"Do I want those luscious lips of yours wrapped around my cock? Am I eager to sink it into your warm, wet mouth? Damn right, I am."

"Since you put it that way." Her eyes locked on his as she took him as deep as she could.

"Oh. My. God."

She pulled back and licked the underside of his length, loving how he grew even harder. She slipped her lips over the engorged head and slid up to the tip and back down to the base. Each time taking him deeper and deeper.

She placed her hands on his thighs and reveled when his muscles clenched every time she took him to her throat. Wielding so much power over him was exhilarating. That she could elicit deep growls from him drove her to please him even more. To feel him tremble because of her. To lose control because of her.

Dalton's hands clamped down on her head, his fingers guiding her movements. His soft grunts had her getting wetter and needier by the second.

"Stop." He tugged her away from him, sliding his hands under her arms. Then he lifted her as if she were no heavier than a feather. "You're very good at that."

"Why?"

"I don't plan on coming in your mouth. Not tonight, anyway." He lifted her to her feet, turned her around, and placed her on the edge of the bed. "Lie back."

Dalton dropped to his knees, lifted her legs, and draped them over his shoulders. He ran his hands up the inside of her thighs, leaning in to nip and then kiss his way to the juncture there. His thumbs peeled her open.

Ashley held her breath, expecting his wet tongue to glide across her skin at any moment. When nothing happened, she lifted onto her elbows to see him studying her.

His smile filled her head with embarrassment and her heart with emotion. "You're beautiful. Soft. Pink. Perfect."

His head lowered, and his mouth found her clit. She gasped. Loudly. His tongue lashed her most sensitive of places, pausing every few seconds to circle it. He pushed her to the edge of an orgasm, but not enough to come. He drove her higher and higher. Seeking every available place to kiss, lick, or touch, he took her to the edge and thrust her over.

Ashley's thighs clamped down over Dalton's ears. White lights engulfed her. Took her somewhere she'd never been. Her body shuddered as tremors of pleasure exploded from within. It was only when the spasms subsided that she realized she'd been holding his head hostage. She pulled her legs off his shoulders, pushed herself upright, and stared down at his smiling face. "Oh my God." She fell back on the bed and laughed with him. "I've never come that hard."

He crawled up beside her, lifted her higher onto the bed, and rolled over on top of her. "That was cataclysmic."

"You should have been inside me." Her body still vibrated inside and out.

"No thanks. I was happy right where I was. Let's try for a couple more."

He captured her in a soft, open-mouthed kiss, moving from one corner to the other before covering her lips with his. His tongue searched out hers, and she tasted herself on him. Her hands slid into his hair as they both became aggressive, touching and dancing around inside each other's mouths.

His lips trailed down her neck, pausing to bite her throbbing vein and run his tongue over the tender spot. Leaning on one elbow, he pulled one nipple into his mouth. Moving back and forth between her breasts, he sucked and licked her hard peaks until her nails dug into his scalp. Her hips lifted, reaching for more.

"Please. I need you inside me."

Dalton lifted his head. "That's my girl."

He guided himself to her opening and nudged the head into her hot passage. Slowly, he pushed deeper until his body was flush against hers. He pulled back, slammed home, and then set a pace that had her grabbing onto his shoulders to keep from being shoved farther up the bed.

"Dalton." His name spilled from her mouth with each thrust as he stroked over that sensitive place inside her. Without warning, another orgasm ripped through her. Her hips lifted and her body convulsed.

He slowed but kept a smooth in-and-out stroke as she fell back to earth from that heavenly plane she'd flown apart on. She opened her eyes and found him watching her. A satisfied, smug grin on his face.

"Oh. My. God," she said, knowing he hadn't come.

"Again." His hips started moving faster, and one hand slipped between them.

"I can't, but you can."

"Three." His thumb circled her clit. Coming closer and closer by the second. When he found his target and pressed down, her body caught fire.

Burning from the inside out, she matched his thrusts, lifting and rubbing against him faster, harder, more frantic. She opened her mouth, but no sound came out.

His hands clamped down on her hips, pulling her against him. "Now. Ashley. Come now."

She felt him swell and pulse as semen flowed from him. The first sensation of him coming deep inside her sent her spiraling off the cliff.

She saw nothing but white. Felt nothing but him inside her. She gave him everything she had.

He rolled onto his side, taking her with him. For a moment, there were no other people on planet earth. He leaned over and kissed her forehead. "I'll be right back."

Ashley was almost asleep when she felt the warm wet washcloth between her legs. He tenderly cleaned up their mess. When he slipped off the bed and returned to the bathroom, a sad truth slammed into her heart.

She cared for him.

Cared more than she should.

Cared enough to know how much it would hurt when they parted.

It wasn't something she'd share with him. He could never know.

She rolled to her side and pretended to be asleep, so that when he returned she wouldn't have to face him. In the morning, she'd be better prepared to believe this was just sex.

Nothing more than two people enjoying each other's bodies.

Chapter 16

Dalton rolled over and ran his hand over the cold spot where Ashley's soft warm body should have been. He'd slept so soundly he hadn't been aware of her leaving the bed. He was disappointed he hadn't found her naked and cuddled against him like she'd been when he'd fallen asleep.

"What the hell?" The double doors to the bedroom had been closed. When had she gone to the living area? He quickly pulled on his pants and opened the doors, expecting to find her at the table peering at her laptop, but the room was empty. Where was she?

He spun around at the sound of the door lock disengaging. She walked in with both hands full. She wore jeans, a red T-shirt, and tennis shoes. Clean-faced, without a hint of makeup, she was outright stunning.

"Let me." He took two sacks from her, and the smell of coffee wafted from one of them. He set them on the small table and turned to her. "You didn't call room service."

"When we checked in last night, I spotted a pastry shop across the street that opened at six in the morning." She removed two large containers of coffee and several individually wrapped delicacies. "Join me."

"You left without waking me."

"I did." She removed the lid of her cup. "So?"

"I can't remember the last time I slept through the night so soundly."

"Wore you out, did I?" Her cheeks flushed at her own joke.

"I've recovered."

Her gaze dropped to his jeans. "I can see that."

He adjusted himself away from the pressure of his zipper. "How long have you been up?"

"Not long." She picked up a bear claw pastry and took a bite. Then she pushed the sack of pastries toward him.

Her eyes tracked his movement as he crossed the room.

"Do you find it odd that you know a lot about my life and family, but you've been very limited with information about yourself?"

"Not at all." Dalton grabbed something large and flaky from the bag. Not knowing or caring what it was, he took a bite. The flavor of butter and honey flooded his mouth. He chewed slowly to avoid answering. He'd already told her more than he normally shared.

"You have to swallow at some point."

He took another quick bite, then leaned back in his chair, taking a second to decide what to divulge. He liked her. Liked how she smelled, her skin, and how she responded to his touch. He took a sip of coffee.

"You're right. I recently bought a house and a few acres outside of Dallas. It's close to the compound. It's where I go to decompress."

"Do you specialize in dangerous cases?"

"Sometimes. Some are simple, some not so much. We work with desperate families with nowhere else to go, and occasionally, we do assignments for the government."

"Will you sell your home and live on the compound in Houston, like Nate and Kay in Dallas?"

"Yeah. Lost and Found is a lifestyle, not a job. The facility will be somewhere outside of town with enough land to provide privacy."

"Did I tell you how proud of you I am?"

"Not that I remember." She was the first woman to ever utter those words to him. "Tell me again."

"Of course." Her head tilted and her eyes filled with questions. "It's a huge responsibility, but there's no doubt in my mind you'll be amazing."

He took another sip of coffee before giving in to share a little of his past. "I didn't have a lot of female influence in my life when I was a kid. My mother wasn't interested in sports, but Dad attended every one of my football and baseball games. Didn't matter if they were at home or out of town."

"She didn't go watch you play? That's sad."

"Not really. She had a lover to keep her busy. My father took her betrayal hard, but he pulled it together where I was concerned. He owned an automotive shop and had men working for him that he trusted to take care of business while he attended anything I was involved in."

Her expression softened and a slight smile lit up her face. "He's still alive?"

"Oh, yeah." Dalton smiled. "He spends most of his time fishing with his buddies. You'd like him." He surprised himself by adding that last part.

She patted her mouth with a paper napkin, stood, and walked to his side of the table. There was just enough room for her to swing one leg over, straddle him, and sit on his thighs. She cupped his face in her hands, lowered her head, and softly rested her lips against his. His heart clenched. It was the sweetest and most tender kiss he'd ever had. His lungs expanded, and warmth filled the cavity.

"I'm sure I'd love him."

Dalton snapped back to reality. "We need to know what and who sent intel last night and this morning."

"Yes, we do." She smiled and stood. "No doubt my inbox is full." Her cell rang. "It's Ash."

Dalton chuckled that she'd used Elvis's song, "(If You're Looking For) Trouble" for her brother's ringtone.

She moved to a chair, placed the phone between them, and tapped the speaker icon. "Good morning. You're up early."

"So are you. I have to assume Carl informed you that the shell casing from George Dawl and Brenna Hawley are a match."

"He did. Have you learned anything that might be helpful to us?"

"That's why I called you. Carl seemed reluctant to share information."

Ashley's smile vanished. "I hate to say it, but he's probably salivating over the accolades he'll get when we catch her. Sorry. That sounded so cynical."

Ash chuckled. "Truth can sometimes be cynical."

"I promise I'll keep you in the loop."

"Same here."

"Keep my offer to join the team in mind," Dalton said.

"Oh. Hello, Dalton. It's front and center. You two are up and at work already?"

Dalton caught the question in Ash's words. Big brother was wondering why they were together so early in the morning.

"I haven't slept late since my first day at Quantico." Ashley waved her hand dismissively, as if her brother could see her. "Do you have anything else for us? We were getting caught up on emails when you called."

"I'm sending you everything we have on Brenna Hawley."

"Thanks," Dalton chimed in. "I appreciate your help."

"Me too," Ashley added.

"Talk soon." Her brother ended the call.

Dalton shook his head. "He didn't buy your excuse as to why we're together in the same room this early in the morning. He's too smart to fall for that."

She tilted her head and jutted out her chin. "It was none of his business."

"I thought you two were close. Even though I don't have any siblings, if I did, and it was a sister, I'd be pretty protective of her."

"We've lived separate lives for a long time, but we're still tight." Her face softened. "Sooner or later, I'll get the third degree from Ash."

"Tell him whatever you want. If it was my brother, I'd tell him to mind his own business."

Her gaze dropped to the laptop she'd opened. "We have travel plans to San Diego. Do we go or stay to look at the details on Mrs. Hawley?"

Dalton considered the question while she scrolled through emails. "It's time to add to our team." He lifted his cell. "What's the name of the victim in California?"

"Don't you keep track of these details for yourself?"

"When I work alone. I don't usually have you to distract me. Besides, you're more efficient on a laptop than I am."

"But now you have me."

"As a matter of fact, I do." He leaned across the small table and kissed her. "Read to me."

"Yes, sir." The tip of her pink tongue slipped out and swept across her bottom lip.

Dalton groaned. "Don't do that."

"Why not? You left your taste on my lips."

"Makes me want to do it again."

"You can do better. Let's try again."

Dalton stabbed a finger in the direction of her laptop. "Read."

She wiped the grin off her face with her hand. "To refresh your memory, Wayne Arber was a single, forty-year-old motorcycle mechanic who had taken over the family business from a long line of Arbers in Cabena, California."

"We need somebody to look into the Hawley murder while we go to California. Reed Ballatori is just back from an assignment. I'll call him."

Dalton walked to the bedroom and got his phone off the nightstand. A glance at the clock there reminded him it was barely seven. "I'll call after I've finished my coffee, had a shower, and brushed my teeth."

Ashley glanced up. "Hmm. I haven't showered yet."

"Then finish reading to me, and I'll wash your back."

"Bossy much?"

"I think I answered that question the first time we met."

She lifted one eyebrow. "You're right. I seem to remember you saying I had no idea. What if I want to see more of your bossy side?"

"Do you want to? Just say the word."

"Maybe." She lowered her gaze to the laptop screen. "A synthetic black hair was found in the empty apartment. No fingerprints."

"Anything from Iain?"

"Hang on." Her fingertips flew across the keyboard. "All the information the woman gave the apartment manager was fake."

"As expected."

"He's finally free to work on the list of Vardon's texts, emails, and phone contacts."

"It's about damn time."

"Sounds like he stays pretty busy."

"He does."

"Which means you'll have to find an Iain for Houston."

Now Dalton's eyebrow lifted. "Are you applying?"

She laughed and her eyes sparkled. "Wouldn't that toast Carl's balls? I'm supposed to bring you back to the FBI, but instead, I go to work for you? He'd have a stroke."

Dalton's thoughts went to Nate and Kay. It worked for them. Then he shoved those thoughts to the far recesses of his mind.

"Read," he demanded.

Ashley complied, and he listened to every communication she'd received. He scrolled through his messages on his cell, finding nothing to add. He leaned back in his chair and propped the ankle of his right leg over the knee of his left. "In other words, we have nothing."

"Exactly," she agreed. "We need to catch a break."

"Most cases are solved because of a mistake. We need her to make one."
He stood and checked his phone. "Time for a shower."

Ashley lowered the cover on her laptop. "You go ahead. I'll take mine
after you're finished."

He laughed full out, his head dropping back as the sound rolled up from
deep in his chest. Then he walked to her, pulled her from the chair, and
tossed her over his shoulder, fireman-style. She squealed like a little girl as he
carried her to the bathroom.

He reached in and turned on the water in the shower before putting her
down. "Strip," he ordered as he shucked his Levi's. His erect cock slapped
against his stomach as he stepped under the water.

****

They checked out of the hotel and headed to the airport. The line at security
was short, and Dalton's smug grin reminded Ashley he'd been right: they'd
had plenty of time. After they'd had sex in the shower, he'd called Nate, and
Reed Ballatori had been assigned to look into the Hawley murder.

They'd each picked up a burger and iced tea before finding a place to sit
at the gate. She put down her drink and then removed her lunch.

"You were right. We had plenty of time, but I hurried and didn't take
time to put on makeup." Not that she cared one bit, not after how he'd
made her feel during their shower. He'd given her the best orgasms she'd ever
had. She'd miss them when their assignment ended. Her chest clenched as
if someone had wrapped a band around her and tightened it to the point of
pain. She didn't want to think about that. Not now. She'd deal with it when
the time came.

"You are breathtaking fresh out of the shower. You can't improve on
perfection." He unwrapped his burger and took a big bite.

Ashley was stunned. Speechless. Her eyes watered. He spoke without
guile, just as if it were a matter of fact. Words formed in her brain. Words
that would tell him how attached to him she'd become. Thank goodness her
mouth was full of food, because she didn't know what to say to him.

His gaze caught hers, and he set his burger onto the wrapper. "Tears?
What did I do?"

She blinked away the moisture sitting on the rims of her eyelids. Why did he have to be so perceptive? "Why are you assuming you did anything?"

He reached over and covered her hand with his. "I've never met a woman who got upset when somebody mentioned she was gorgeous."

She breathed easier. He'd solved the problem as to why she misted over. He was wrong, but she could live with that. Unless they caught a break, they still had a lot of time left together. She didn't want him to know she was already missing him.

"Thank you. I'm flattered, and truly glad you think I'm beautiful."

He picked up his sandwich and took another bite. They finished eating in silence and boarded without talking. Dalton seemed to be lost in thought, and Ashley didn't want to interrupt him. Once they settled in the first-class seats, she had to address his extravagant spending.

"Doesn't your boss review your travel expenses? Carl would flip his lid if I flew first class."

"Nate won't say a word." One side of his mouth lifted in a hint of a smile. "Besides, your boss is paying for my time and expenditures. Most of the time I pay for my upgrades."

A flight attendant stopped at their seats. "Would you like something to drink before takeoff?"

Dalton turned to Ashley. "How about it? A glass of wine, maybe?"

A smile spread across her face. "That's a great idea. Red, please."

Sitting in the aisle seat, he looked up at the flight attendant. "I'm good. Red wine for the lady."

"Sure thing." The flight attendant stared at him for a second. Then she turned and bumped into a silver-haired female passenger who was struggling to lift her heavy bag up and into the overhead.

"Can you help me?" the woman asked.

In seconds, Dalton had unbuckled and was on his feet. His hand touched the flight attendant's shoulder. "I'll get it. Neither of you two ladies should be lifting that bag overhead."

Both women beamed up at him. The older woman, her blue eyes sparkling, said, "Thank you, young man."

"Thank *you*." He winked at her, bringing a big smile to her face. "For calling me young." He slid the suitcase into place and closed the compartment.

She turned her bright smile toward Ashley before sitting in the seat in front of Dalton. "Your husband is a gentleman."

"We're not married," she and Dalton answered at the same time.

Everyone in first class heard their outburst and laughed. Dalton quickly retook his seat. Shaking his head, he spoke to the flight attendant. "Make that two red wines."

Without so much as a smile, she said, "Coming right up."

Ashley was glad when things settled down, people went back to talking amongst themselves, and the plane taxied onto the runway. She reached under the seat in front of her, dug her air pods out of her bag, and settled in for the three-and-a-half-hour flight to LAX.

"What are you listening to?" Dalton leaned his elbow on the armrest. A slow smile lifted the corners of his lips.

She removed an earbud. "Say that again."

"Your audiobook. Is it erotic? Have handcuffs and whips?" His grin was positively evil.

"Do you really think I'd tell you if it were? This one is Kym Roberts's latest historical romance. I've read everything she's ever written."

He rubbed the backs of his knuckles over her jawline. "I would've liked this conversation better if your answer had been yes."

"Ssh." Heat flooded her cheeks. "I have a few erotic books. Want to listen to one?"

He chuckled. "I'd rather you read one to me later." He lowered his tray and took their wine from the gorgeous blonde serving them without so much as a glance at her. He handed Ashley's to her. His long, thick fingers lingered over hers.

"Thanks." She took her drink and toasted him.

He rested his hand on her thigh, rubbing circles with his thumb. The heat his body put off was unbelievable. He leaned his head back and closed his eyes.

Ashley forced herself to look away from his profile. His strong jaw, stubborn chin, and soft lips made her want to lean over and kiss him. She didn't. Instead, she turned her attention to the narrator, but had trouble paying attention.

Dalton had changed a lot since she'd met him in Monterrey. He was more relaxed and had shared a little about himself. When he smiled, she melted. This side of his personality was warm and endearing.

****

Angel's hand trembled as she patted her pocket, where she slipped her name tag after realizing who'd boarded the plane. Calming herself with deep breaths, she strapped herself into her seat and waited until the pilot signaled it was safe for her and the rest of the occupants to move about.

The feeling of déjà vu slammed into her. How the hell in a world full of airplanes did he wind up on her flight? Dalton Murphy was sitting less than five feet away from her. Her heart pounded against her ribcage with the thrill of having him so nearby. She didn't quite understand why, but seeing him so up close was exciting.

The odds of her being on this flight with the very agents looking for her were astronomical. This wasn't her run. She wouldn't have been here if she hadn't swapped with a coworker so she could work the flight to London.

It wasn't fear causing her nerve endings to react like fireworks on the Fourth of July. Nothing truly frightened her. She sometimes wondered what else had been omitted while she'd been forming into a human. The woman who'd birthed her hadn't loved her. Angel had always been in the way. A burden. A mouth to feed.

Then he'd come along, and her mother had found a way to get rid of the burden.

Leaving her with a monster.

No. Angel had no compassion. None. She gave less than a damn about people in general. Especially men who had assumed they could put their hands on her. Touching led to beatings and rape.

Her coworker unfastened her seatbelt and stood. "Do you know the guy in 2B?"

"No." Angel shrugged. "Why?"

"You've been staring at him since we buckled in for takeoff."

"I'd be willing to bet he's used to women staring."

Angel unhooked, stood, and readied herself to offer drinks and snacks to those who'd paid extra for more legroom and instant attention.

She could see Dalton from where she was standing, and he appeared to be asleep. The woman was watching him. Her hand lifted as she stroked his cheek. His eyes opened and he caught one of her fingers with his teeth. His lips closed and his cheeks sunk slightly.

A sizzle of heat zipped up Angel's spine. He was gentle and affectionate. The sight set off a series of flashes that almost blocked her vision. The scene she was seeing confused her. Had she found a man who didn't use women? Who didn't think a female was theirs to abuse?

Her knees buckled, and she gripped the drink cart handle to steady herself. She watched as he pulled those fingers from his mouth and one by one, licked them clean. Then he leaned his head back and closed his eyes.

Angel helped prepare the trays for the in-flight meals for the first-class passengers. She couldn't stop herself from taking an occasional peek at him.

She averted her gaze when Dalton woke. He rolled his shoulders, unhooked his seat belt, and stood to stretch. The muscles in his back rippled against the material of his shirt.

The old woman he'd helped with her suitcase tripped coming out of the restroom and fell forward. Before Angel could react, he caught the woman and pulled her to his chest. He calmed her and helped her return to her seat. Angel had never seen anyone with reflexes that fast.

"Thank you, again." She gave him her best smile. "You prevented a horrible accident."

"No problem."

Angel didn't want him as an adversary. For his sake, she hoped he wasn't like most men. Men who thought they could touch without permission. Men who forced her to do things. What if...

She refused to let her mind wander that far back. Back before she knew men were disgusting animals. Back before she learned how to punish them.

"Excuse me, doll!" the passenger seated in row three called out. "I'm still waiting for my drink."

"Coming right up."

Chapter 17

Dalton put both their bags in the trunk of the rental, stopped, and took a call from Iain as he got in and buckled up. Facing Ashley, he asked, "What do you think?"

"About?" She lifted one perfect eyebrow. "Do I think you're too extravagant?"

"No. Top up or down?" His fingers hovered over the button on the dash. "We're taking the scenic route out highway 101."

"101 is the coastal highway." She perked up, digging through her handbag and pulling out a pair of sunglasses. "Down."

"That's my girl." In the blink of an eye, he'd readied the car and set the directions to Santa Barbara. "Say something when you get hungry, and we'll find somewhere to eat."

"Wait." This time both her hands dug into that wasteland women called their purse. A few seconds later, she held a hair band and pulled her hair back into a low ponytail. She turned her face up to the blue sky. "Now I'm ready."

Adorable wasn't a word he remembered ever using before, but it fit her. She was fucking adorable. He bit back the urge to unhook her seat belt, drag her across the console onto his lap, and taste those sweet lips of hers. Instead, he put both hands on the wheel and pointed the convertible toward the highway.

There wasn't a lot of conversation as they traveled. The scenery was lush and green, and he wanted her to take it all in. He couldn't wait until they reached Ventura. The highway ran along the coastline, giving her the perfect view of the Pacific Ocean.

"California is your home state. Isn't it? Does your dad still live here?"

"You have a good memory. Yes, he does."

"How far away are we from where he lives?"

He glanced at her just in time to see a strand of wheat-colored hair escape its bondage and allow the wind to whip it around her face. Her hand went to her head, trying to capture the errant lock, but it deftly avoided her grasp.

The breeze caught her laughter and blew the sound away from him, but he felt her joy. Her face, which was covered with a wide smile, reaffirmed his decision to reserve a convertible.

"He's a couple of hours east of Cabena. When we finish this interview, we'll have the entire weekend. I figure we'll have time to visit."

She slapped his arm. "Figure? How would he feel if he knew you were that close but didn't come see him?"

He scowled at the thought. "Depends. If it was work, he'd understand. If not? He'd be royally pissed, and I'd hear about it."

"I like him already." She leaned her arm across the seatback and stroked her fingers over the top of his ear.

After a few miles, she hadn't moved, and he wondered if she'd dozed off. It was hard to tell with the aviator sunglasses she wore. Oddly enough, he felt at peace in her presence, even when she was asleep, as if all was right with the world. She was smart, sweet, strong, and compassionate. Not to mention so very responsive to his touch.

It pissed him she'd been tasked with bringing him back to the agency. That she'd been honest and had told him made him respect her even more. He had to figure out a way to ensure his refusal wasn't held against her. She'd been given a taste of working in the field, and he knew she'd never be happy sitting behind a desk again.

He slowed the car when the Pacific came into view. Ashley had slid down in her seat and dozed off. He reached across and squeezed her knee. "Wake up, sleeping beauty."

"I'm not asleep. I'm daydreaming."

"You can tell me about this daydream later. For now, I think you should look over your left shoulder."

Shaking her head, she chuckled. "I'm not sharing my X-rated musings with you." She straightened her seat and glanced past him.

He would've given anything for a photograph of her face. Her mouth opened and she dragged her sunglasses down. Ashley's reaction mirrored the scene from *Jurassic Park*, where the heroine saw the live Brachiosaurus for the first time.

"It's stunning. Beautiful."

"Yes, it is. This view of the ocean never gets old."

"I've been to the Gulf of Mexico, but it's nothing like this. Let's stop somewhere for lunch that has a view."

"I know just the place." Thirty minutes later, after learning his favorite place to eat years ago had permanently closed, they were at Toby's Fish House. Ashley was thrilled they'd been seated on the wraparound patio, which offered a sweeping oceanfront view.

"My dad and I spent a lot of time on this stretch of the highway. During the off-season, or when I didn't have a game, we'd drive down. He loves to go deep-sea fishing."

"He sounds like a great dad."

"Now that I'm old enough to realize it, I can see how he tried to be both mother and father. I didn't appreciate it enough back then."

"I'm sure he knows you appreciate everything he did." She dipped a bite of lobster into clarified butter. "Oh God, that's good."

"Speaking of dads, why hasn't some guy tucked you away in a house with a white picket fence and a couple of kids?"

She shrugged her shoulders. "I dated this one guy in college for a while. We had different wants and ambitions. It didn't help we were on separate ends of the political scale."

"You ended it?"

"He did, but I agreed. The closer we got, the more we realized we worked better as friends." She put the bite of lobster dangling from her fork into her mouth. "My dad was over-the-moon pissed at me. He thought I'd be better off married with a family."

"What an ass." Dalton's tone left no room for argument. "It's hard to believe anyone alive still thinks a woman doesn't have the right to do whatever she wants with her life." He reached across the table and wiped a spot of butter off her bottom lip.

Her tongue popped out, tagging the tip of his finger, sending all sorts of dirty thoughts through his mind. "For what it's worth, I think you're very capable. You can do anything you believe you're big enough to do."

"Thank you." She folded her napkin and put it on the table. "The food was delicious. I'm stuffed."

"Me too. We should get back on the road." Dalton signaled for the check, dropped cash on the table, and then walked around behind her. He leaned down and placed a kiss in the hollow beneath her earlobe before gripping the back of her chair to help her to stand. "Never get so independent you can't allow a man to show you respect."

Her fingers brushed over the spot where his lips had touched her. "I will never forget this day." She stopped next to the car, turned to face him, and put her hand on his cheek. "You're a good man."

"Thank you. I'll admit to having a few morals and ethics, but I'm also a selfish bastard." His gaze locked on hers. Did she get it? The first time they'd kissed in the conference room of the Lost and Found compound, he'd been honest with her.

She squirmed under his scrutiny. "I think we're all a little self-centered."

Dalton stepped closer, backing her up until she was leaning against the passenger side door. His hard body pressed against hers. As had become his habit, his hand cupped the nape of her neck. His thumb stroked her skin. "Let's get you in the car before I do something extremely embarrassing right here in the parking lot."

He caught her hips with his hands and moved her far enough to open her door. Then he leaned down and captured her lips with his. His tongue slid into her mouth while his hand gripped her ponytail, pulling her head to just the right angle. "I wasn't thinking about just a kiss."

He walked around to the driver's side. With his back to the open-air patio, he adjusted himself before getting in and starting the car.

Neither spoke as he drove onto the busy highway, the wind cycling through the convertible to cool both of their desires. "Why don't you let the Arbers know we'll be there right on time?"

****

Ashley liked the Arbers's house. The white bungalow with black shutters on the windows seemed inviting. Set back off the road, a huge post oak tree gave relief to the bright sunshine. The front yard had five lawn chairs placed in a semi-circle near a firepit and a cornhole game sat nearby. A wooden bullseye target had been mounted midway up the trunk.

A brown-and-tan speckled dog rose from the porch and slowly walked over to greet them. Thin, with its ribs sticking out, the poor thing walked to the passenger side of the rental car, stopped, and looked right into her eyes. Her heart skipped a beat. Its dark brown gaze spoke to her. The animal was asking her for help. Tears flooded her eyes.

"I'm taking the dog with us."

"What? How would you get it home?" Dalton had been scanning the area and probably hadn't seen the animal. He unbuckled and leaned over next to her shoulder. A scowl crossed his face. "Fuck."

"You see it, too. I'll buy this dog if I have to."

"Stay on task and let me handle the dog."

She looked at him, questioning his tone of voice.

He caught her chin with his finger and thumb, turning her head to face him. "I'll take care of it."

The front door opened, and a middle-aged couple stepped outside. They didn't approach, but waited.

"I have a feeling they're not going to be helpful."

"Sure they are." Instead of walking to the porch, Dalton swung by the firepit, picked up an ax, and tossed it. He hit the target but missed the bullseye. "I've got this."

****

Dalton put the top up, then Ashley settled the dog in the back seat of the car. She'd spread the animal's tattered blanket out and watched as the poor thing made two circles before settling down. She appeared to be content. The Arbers had been willing to part with the dog when Dalton offered to take her instead of the fifty dollars he'd won after challenging Mr. Arber to an ax-throwing contest.

Mrs. Arber had gotten emotional and fled to the inside of the house when her husband started talking about their only child. Dalton remembered reading the report saying the man had never been in trouble with the law, had never married, and was a well-respected mechanic.

The son's involvement with a motorcycle club had caused a rift between mother and son. Unable to convince her that he hadn't joined a criminal gang, but a club that did good things for the community, he'd gone to work at the club's garage and moved onto their compound.

The fact that Wayne had paired up with one of the "sweet butts" who hung out with the gang had just about severed the relationship between mom and dad. They had assumed one of those women had killed and mutilated their son until they'd heard the news linking his death to two others.

Dalton and Ashley said their goodbyes and drove away without learning anything that would help identify the killer.

The couple had denied knowing why the dog was limping or why her ribs were showing, but the dog had avoided Mr. Arber, giving him a wide berth.

"How did you know you'd win or that Mr. Arber would accept the challenge?" Ashley asked, getting comfortable in her seat.

Dalton glanced at her with a question in his eyes as he got in, buckled up, and started the car. "You doubted my ability?"

"Well, yeah," she laughed. "Who knew you could throw an ax like Paul Bunyon?" She stretched across the console and kissed his cheek. "But I'm glad you did."

"Me too, but I think we'll drive straight through to my dad's house. The dog might not do well inside a motel room all night."

Ashley reached back and stroked the dog's head. "I know I created a major problem, but she was begging me."

"If I hadn't seen her eyes locked on you, I wouldn't have believed it. We'll ask my dad. He might know someone who will take her. That is, unless you plan on taking her to Texas. Then we have to get creative."

"I'm hoping we'll find somebody who will give her a good life. Marcus and Diablo seemed devoted to each other. Yet, he goes on assignments. How does he manage?"

"His wife, Chris, owns an animal rescue in Dallas. After Diablo saved her life, they bonded. They're fine without Marcus while he's on assignment."

"The dog saved her life?"

"Chris had been kidnapped, and when Marcus and I found where she was being held, we went after her. There was no way of slowing him down, and he went in ahead of me. The bastard had a knife to her throat, so Marcus started trying to talk to the guy. I stayed at the door with Diablo, but before I could stop him, he was in motion. He flew across the room and attacked the bastard."

Dalton's cell vibrated. "That's Reed. I'll pull over so we can hear. Put him on speaker."

She picked up the phone. "He's the hot guy, right?"

A sharp stab of jealousy punched Dalton in the chest. "Just answer the damn phone."

She held the cell up so they both could hear, and then accepted the call. "Hi, Reed, you're speaking with both of us."

"I'd rather talk to just you. You're much prettier than he is."

"Just tell us what you found," Dalton growled.

"I decided to take a look at Senator Hawley. He's on every news station talking about how much he loved his wife and shedding a tear when he asks the public for help catching her killer. I'd wager good money he paid to have her killed.

"At the end of his workday, he went home for a couple of hours and then drove straight to a motel about a half-hour drive outside of Houston. He's having an affair with his campaign manager's wife. When they came out, I followed her instead of him."

"Reed, call my brother and tell him what you've learned."

"Already done. You need anything else from me?"

"Yeah," Dalton said. "Do you have a dog?"

"No. And don't want one. Why?"

"No reason. Talk soon."

As if the dog knew she had been mentioned, she wedged the upper half of her body between the front seats and lay down on the console.

Ashley leaned across and patted Dalton on the cheek. "You were jealous when I said Reed is hot."

He glanced at her with one eyebrow raised. "I was not."

"Then pretend you were, because I liked thinking it."

"I was jealous as hell."

"That's better."

Dalton started to pull onto the highway but stopped. He scrolled through his cell and found his dad's number. "I should let him know we'll be there around three."

"What's his name?"

"Scott."

"Scott," she repeated. "I like it."

She took his cell, leaned back in her seat, tapped the number, and changed to speaker.

"Son!" The male voice was deep and slightly gravelly, like Dalton's. "I'm glad you called. How's it going?"

"He's fine, Mr. Murphy. He wanted to let you know we'll be there around three this afternoon. Does that work for you?"

Dalton shook his head and laughed. "You're going to give him a heart attack."

"What was that? I didn't hear what he said," Mr. Murphy said.

"I think Dalton's afraid you're going to think he's bringing a surprise wife to visit."

"Well, that would be good news. Is he?"

Dalton snagged the phone from her hand. "No, Dad. She's my partner."

"Oh. I'd still love to meet her."

Dalton could hear the confusion in his dad's tone. "Not life partner. Temporary work partner."

"Either way, she's welcome. I'll have a fish fry pulled together by the time you get here."

"We have a dog with us. She needs to see a vet."

"Got you covered. One of my newest fishing buddies is a veterinarian."

"Great. See you soon."

****

Angel changed into the dress and shoes she'd bought at a boutique near the hotel. The charity auction she was going to attend required her to fit in, yet go unnoticed, which meant her gown had to be lovely, but nothing anyone would remember as she moved through the crowd.

She secured the red wig, rearranged the bangs so they would look natural, and finished her makeup. Satisfied, she took the stairs down to the lobby, hoping to avoid a chance meeting with a coworker in the elevator. She'd begged off meeting for drinks, claiming a headache, and it wouldn't do to be caught in the lobby dressed as if she had an audience with the queen.

A taxi took her to the cigar store on Regent, London's most popular high street, where she picked up a box with Kyle Beltrane's name on it. She paid the clerk and hailed another cabbie. On the way to the Discovery Centre, she opened the box and removed a knife and invitation to the ball.

Shorter than the stiletto knife she usually carried strapped to her thigh, this bad boy had an eight-inch blade and a stylish black marble handle. She slipped the weapon, butt-end first, under the right cuff of the long-sleeve gown she wore.

This situation didn't sit well with her. Twice now, she hadn't been allowed to determine when, where, or how to kill a mark. But Kyle had been very explicit in his instructions. And like with the pistol she'd kept; she'd been told to ensure the weapon couldn't be found after she'd finished the job.

The cabbie stopped, and she exited, staring up at the huge building.

"Hey, lady!" the driver called out. "You forgot your package."

"Keep it." Carrying the invitation in her hand, she leaned down and looked through the cab's window. "I bought my husband his favorite cigar, but in retrospect, he doesn't deserve a gift."

She spent the next hour perusing the items laid out for the silent auction and observing the movements of the woman whose life would end tonight. Not that she cared what the target had done. This was a job. Not as rewarding as her newest pastime, but it paid well. So well, she was going to take a sabbatical from both jobs when she returned to the States. She deserved some time to herself.

The target said something to the man next to her, then turned and walked away. Angel waited a few minutes and then followed her to the restroom. She stepped into the stall three doors away from the target, unbuttoned the cuff of her sleeve, and let the stiletto slide into her hand. She waited until she heard the water running before exiting.

She took the time to ensure they were alone, then stepped behind the target and quickly slid the blade under her shoulder blade, straight into her heart. The woman didn't make a sound. Her mouth moved like a fish out of water.

There was no time to waste. She shoved the shocked and dying woman back into a stall. She sat her on the toilet, wiped the handle of the knife clean, and then tucked a queen of diamonds card in the now-dead woman's hand.

She left the building, snagged a lurking black cab, and as a precaution, requested a ride to a hotel near the airport. She then took a second taxi back across London to her hotel.

The ride gave her time to go over the night's events. It was an amateurish kill. Too many things could've gone wrong. Someone could've come into the restroom. Kyle assigned this hit to her knowing the risk of being caught was great. Had he hoped she'd get caught?

He'd be furious that she'd left her calling card. Too bad. Why shouldn't she be world famous? It would surely impress Dalton.

She carefully made her way back to her hotel room. Once she'd removed the wig, she changed into black leggings, a multicolored tunic, and ankle boots. Satisfied with her appearance, she went down to the bar and joined the flight crew in time for one drink before closing, claiming her headache had disappeared after she'd had a nap.

****

The nine-hour flight home had been uneventful. Most of the passengers had slept, giving Angel's coworker time to go on and on about the UK Secretary of Transport's wife who'd been brutally murdered.

Angel rolled her eyes. That kill was one of the kindest she'd ever pulled off. Wouldn't they be surprised to know she'd wanted to castrate every single one of those bastards who'd hurt her? Not once did one of them have second thoughts. They were like a pack of animals circling their prey, waiting for their turn to destroy her.

****

Angel made her way to her car, started the engine, and then called Kyle. She had to tell him the package had been mailed, letting him know the job had been done. He answered on the first ring.

"I need to see you. Now." The anger rolling off him made its way through the airways.

The hair on her arms stood. Killing him would be fun, but he had connections with too many powerful people. She wasn't the only person he used when someone needed to die.

Before Dalton, she wouldn't have cared if a contract had been put on her. Even now, she wasn't sure she gave a damn. "I just got into my car. I'm tired and I'm going home."

"I'm not sure that's a good idea."

"Why not?" She knew he was pissed she'd left her card, but she cared little about what upset him or didn't.

"Because I'm not sure you're safe there. International fame may have cost you your life."

"Let me worry about that." Angel was tired to the bone. Maybe even tired of living. Tired of hating to go to sleep for fear the nightmares would return.

"I warned you about leaving that fucking card." Kyle's voice had risen a couple of octaves. "Jesus. Now I'm worried about myself."

Leaving the queen of diamonds card on her stepfather's body had made her feel powerful. Granted none of the bastards she'd carved up had been as bad as the animals who'd laughed and leered while she'd been passed from man to man. The card was supposed to send a message.

Why had she started leaving them on paid hits?

That was just for fun.

"Our primary customer has expressed extreme displeasure at your ever-growing vanity. This one has put us both in the crosshairs."

"And you know I don't give two fucks what the mafia boss thinks. Tell me his name and I'll make sure he doesn't send someone for either of us."

"You really don't care if you die, do you?"

Her fingers drummed on the steering wheel. "I'm already dead."

"I'm not. I want to live to a ripe old age."

"Tell him people will die if they come after me."

"Are you coming in as I asked?"

Did he think she was that stupid? "No."

Angel ended the call. She sat in the parking lot and thought about Kyle's words. If he truly believed his life was in danger, he'd give her up without a second thought. He'd share her address and everything he knew about her to save himself.

What he didn't know was she'd prepared for trouble a long time ago. Purchasing the small hideaway outside Dallas was finally going to pay off. All she had to do was get there safely.

She started the car and headed outside the city, making sure she wasn't followed. An eerie calm came over her as she lay out the path ahead in her mind. Angel was comfortable with the fact she'd probably die a violent death, but not yet. She had a couple of allies, who for the right amount of money, would do anything she asked.

Once safely tucked away in her cabin, she emailed her resignation to her supervisor. Next, she sent a text to Axel. They had a lot to go over, but with his help, she'd know where Dalton was at all times, and what he was doing. She wanted to meet him. Spend time with him.

Had she truly found the perfect man?

****

Ashley put the last plate in the dishwasher, dried her hands, and turned to Scott. "Mr. Murphy, the fish was amazing. I've never eaten anything cooked in an outdoor deep fryer."

"Call me Scott," he said, glancing over his shoulder. He watched out the window as his son drove away.

He'd sent Dalton to the store for ice cream, and she had a feeling Scott wanted to chat with her.

"Cooking and eating outside makes everything taste better. Let's go out back and sit with the dog and watch the sunset."

"Good idea." She trailed along behind him to the patio, giving him time to sit and stretch his legs out before she sat in the chair next to him. The dog trotted to them, and Ashley scratched behind her ears.

"What's her name?"

"I've been calling her Lucky. It's not very creative, but her luck has taken a turn for the better." She smiled as the dog sniffed Scott's hand for a second before dropping to the ground right next to his feet. "Thank you for calling your vet friend."

"She has an appointment with him in the morning. He'll get her fixed up. I've decided to keep her. It's been too long since I had a dog. She'll put my backyard to good use."

"Thank you. Dalton and I just couldn't leave the poor thing behind."

"He likes you."

She had known Dalton would come up in their conversation. Knowing hadn't kept her blush reflex from kicking in, though. She turned toward Scott and spoke the truth. "He is a great guy."

"I've never seen my son look at a woman like he does you."

"Never?"

"No. Never."

"I like him, too."

"But?" Scott's eyes were filled with interest.

"Dalton is nothing if not honest. He has no interest in a relationship."

"That's my fault. What happened between his mother and me had nothing to do with him, but I didn't help him understand. He started keeping people at arm's length, never letting his friends get too close. After his divorce, he just shut down his emotions. I think he doesn't get attached so he won't be hurt again."

"He loves you very much," she said to reassure Scott. "When he shared memories of his youth and how you were always there for him, I could see and hear his affection for you."

"I've worried he'd never open himself up to love again." Scott smiled down at her. "You may be the key to unlocking that wall he's built around his heart."

"I don't know about that. He doesn't open up easily."

"Did my son tell you he's the one who walked in on his mother and her lover?"

Ashley's heart dropped to the bottom of her stomach. "No, he didn't." She struggled for a breath. "That's why he doesn't trust anyone enough to let them get close to him."

"He felt his mother didn't love him enough to stay. To him, it meant he wasn't worthy. From then on, he was always trying to prove himself. Had to be the best at everything. It didn't surprise me that the FBI recruited him right out of college."

Ashley remained silent, letting Scott's words sink in. "Between you and me, I'll miss him when this case is over."

The sound of a car engine ended their talk. Both of them stood, and Scott stepped between her and the door. "I'd appreciate it if you don't tell him about our conversation."

"I won't. Maybe someday he'll trust someone enough to share the whole story." Ashley walked out front to meet Dalton. His dark eyes searched her face when she blocked his path. She reached up and pulled him down for a kiss.

His free arm slipped around her waist and held her against his rock-hard body. "Careful kissing me like that. I'll have a hard-on when we walk inside. And it will be your fault." The sound of the door opening ended their moment. He released her and grinned over her shoulder at his dad.

"I would suggest you two get a room, but you've already got one here." Scott's laughter was genuine, and Ashley did her best not to blush.

"Ice cream's melting." Dalton's grin was pure sex as he caught her hand in his and led the way back inside.

Scott dished up their dessert, and the three of them moved to the living room. They were almost finished when their cells started buzzing. Ashley was the first to end the call, and met Scott's sad gaze.

He stood, picked up their bowls, and set them on the kitchen counter. "Another murder?"

"Yes." She shook her head in confusion. "In London."

Dalton stood and slid his cell into his hip pocket. "Yeah. A United Kingdom cabinet member's wife."

Scott's eyes were wide. "And it's connected to the ones you're working on?"

"Nate said the killer left her calling card," Dalton said.

Scott scratched his chin. "Sounds like you're looking for a pilot, traveling salesman, or flight attendant."

"Dad," Dalton said with a nod. "You might be right."

"Could flight records tell you anything? Can that even be done?"

"With all the flights going into London from all over the world?" Ashley responded. "That search would be the proverbial needle in a haystack."

"Iain might quit if we asked him to try that search. Who knows?" Dalton winked at her. "Has Carl been in contact with the Metropolitan Police?"

She nodded. "We'll hear more as soon as he knows something."

Scott had scooted to the edge of the couch, and his gaze was flitting back and forth between Dalton and Ashley. "Is Carl on your team?"

Dalton turned to his dad. "We worked out of the same office years ago. He's been promoted, and Ashley reports to him."

"Are you going to London?"

"No, Dad. You're stuck with us until morning."

"Then the logical question is, who's ready for more ice cream?"

19

Dalton had put both of their suitcases in his old bedroom. His dad hadn't as much as lifted an eyebrow, but Ashley hesitated to enter when Dalton opened the door. He held back a smile as he extended his hand. "You coming in?"

"You're sure your dad is OK with us sleeping together?"

"I'm sure he thinks we're old enough to make our own decisions." His eyes darkened, filling with lust. "Now get your ass in here before I throw you over my shoulder and haul you in."

"You wouldn't dare."

"Wouldn't I?" He stepped toward her, and she ran past him, laughing and stopping at the foot of the bed.

He shut the door and then closed the distance between them. His fingers cupped the nape of her neck before sliding up to gather a handful of hair. He tugged her head back. "I'll give you five minutes in the bathroom before I join you."

He laughed as she looked around, as if someone else was in the room. "Here? With your father down the hall?"

"Here. Now." He pulled her closer and ran his tongue across her bottom lip. "Four minutes."

"Give me three and you can join me in the shower."

His hands dropped to his sides. "Go."

She slid between his body and the wall and then sprinted to the en suite bathroom, closing the door behind her.

He placed his cell on the nightstand, watching the time while he toed off his boots, removed his socks, and placed them on the floor next to the bed. Hearing water running had him jerking the rest of his clothes off at record speed. His entire body tightened just knowing she was ready for him to join her. He was already so hard, his dick almost hurt. Taking himself in his hand, he squeezed, trying to slow down his need to be inside her.

He opened the door to find Ashley standing in front of the sink. She turned to face him. Her eyes flared as she watched him stroke himself back and forth.

"You are so beautiful," she said, crooking her finger, motioning him to come closer.

"Men aren't beautiful," he growled.

"You are." Her fingers trailed across his cheek. "You have a strong jaw. I like it."

"Is that all you like?"

Hell yes, he was baiting her, but he couldn't help himself. Hoping she'd bypass the rest of his body and go straight to where he needed her most, he stood very still.

No such luck.

Her hands moved to his pecs, dragging her nails slowly to his abs.

"I think your Adonis belt is sexy."

"So you've said. I've noticed you like it." At this point, he was holding his breath.

"You're very well endowed, and I'm growing fond of the rest of you." She dropped to her knees, moved his hand, and replaced it with her tongue. She licked the tip like it was a lollypop and she was hungry. His knees damn near buckled.

"Fuck." He wanted her to lock her lips around him and take him deep. Instead, he caught her arms and pulled her to her feet. "I promised to wash your back."

It took all the strength he could muster to take her hand and help her stand. She turned and lifted to her tiptoes. She placed a soft kiss on his lips before stepping under the water.

Dalton followed and stood behind her, pressed against her soft warm skin. He reached for the soap, lathered his hands, and washed every inch of her body. Turning her to face him, he lifted her left leg and placed her foot on the small bench. He dropped to his knees and looked up at her. "If you don't want my dad to know what we're doing, you'll have to keep those sexy noises you make to a minimum."

Ashley's eyes narrowed. "I don't make noises."

"Yes, you do. And I love them. When you make those sounds, I know I'm doing something right." He opened her folds with his thumbs, flattened his tongue, and licked her from back to front.

Her low moan was like a shot of adrenaline to his body. He moved one hand to her mound and pulled the hood back from her clit. Her fingers threaded into his hair, pulling hard, and he growled against her flesh. When he pressed down on her little button, she muttered something he couldn't understand, but it didn't matter. She was pleased, and he was right where he needed to be.

He slid one finger into her tight warm passage. Damn, he was dying to get inside her. He needed to feel her body stretch and accept him. That could wait as he devoted his attention to lashing her clit until she tightened her grip on his hair and his scalp tingled.

Dalton stood, pushing her back against the tiles. Then he lifted her, pulled her legs up around his waist, and slammed his cock inside her.

"Yes!" she cried out as her inner walls squeezed, as if trying to pull him even deeper.

He slid in and out, relishing the feeling of being one with her. He covered her mouth with his to muffle the unintelligible sounds coming from her. Her hands cupped the back of his neck and pulled his head back until just their breath separated them. Her eyes, full of need, were almost green.

"What do you need, baby? Tell me, and I'll make it happen."

Her gaze locked with his. "I want to feel you come inside me."

"Fuck. Hang on." Her words opened the damn inside him, and he pounded into her again and again. He held back his release until her mouth fell open in a silent cry and she pulsed and spasmed around him. Then he exploded inside her as jet after jet of his cum mingled with hers.

He held her, still pressed against the shower wall, until their minds drifted back to earth.

"Dalton?" Her words were spoken so softly he barely heard them.

"Hmm?" It wasn't a good response, but was all he had at the moment.

"Thank you."

"For?" he asked, as he set her feet on the floor.

"Being you."

Not sure how to respond, he stared at her as she relaxed her legs and moved him back a step. She picked up the soap, lathered her hands, and slowly washed his body. When the water started to cool off, he stepped out and grabbed two towels. Draping one around his neck, he slowly dried her and then himself. By the time he was finished, he was hard as steel.

He had to kiss her. His tongue took control of her mouth. Her body dissolved in complete surrender. Standing naked in his father's bathroom, their bodies had become one. Complete. As if one wouldn't exist without the other. That startled him. Scared the fuck out of him.

Why had he allowed this to get so far out of hand?

He released his tight grip on her, backed up, and stared down at her. Her gaze held his for a long moment. Her beautiful eyes slowly lost their sparkle. It was as if she could see inside his brain.

"Relax. I didn't hear wedding bells. Did you?"

The tight band of nerves constricting his chest relaxed. "It's a little scary that you can read my thoughts."

She scooted around him, turned down the bed, and got under the covers. "We have a busy day tomorrow. I need some sleep."

Dalton climbed in next to her, instantly realizing the full-size bed was smaller than he remembered. He turned off the light and rolled toward her, quickly noticing he couldn't feel the warmth of her body. She'd scooted as far away from him as possible and turned her back to him.

He'd hurt her. It was the last thing he'd wanted to do. He administered an invisible head slap to himself. He moved closer, slid his hand around her waist, and pulled her off the edge of the bed. Their bodies were spooned, and she didn't pull away, which he saw as a good sign. "Hey."

"How many times do I have to tell you I'm not in the market for a husband before you believe me? No. Don't answer me."

****

Ashley lay perfectly still until Dalton's breathing slowed and the muscles in his arm relaxed. Just his nearness had heat racing through her veins. His warm hard body pressed against her back made her feel wanted and safe.

She understood his reluctance to get involved with anybody. He'd been hurt twice. Once by his mother, and then again by his wife.

Telling him she wasn't looking for a husband had been the truth. She'd planned her future very carefully. Starting the day she spoke with the FBI recruiter. She'd known exactly what she wanted to do with her life. She wanted to make a difference, and she'd accepted that she'd have to sacrifice some things to achieve her goals. From forgoing nights out with her college dorm mates so she could cram knowledge into her brain, to pushing past her insecurities to be in the top ten at Quantico. Then she'd executed every assignment with diligence once she'd been assigned to an office.

She'd dated in high school and college, but time spent with the opposite sex had been limited. The one time she'd opened herself to what she thought was love had proven her ability to judge a person's character wasn't as good as she'd thought.

Ashley wouldn't allow herself to fall in love with Dalton. She hoped someday a man like him would care for her, but it wouldn't be him. Not when she knew when the case was solved, all she'd have left were memories and a broken heart. She drifted off while trying to convince herself she hadn't already fallen in love with him.

****

Sunlight streaming across Ashley's face pulled her from a deep sleep. She rolled over only to find Dalton's side of the bed empty and cool to the touch.

She got up and pulled the curtains closed. For a few seconds, she considered the merits of getting back between the sheets and just lounging for a few minutes. Sounds coming from somewhere in the house got her attention.

She made a quick trip to the bathroom, and then slipped on jeans and a fresh T-shirt. Barefoot and hair pulled up in a loose bun, she stepped into the hall and walked toward the sound of Scott's voice.

"Your girl still asleep?"

"Dad." Dalton's tone rang with frustration. "She's not my girl."

****

Dalton hoped a lecture wasn't coming.

"She's the first woman you've ever brought home." Handing his son a cup of black coffee, Scott continued. "I watched you two last night. There's something there."

Dalton was dumbfounded. They'd never discussed women or serious relationships. Sure, they'd had the sex talk, but this discussion was strange. "To be honest, I don't have any long-term expectations. Ashley's life is with the FBI. I think she's as dedicated to the job as I was. After this case is closed, her career is going to take off.

"What about you, Dad? You were what, thirty-six when you divorced mom? Why didn't you ever date? Re-marry?"

His dad grinned. "Nice attempt to sidetrack me. Don't let your feelings about your mother interfere with what could be the love of a lifetime." He held his hand up to stop Dalton's protest. "In answer to your question, I wish I had found a woman I wanted to spend the rest of my life sleeping beside. Unfortunately, that hasn't happened, but I assure you, I haven't lived the life of a monk." He refilled his cup. "Just be careful with Ashley, son. Don't hurt her."

The door to Dalton's bedroom closed. Thankfully, it would end this conversation. "Incoming," he said, loud enough for her to hear.

"Coffee's hot," his dad said as Ashley entered the room.

"Good morning, and yes, please." Barefoot, hair tangled into some sort of a knot at the top of her head, she wore jeans and the shirt he'd worn yesterday. Her gaze scanned across his dad before settling on him.

"Sleep OK?" his dad asked.

"Like a baby." She accepted the cup, held it close to her face, and took a deep breath. "Thanks, Scott." She turned and started walking back down the hall. "I'll be ready to go in fifteen minutes. You know how dedicated I am."

The door closing felt like a ton of bricks had just landed on his chest. "Fuck."

20

Ashley had frozen in her tracks when she'd heard Scott ask Dalton if his girl was still asleep. She'd opened her mouth to let them know she was in the hall when he'd corrected his father with a brisk and flat statement that she was nothing more than a coworker to him. She'd blinked back the stab of pain in her chest before opening and closing the door to Dalton's room. It was a warning that she was awake and about to join them.

Maybe she shouldn't have paused and listened, but she'd been the topic of their conversation.

Maybe she shouldn't have waited so long before she'd alerted them to her arrival.

Maybe hearing Dalton snap out the words, "She's not my girl," with such venom shouldn't have upset her.

But it did. Hearing him write off the past few nights as if they hadn't happened had cut her to the core.

She'd dressed in jeans and a bright yellow and purple Los Angeles Lakers T-shirt she'd bought at a gas station on the way up the coast. The display had offered a selection of team shirts, but she loved bright colors, so she'd bought that one. She spent a few minutes on her hair, swiped the mascara wand over her lashes, and added lip gloss. She was tying her sneakers when Dalton entered the room.

He sat next to her. She stood and grabbed her bag. "I'm ready when you are. I'll be in the back with Lucky."

"Lucky?"

"The dog. Your dad is keeping her."

As she walked past, Dalton caught her hand with his. "How much did you hear?"

Without looking at him, she answered, "Enough." She looked down at her small hand in his. She tugged herself free, grabbed her bag, walked through the door, and then straight to the backyard. Kneeling, she hugged Lucky to her, whispering about what a wonderful life she was going to have living with Scott.

She hadn't known what to say to Dalton. Hadn't she reaffirmed the fact she wasn't looking for a husband? So why had hearing him state there was nothing between them hurt so much?

Scott joined her, sitting on one of the steps. "I think that dog is going to miss you."

"She desperately wants affection." Ashley scratched behind the dog's ears, laughing at how her entire backside wiggled when she wagged her tail. "Just because I've been calling her Lucky doesn't mean you can't change her name to anything you want."

"Lucky is a great name. I'm sorry if I caused problems between you and Dalton. Probably shouldn't have asked such personal questions. I guess I got too excited that maybe he'd learned to trust again."

"I don't know him well enough to comment on that. You know, he's right about us. We don't even live in the same city, so there's no reason to expect that we'd see each other after the case is over." She stood, and Scott did the same.

"I'm ready when you are," Dalton said, holding the screen door open.

She extended her hand to Scott, thought better of it, and hugged him instead. "Thank you for your hospitality."

"Come back any time."

He walked them out to the rental car. Wrapping his arms around his son, he patted him on the back. "I love you."

Dalton's face lit up with a smile. "Love you too, Dad."

Watching father and son openly show affection for each other tugged at her heart so hard Ashley had to blink back the tears welling in her eyes. She couldn't remember receiving any terms of endearment from her dad. She'd survived just fine without it.

She gave one last wave to Scott, tossed her bag in the back seat, and got in the car. Dalton followed, driving away without uttering a word. The silence suited her as she thought back through the last few nights she'd spent in his arms.

Had she overreacted to words meant for his dad's ears and not hers? Of course she wasn't his girlfriend, but they were or had been in some sort of a relationship. How did you have sex again and again with such passion with someone who meant nothing to you?

Apparently, he could.

It was best if she stuck to facts pertinent to the case. "Our flight is on time and leaves at 3:15."

"We'll make it." Dalton's tone was cool.

Ashley opened her laptop. Seconds later, she was scrolling through her emails. "Way to go, Iain," she said. "He's sent information on Vince Vardon's Grand Cayman bank account. Sizable amounts are going into the account from foreign entities."

"That information needs to go to the ATF."

She ignored the interruption. "Iain also found an anomaly he thought might be interesting. A few months ago, Kyle Beltrane made a fifteen-hundred-dollar electronic deposit to Vardon's account."

"Who the hell is Beltrane?"

"If you'll let me finish reading, I'll tell you."

Damn him. She could be as cranky as he could.

"Sorry," he snapped.

"Sure you are." Her fingers dug into her palms. He had no reason to be pissed.

The car took a quick dive into a gas station parking lot. He drove around to the side, slammed on the brakes, and parked.

Dalton exited the car and then marched around to the passenger side. His expression sent cold shivers up her spine. His mouth was drawn into a thin line and the nerve in his jaw was pulsing. He opened her door and pulled her outside so fast she was stunned and then even angrier.

"What the hell are you doing?"

His answer came when his lips slammed down on hers. Ashley held back her response for maybe two heartbeats before she relaxed into him and kissed him back. Anger gave way to lust as his tongue gained entrance and swept inside her mouth. One hand gripped the back of her blouse, holding her tightly against him, and the other wrapped her low ponytail around his hand, tilting her head to whatever angle suited him.

She wasn't sure how long the kiss lasted, but when he lifted his head, her legs had turned to rubber and her brain was fried. Somewhere in the back of her mind, she wondered what had just happened, but couldn't seem to form the question.

"Will you stop being pissed at me?" His words growled through gritted teeth. He didn't wait for an answer, although her mouth was open, ready to speak. "What did you want me to tell my father? That we've been fucking like rabbits? That this was the first time in years I've had sex with the same woman more than once?" His mouth clamped down and his eyes slammed shut, making it obvious he hadn't intended to reveal that last little tidbit.

She tried but failed to hold back the smile creeping across her face. She lifted onto her tiptoes and gently kissed his soft, sexy lips. "I kind of like what you just said."

His eyes opened to slits. "Which part? The rabbit fucking or repeated sex?"

"Both." She wrapped her arms around his chest. "And I'm not mad anymore. I overreacted. I know we're not in a committed relationship, but I'm glad to be the first woman in a while you wanted to have more than once."

His entire body seemed to relax under her hands. A split second later, his muscles tensed. "We gotta go or we'll miss our flight."

Back on the road, she continued reading. "Beltrane is an attorney. Iain is looking into him as soon as he can. Then we'll send facts to the ATF."

****

The plane's landing gear groaned as if in pain, and woke Ashley from a comfortable nap. She felt Dalton's hand cup her cheek as he kissed the top of her head. He'd lifted the armrest between them before takeoff, giving her room to lean on his shoulder, and she'd gotten comfortable enough to fall asleep.

She tilted her head up and smiled as a second kiss landed on her forehead. "You make a wonderful pillow."

"I must, since you fall asleep on me every time we fly." His thumb brushed a loose strand of hair off her face. "I like holding you while you sleep."

Ashley pushed off his chest, rolling her head in circles. "Time to reenter the real world."

"What does that mean?"

"We've interviewed every person we could and came back with nothing more than a note from the killer to you. Carl may pull me off the case."

"He won't."

"He might." Her heart hurt at the thought of failing, but sooner or later, she'd be called back to San Antonio.

"Not until I say we're through with this case." Dalton ran his hand through his hair, shoving back that one lock that seemed to be intent on falling onto his forehead.

"We need an update from Reed and Iain."

"Will they be at the compound this late?" Their flight had been delayed three hours while they waited for a maintenance crew. Ashley was happy they'd finally arrived and would be on the ground in Dallas soon.

"Somebody's always around, but I think we should wait until morning. We can work from the office at my house, get some rest, and go to the compound in the morning." Dalton put his tray up and tucked the book he was reading in his bag under the seat. "That sound OK to you?"

21

Dalton unlocked the front door to his house and dropped their bags just inside. "I'll give you a tour later." He walked into the kitchen and grabbed a couple of plates from the cabinet and placed them on the breakfast bar. "Let's eat first."

He pulled two ice-cold beers from the fridge while Ashley opened the pizza box and put two slices out for him and one for herself. He straddled the stool and ate the first one in three bites.

"You were hungry," she laughed, taking a huge bite. "Hmm, so am I."

"Sorry, it's barely warm. Want me to nuke yours?"

"No thanks. It's perfect."

Her lush lips covered the tip of her wedge and he almost groaned. Watching her eat shouldn't be sexy.

Dalton took a long pull of his beer, then attacked the second piece. She ate with way more manners than he did as he emptied his plate and took another helping. Her eyes sparkled with humor. He shrugged off the tightness in his chest.

She'd read the emails to him while he drove, but he hadn't paid enough attention to her. That alone irritated the hell out of him. His libido had been too busy thinking about having her in his bed again tonight.

Not paying attention was a surefire way to get your ass killed. That crap just wasn't acceptable.

"Tell me Iain's come up with something helpful."

Ashley retrieved her laptop and logged on to her email. "Here's more. This Beltrane person is an attorney and a gun lobbyist. His office is in Boston, and Iain's digging into his background."

"And Reed?"

"You really don't read your emails, do you?" She took another slice of pizza, and Dalton got two more beers for them.

"I told you there was no need." He placed her drink in front of her, leaned down, and licked a spot of sauce off her upper lip. Her head lifted slightly, giving him better access. "I have you."

"Why, yes. You do."

Damn, he was instantly hard. He sat and willed the swelling against his zipper to go away. Her fingers flew over the keys ten times faster than his would. He liked watching her work. The set of her jaw left no doubt she was in serious mode.

"Reed says Ash questioned Senator Haley and his staff. There was trouble in paradise, but Haley has an airtight alibi. They haven't connected him to the murder."

"Let's get some rest. Tomorrow we ask Iain why he was so interested in that attorney Beltrane."

"Are we going to Boston?"

"Maybe. If nothing else, we may solve some of your old boyfriend's cases for him." Dalton gathered the pizza box and tossed it in the trash, then offered Ashley his hand. "I'll give you the grand tour on our way to bed."

"Sounds good." She followed as he walked through the living room. There wasn't much to look at except a massive TV, his brown leather couch and recliner, but she stopped and turned a circle. "Dalton?"

"Yes?" He had no idea what she'd ask. Surely she hadn't expected lace curtains or bright colors. His white walls suited him just fine.

"Why are there no pictures in here?"

"What do you call the one over the couch?"

"A Dallas Cowboys poster from the sixties."

"Exactly."

She gave him that sexy smirk that made him want to kiss it away.

"It was my dad's. He mailed to me when I bought this house."

"Oh. Then it's lovely."

Dalton sighed, walked over to her, and tossed her over his shoulder. She squealed and pounded on his back. Ignoring her, he locked one arm around her legs. "Forget the tour."

"Put me down."

He smacked her bottom while striding down the hall. "When we get to the bedroom. I can't wait for your critique."

"You're going to be sorry." She was laughing so hard it was hard to understand her.

"And why is that?"

"Because I need to pee."

He slid her to the floor and pointed at a closed door. "Bathroom."

He chuckled to himself and walked into his bedroom. "She's gonna love this." The room was as plain as the living room. A bed, dresser, bookcase, and a nightstand. That was it. Like the rest of the house, there were no curtains. Blinds were all he needed.

Her hands suddenly slid around his waist from behind.

He took one hand and pulled her around to face him. "Better?"

"Much." She tilted her head and look up at him. "You've changed over the last few weeks."

"Have I?" He scowled as she shook her head. "How so?"

"You're not as cross and grumpy."

"And you're going to take credit for that?"

"I am."

He snugged her against him, sliding his leg between hers, feeling the heat coming from her.

"Great sex always puts me in a good mood."

"If you're lucky, after we shower, I'll put you in an even better mood."

She roared with laughter when he tossed her back over his shoulder again and marched them into the bathroom. Dalton reached in and turned the jets on, and then set her on her feet. "Get naked."

Ashley patted her heart. "You are such a romantic."

He arched an eyebrow and reached for her, but she backed away. Her fingers caught the bottom of her pullover top, and it was quickly dropped at his feet.

"On second thought, I'll do it myself." He grabbed the waistband of her jeans and popped the snap and lowered the zipper. The rest of their clothes came off in a flurry. He stepped back and watched as she stepped under the spray. Water sluiced down her back and over her shoulders, streaming down her chest, and then flowing over those rose-colored nipples. "You are too perfect to be real."

"Oh, I'm real all right."

"Yes, you are." He undressed and joined her. Reaching around her, he grabbed the soap, lathered his hands, and washed her from her neck to her toes.

After he'd given her two orgasms and had one for himself, he turned off the water, pulled her out onto the rug, and toweled her dry. He quickly dried himself while watching her. Pleasure washed through his system at the dreamy expression on her face. She appeared to be extremely satisfied.

He pointed her toward the bed and smacked her bottom. "I need to shave, and then I'll join you."

Ashley cupped his cheeks with her hands. "You're not going to shave that stubble off completely, are you?"

"I was. Figured it might be too much on your thighs."

"It's not." She caught his hand and led him to bed.

If she liked hair on his face, he wasn't going to disappoint her. Hell, he'd probably grow a full-blown beard if that's what she wanted.

Dalton joined her on the bed. Sitting against the headboard, he pulled her between his legs. Her back to his chest, they relaxed into each other. He touched her cheek with the tips of his fingers. Gliding them downward, he mapped the soft skin of her neck, onto the lightly flushed flesh across her chest, to the cleft between her breasts, then across her rib cage and down to make circles around her belly button. "Tell me a story about a summer you remember with fondness."

She tilted her head. Her eyes filled with curiosity as her gaze lifted to meet his. "Fondness? How did that word get in your vocabulary?"

"You know what I mean." He stopped the movement of his hand, resting it low on her stomach. He waited. "Go on. Tell me."

Ashley was quiet for a minute. Was she uncomfortable with his request? Or retrieving something from years ago?

"My mom and I had been to the grocery store and were headed home. It was August, and incredibly hot. She'd taken me to Dairy Queen and bought me an ice cream cone. On the way home, I saw a tiny kitten under a broken-down old car on the side of the highway. I begged her to turn around and go back, but she hesitated. She said Dad wouldn't be happy if we brought a cat home. Being ten and soft-hearted, I started crying." Ashley closed her eyes and tapped her lip with her finger. A soft smile ghosted across her face.

"Go on," Dalton encouraged her.

"Mom surprised me by making a U-turn and going back. I didn't give her a chance to rethink it. The second we stopped, I was out and running. The little creature was skin and bones and drinking from a puddle of something that had dripped from the old car. I wound up on my belly, trying to sweet-talk the kitten to come to me, but it was too scared. I was still holding my treat in my hand, so I slid under the car far enough to let my ice cream lure the little thing out. When it emerged, I was so excited at the rescue we'd pulled off. I gathered it in my arms and let the little bundle of fur eat the rest of it." Ashley sighed, obviously having enjoyed the memory.

Dalton thought she'd never been more beautiful. He smoothed his hand over her forehead, spreading her hair across his arm. "Go on. Was it male or female? What did you name it?"

"She was a tiny yellow tabby, with white socks all the way around. I named her Berry after my strawberry ice cream she'd eaten, which she'd thrown up minutes after we got home. Mom said she'd been expecting that to happen." A dark cloud seemed to drift across Ashley's face. She reached up and took his hand "Anyway, that's my memory. What's yours?"

Dalton shook his head. "You're not getting off that easy. Did you think I'd miss that burst of sadness that darkened your eyes? What happened with the cat?"

"That was the end of the good memory."

"But there's more. Did you get in trouble?"

Ashley sighed, and then continued her story. "Dad didn't believe in feeding an animal that didn't earn its keep. He could turn a profit on cattle and horses. A cat, dog, goldfish, anything that didn't earn its keep, had no place at his house. I tried the theory that cats killed mice, but Berry was an inside cat."

Dalton bit back a nasty remark about her father. "You dad wouldn't let you keep it?"

"He never came right out and said no, but I heard him and Mom arguing about having an animal in the house. A few weeks later, I came home from school and Berry was gone. Dad said she'd run out the open door and disappeared. Ash went with me while I hunted and called Berry's name. We walked for a long time. Mom finally came after us and took us home. I knew Berry was dead, but I had to look for her just in case."

"I'm sorry." Dalton had no idea what to say. "I didn't intend to make you sad."

"It's history." Her hand covered his, moving it back to her navel, where it had been when he'd started this conversation. "But you can replace that memory with a new one."

"I like the way you think." He rolled her to her back and moved between her legs.

"Keep in mind you owe me a story from when *you* were a kid."

"Hush. I'm about to give you that new memory." Dalton felt electric shockwaves burn through his system when his tongue touched her skin. Her deep moan said he'd found the exact spot he needed. Her hands dug into his hair, fingernails almost piercing his scalp. That didn't deter him from his mission. He intended to obliterate her sadness. His hands gripped her thighs, holding her still as he feasted on her soft wet folds.

"Dalton," she said in a whisper.

He kissed his way up her body, stopping long enough to suck and nibble her breasts. He'd been holding her back from her orgasm that was lurking right below the surface. "Yes?"

"I need you." Her blue eyes, flecked with tiny bits of cinnamon, flared as she spoke.

"You have me."

22

Ashley held Dalton's weight for a few seconds while they both caught their breath. He lifted onto his elbows, kissed her forehead, and smiled.

"Am I crushing you?"

"Only when I try to breathe." In the quiet, while looking into his eyes, she realized something. Her heart ached as if he'd reached inside her chest and squeezed it. She'd never experienced this feeling before. This was more than passion that rushed to the surface to satisfy a deep sexual need. It was something she couldn't allow.

He turned them to their sides. "What just happened?"

She mustered a fake chuckle from somewhere. "You don't know? Do I need to tell you the story about the birds and the bees?"

"Something heavy just crossed your mind." He stood and started toward the bathroom. "Hold that thought."

Ashley listened to the water being turned on. That he always gently cleaned her had been endearing from the start. Now it gave her a minute to come up with a believable response. She knew she'd need one, because Dalton didn't ask questions unless he wanted an answer.

She lowered her lids while trying to block out the crazy thoughts racing through her mind. A damp warm rag between her legs forced her to open her eyes. "Thank you."

"You're welcome. I like taking care of you." He tossed the rag across the room and rolled them on their sides, facing each other. He held up his hands in surrender. "I know you can take care of yourself. In this situation, I'm in charge, and you'll just have to get used to it."

"I'm going to have to wash clothes in the morning before we go to the compound or buy a whole new wardrobe." She'd said the first thing that had popped into her head. "Oh, remind me to call my apartment manager and ask him to get my mail."

Dalton blinked a couple of times. "If you're thinking about shopping right after we had mind-blowing sex, I'm not doing it right."

"It was mind-blowing."

"Really? Give me a minute, then we'll do it again just to be sure."

****

Ashley waved at the guard at the gate as they drove away from the guard shack toward the main part of the compound. The man had stepped out into the Texas heat to say hello and congratulate Dawson on being the new head of the Houston office. He'd also mentioned that he was happy to transfer and or travel.

"If Iain has found something interesting, maybe we should take a trip to Boston. We're not getting anywhere with the card case."

"I agree." Dalton parked and followed her into the building. "Something has to break, and soon."

"Welcome home," Kay said, leaning against her husband's desk. She stood and joined them in the hall. "I'll see you two at lunch."

"Come in!" Nate's deep voice called to them. He stood and shook hands with her and then Dalton. "Welcome back. You two are racking up the frequent flier miles and still aren't finished."

"That's the damn truth. We haven't learned jack shit."

"That's not true," Ashely said with a grin. "We know we have a murderess who's infatuated with Dalton."

Nate's handsome face lit up with a grin. "I knew I liked you."

"Thank you."

"Does Iain have anything else for us?" Dalton asked.

"I don't know. He's stretched pretty thin. I've put out the word we're interested in an assistant for him."

Dalton stood. "We need two. One for you and one for me."

"That's true. I also need a good female agent on my team." Nate tilted his head toward Ashley. "Dalton, don't you agree?"

Dalton crossed his arms over his chest. "Don't ask me to help you recruit her to work for you."

Nate winked at her. "I'm not asking you to convince her."

Dalton snarled. "If she works for anyone besides Carl, it will be for me."

Nate's gaze locked on Ashley's. It was obvious he was holding back a smile. "What have you done to him? He's still a grouch, but he's speaking in full sentences."

Dalton dragged a hand down his face. "We'll be in my office with Reed and Iain. Probably flying to Boston before the day is over."

"Wrap this case up. The ground in Houston is prepped and ready for construction to begin. The architect and contractor are both chomping at their bits, asking for a meeting to go over what they've put together. This baby is yours. You'll want to be involved from the ground up."

"Set a date and time agreeable to all parties, and I'll be there."

"Good." Nate glanced at Ashley. "Maybe Reed can make the trip to Boston with you. You could give us some insight on how Reed would handle working with a woman on the team."

She'd been pretty quiet until both men's heads swiveled toward her. Nate's eyebrows were lifted in question. "Uh," she stammered. "Sure thing. I don't have a problem working with Reed. But he works around Kay. What does she think?"

"Kay is married to the boss." Nate glanced at Dalton. "One of the bosses. All the men here treat her like royalty. She's gone to town with Marcus and Chris to a fundraiser. Now it's Kevin's naptime, and I promised to read him a story." He stood, ending the meeting.

Ashley followed Dalton into the hallway and down to his office. He stopped and seemed undecided for a minute. His brows were pulled together, and his lip was curled into a slight snarl. She put her arm on his bicep and the muscles tightened. "What's wrong?"

He shook his head. "Let's use the conference room instead of my office. Meet with Reed and Iain at the same time."

She walked with Dalton down the hall and into the area they had been working out of. After they reached the table, he texted both men and then sat down across from her. "They'll be here in a minute."

Ashley opened her laptop and clicked on the email icon.

"Maybe another pair of eyes on your case would be helpful." Dalton shifted in his chair. "I'm going to make a run to the bank soon. I need to get Nate his check today."

"You trust him, don't you?"

Surely Dalton wouldn't bail on the case.

"Trust who?" Reed had entered the room without them realizing it.

"Nobody," Dalton snapped. He glanced at Ashley. "Appearing out of nowhere is why he earned the nickname Ghost. Have you learned anything new about the illustrious senator?"

"Other than his campaign manager, who he's been fucking, sorry Ashley"—she waved him off—"is pregnant. The news vultures haven't uncovered it yet, but it won't be a secret for long. She just passed the second trimester."

Ashley was impressed he'd dug out a fact that hadn't previously surfaced. "Are you sure about your information, or is it a rumor?"

Dalton nodded his head. "Good question."

"Call it a rumor if you like, but I had a few drinks with the campaign manager's assistant the other night. She happens to sit right outside his office, and heard the entire conversation. Poor thing is underpaid and not appreciated. She just needed someone to talk to who understood." Reed smiled, displaying deep dimples in his cheeks. "I let her unburden herself on my shoulder."

"I'll bet you did." Dalton chuckled, pulling Ashley's gaze back to him. "Did you tell Ash?"

"Of course."

Iain burst into the room. "Sorry. I had a last-minute request from Tank. He's on location and needed information stat."

"No problem. Talk to us about Kyle Beltrane."

"All I know is what I sent you. The fifteen hundred dollars was a pittance compared to the other deposits made into his account. It caught my eye." Iain passed a sheet of paper to Dalton. "Those are the dates and times the calls were made."

Ashley leaned over and scanned the page. "What about Beltrane's personal life?"

"He's an attorney who hasn't handled a single case that wasn't related to weapons in seven years."

Reed leaned forward in his chair. "What are you saying?"

"Occasionally, a personal lawsuit is filed against a weapons company, claiming a death or injury was their fault for making and or selling the particular gun. Most never go to trial because the protection of lawful commerce in the arms act shields the gun industry from nearly all civil liability for the dangers their products pose. A few get through, and Kyle Beltrane is the attorney of record for one of the largest manufacturers in the country. His office is conveniently located one floor below their corporate office. He reps the company against those claims. Sometimes the manufacturer decides it's a nuisance case or they don't want the publicity and Beltrane negotiates a payoff with the complainant." Iain leaned back in his chair and took a breath.

"He's single, never been married, and has a great credit rating. I downloaded his credit card purchases for the past five years." Iain removed a flash drive from his shirt pocket and placed it on the table. "I'm sorry I haven't had time to work through them all."

Reed reached across and picked it up. "I'll look through them. See how far I can get today and tonight."

"I didn't hack into Beltrane's U.S. bank records. I don't want to go to jail, thank you." Iain pushed back from the table. "I've got to get back. My boy Tank needs me."

Dalton frowned. "Is he in danger?"

"It's a parental kidnapping. If we get this job done right, a very frightened little girl will be reunited with her mother tonight." Iain paused, placed his hand on Dalton's shoulder, leaned down, and whispered, "Congratulations. We're going to miss you around here."

Dalton nodded. "I'll miss all of you. But especially you."

A feeling of pride welled in Ashley's chest. No doubt Dalton's move to Houston would leave a hole in the dynamics of the Dallas team. Nate and Kay had built the company and grown their own tight-knit family.

"I'll ask Carl about a warrant, but I'm sure we need more than a fifteen-hundred-dollar deposit from Beltrane to Vardon to get one."

"Pressure him," Dalton said. "Tell him I said to use that magic touch he claims to have."

Nate tapped the doorjamb. Dalton turned to face him. "Come join us."

Nate shook his head. His white shirt fit as if it had been tailored to his muscular frame. "You and me in Houston tomorrow. This initial meeting shouldn't take more than one day. That work for you?"

Dalton nodded his head. "You're the boss."

Nate laughed. "Not for long."

Dalton waited until Nate had disappeared down the hall. "Reed, you and Ashley go to Boston and find out exactly what Beltrane knows. My gut tells me if it's a lot, the ATF will love us for giving him to them."

Then Dalton turned to her. "Lean on him. Beltrane has no idea what you know or don't know."

She felt a heavy weight on her chest. "We have virtually nothing."

"My nonna would say we're going in on a wing and a prayer," Reed said. "Means little chance of success, but I think we should try."

"You're right," Dalton agreed.

"You want to leave this afternoon or in the morning?" Reed's question brought Ashley's attention back in line.

"I'll check flights." Her fingers flew over the keyboard, pulling up information. Her breath froze in her chest and a sickening feeling formed in her stomach. Dalton was leaving, and there wasn't one hint of concern in his eyes.

Would Carl yank her from this assignment if he heard Dalton was now a partner and moving to Houston? This might mean she only had one more night with Dalton.

"Are you all right? Reed's voice snapped her attention back to the case.

"Yeah." Her brain scrambled for a longer response. "I got a little light-headed, but it's gone now."

She felt Dalton's gaze boring into her. "We've been pushing hard," he said with a nod. "Maybe you should get some rest."

She glanced at him, knowing he was lying. When they weren't spending time with his father, they'd spent the weekend making love. No, fucking like rabbits. Did he want her to stay here with him tonight? She nodded and turned her gaze to Reed. "That's almost a four-hour flight. We can leave early in the morning and be at his office before lunch."

"Works for me." Reed stood, shoving his chair back in place. "I'll tell Kay we need tickets on the early bird, and I'll meet you here."

"That's perfect." She sat silently for a minute. What had she been thinking? She'd chosen her personal feelings over her job. "Was I wrong?"

"Wrong?"

"Selfish? You know why I didn't want to leave today. Was it for the wrong reason?"

He studied her face. "By not flying to Boston today?"

It was painfully obvious he didn't want to talk about it. She closed her laptop. "I need to see if Kay has gotten back. Maybe she has time to take me shopping."

"I can take you."

"No, thanks." She all but ran from the room. She found Kay in Nate's office and asked if she had time to go shopping. Kay loved the idea, handed Kevin to Nate, and ran back upstairs to change clothes.

Ashley turned to him. "You don't mind me running off with your wife?"

"I'll admit to being busy, but today at the fundraiser was the first time she's been away from us for way too long." He sat his son on his lap. "We can muddle through for a few more hours."

23

Ashley checked the price tag on a pair of skinny jeans and smiled. This boutique would normally be out of her price range, but Kay had promised the sale rack was always full of bargains. "I'm trying these on for sure."

"You'll look hot in those. We need to visit the shoe store for you a pair of boots to wear with them." Kay pulled a white blouse off the rack and held it against Ashley's chest. "This is made of organic cotton. I love anything that's wash and wear. No wrinkles. What do you think?"

The boatneck short-sleeve top was perfect. She could wear it with her new jeans or for work under her blazer. "It's perfect. If it fits, I'll buy a couple for work."

"No way. You can buy one white blouse, and then we're putting some color in your wardrobe." Kay moved to the next selection.

Ashley took the tops and jeans she'd selected to the dressing room. She had to laugh at Kay's exuberance. "I have plenty of clothes at home. Except for the jeans, this is to get me through until the case is closed, so I don't have to wash every few days." She liked the two blouses she'd tried on, and the jeans fit perfectly. It surprised her when Kay opened the door a crack and shoved a dress at her.

"Try this one."

Ashley slipped on the pale-yellow sundress with a square-cut bodice. She turned and looked at herself in the mirror. The fit was perfect and super-flattering, but soon she'd be back at a desk with no reason to wear it. "It's cute."

"I want to see."

Ashley opened the door and walked out.

"Oh. My. God." Kay clapped her hands together. "You are gorgeous. Who knew you had legs like that?" She walked all the way around Ashley. "Dalton is going to like seeing you in this dress."

Ashley ran her fingers down the bodice, and tears swelled in her eyes. He would never see her wear it. Never comment that yellow looked good with her coloring. She quickly returned to the dressing room. She unzipped the dress and stepped out of it. Taking deep breaths in and out, she forced back the sadness that had taken over.

She took her selections to the counter, and Kay noticed she'd left the sundress behind. "I thought you liked the dress."

"I did, but I would probably never wear it."

"You really don't want it?"

Unable to speak, Ashley shook her head and paid for her purchases. "I'll be right back."

She hurried to the restroom, splashed water on her face, and ran her damp hands over the flyaway hair that had slipped out while she changed clothes.

Kay was waiting at the front door. She wrapped her arm around Ashley's shoulders and led her across the mall parking lot. "Let's find you the perfect pair of boots and then have a slice of Mama Bailey's Irish cream cheesecake."

The selection and payment for the boots took some time, but once that was done, Kay took Ashley's hand and pulled her a couple of doors down to a cake and pie shop. Ashley knew what was coming. A question-and-answer session about Dalton.

"I know you want to ask me something," Ashley said, pulling her cup of coffee to her mouth for a sip. "Go ahead. It's just us girls."

"Nate warned me to stay out of it. That you and Dalton are none of my business, but I can see you're hurting. Do you want to talk about it?"

"There's nothing to say except it's over when the case is solved. I knew going in he wasn't interested in a long-term relationship. With the new compound coming, there's no room left for doubt."

"But you fell in love, didn't you?"

Ashley opened her mouth and took a bite, but couldn't taste anything. "Is it that obvious? I hope it's not to Dalton. It would just push him further away."

"Then you'll have to force him to admit he loves you, too."

Ashley choked on her sip of coffee. "Is that what you did with Nate? You two seem so happy together. You both must have been ready to settle down."

Kay laughed hard enough that the couple at the table next to them turned and stared. She glanced at the time on her phone. "Let me tell you a quick story."

"I know he saved your life."

"He also broke my heart. I fell in love with Nate while we were in college, but he'd heard the call of the ocean. He was going to be a SEAL. That, by the way, was never discussed with me. After graduation, the asshole up and joined the navy. Left me behind, wondering what bus had just run over me. I hated him for it."

Ashley couldn't help but smile. "Hated?"

"Oh, hell yes. Ten years later, he and the boys saved my life, but I wanted nothing to do with Nate in the beginning. He'd just retired from the SEALs and returned to Dallas. He was going to protect me, whether I wanted him to or not." Kay closed her eyes and her cheeks flushed red. "I was pretty mean to him at first. Forgiving him took a little work on both our parts."

"But you eventually forgave him."

Kay lifted her shoulders. "I'd never stopped loving him."

"Thanks for telling me. But there's nothing in our past that ties me and Dalton together."

"I've never seen him with a woman, and don't know why he has been such a loner since joining us, but I've seen the way he looks at you."

Ashley's heart stuttered. "How does he look at me?"

"Honey, there's so much heat in his eyes, he could melt the biggest glacier in existence. Don't give up on him."

"It won't make a difference. He'll be in Houston, and I'll be in San Antonio."

"I'm sorry. Maybe Dalton will figure out he loves you."

Ashley nodded. They finished their cheesecake and walked next door to the shoe store.

"Shoe shopping is my favorite sport." Kay tried on about five pairs before making her selection and concentrating on boots for Ashley.

Happy with her purchases, she followed Kay back to the car. They loaded the back seat with sacks and talked all the way back to the compound. To Ashley's relief, the conversation had moved on to Kevin and his antics. She'd never noticed that look of Dalton's that Kay had referred to.

Kay parked in the empty spot right in front of the office door. "I'd better get inside. Kevin's nanny is off today and Nate's probably ready to pull out his hair."

Ashley dropped her purchases in the empty conference room. Reed looked up from his laptop.

"Uncover anything interesting?"

"Not yet. There are a lot of charges on his cards. I'm going to narrow it down by taking out automatic monthly debits and clothing stores."

"I don't know if Dalton or Iain has sent you anything on the case, so I'm going to forward everything I have."

"Thanks." Reed leaned back in his chair. "I liked meeting your brother. He's blunt and straightforward. A take-no-prisoner kind of guy."

"He's the best."

"We kept getting interrupted. Somebody needed his attention every few minutes. I got the impression he was tired of being pulled in different directions."

"Tell that to Dalton. He'd love to have Ash work for Lost and Found, Houston."

"I hope he feels the same way about me."

"He specifically said he wanted you to help on this case."

Reed turned on his hundred-watt smile. Ashley could easily admit he was gorgeous. And it wasn't a shock to her that not one part of her body tingled or tightened when he smiled.

"Good. You're back." Dalton stepped into the room with an overnight bag in his hand. He walked to the table and put a key ring in front of her.

"I am. You going somewhere?"

"Yeah. We were waiting on you and Kay to get back. Our meeting is at eight in the morning. We're going today so I can spend some time going over the plans with him without interruption."

"I don't need these." She pushed the keys away. "I'm sure Kay won't mind if I stay here. I'll ride to the airport with Reed." She'd tried to sound unconcerned, but her throat had gone bone dry, and her words were raspy.

Reed's eyes cut toward Dalton's for a split second before turning to her. "I've got her covered."

"What about your makeup and clothes at my house?" Dalton questioned. One dark eyebrow lifted. "You'll want them."

"You're right. I'll get them and leave your keys on your desk." She was proud her words sounded calm. "Reed, I'll meet you in the break room in the morning."

Dalton scowled. "Keep me updated."

"I'll take care of your girl," Reed said.

"I'm not his girl." She'd said it without thinking. She glared at Reed, who was grinning at Dalton.

His expression darkened, his lips pulled into a thin line, and his brown eyes turned almost black. He opened his mouth, snapped it shut, turned on his heel, and walked away shaking his head.

"That man needs to pick up a sense of humor while he's gone." Reed cut his eyes to her. Seeing the lost look on her face, his chuckle died. "Sorry. He's usually OK when one of us yanks his chain."

Why had she lashed out? She had to get out of there before she started crying and made a fool out of herself. "I'm taking off. I need to wash my clothes and be ready for the morning." She stood, gathering her things. "I'll have my laptop, and will work remotely."

"Sure thing. Now that Kay's back, she can make flight arrangements for us."

Ashley smacked her forehead and plopped back down on her chair. "I'm sorry. Give me your information, and I'll do that myself."

"Great. I don't think we need to reserve rooms, do you?"

Ashley shook her head. "If we need more time, we can take care of it then." She quickly handled the airline reservation and emailed Kay and Reed the confirmations. "I hope all hell breaks loose and we have to stay because of the amazing information we learn. But here, lately, getting anything that helps hasn't been the case." She grabbed her laptop, purse, and sacks holding her new purchases. "See you in the morning."

She hurried out of the building and started toward Dalton's pickup. Her packages blocked her view and her foot slipped off the curb. She stumbled forward. Off-balance, she tried to get her feet back under her. Clutching her laptop close to her chest, she reached out with her free hand and grabbed for the grille on the pickup. She missed and her knees hit the pavement a second before her right cheek bounced off the hood.

She pulled herself up, unlocked the door, and climbed inside, collapsing against the seat. The heat inside the cab was stifling, so she started the engine and set the air conditioner on high.

Her knees and cheek were in pain. A glance revealed both pants legs were torn, and she had slid on the surface enough to leave scratch marks. She pulled down the sun visor and took a peek at her cheek in the mirror. That was going to leave a bruise.

Ashley dropped her head in her hands.

God, even the inside of Dalton's pickup smelled like him.

What had she wanted from him? Had she expected him to refuse to leave her? For him to pull her somewhere quiet and tell her how much he'd miss her? Sheesh. Why had she overreacted to him leaving with Nate? Why was she inventing problems?

Dalton had explained to her why he'd told his father she wasn't his girl. And the fact was, he'd spoken the truth. There could be no relationship between them. His life would be in Houston. The pain in her chest was crushing, and it was all her fault for allowing herself to care about him.

She waved at the guard as she left the compound and had driven to the main road before the tears broke and ran in tiny rivers down her cheeks. Her vision blurred badly. She pulled to the side, opened the door, and ran into a row of thick trees.

Stupid. Stupid. Stupid. The words rolled through her brain.

She stood there in the shade, trying to gain a semblance of control. If he wanted her, he'd have to come to her.

She would survive this.

24

Locating the Lost and Found compound and Dalton's home address had taken some drilling down, but Angel finally had the information she needed. She'd felt compelled to know everything about him. Once she had that information, she'd hired Axel to surveil Dalton.

She and Axel made an odd pair, him a member of a local motorcycle club, and her an untouchable woman. Their relationship was strictly business, though. He respected that, and she respected his loyalty.

He'd recommended she hire him and a friend, but she'd stupidly insisted on taking the day shift. Her decision hadn't been smart, because she'd spent two of the hottest days of the summer sweating her ass off in a rental with a lame air conditioner.

Her cell had been in her hand to call Axel and take him up on his offer when a black SUV rolled to the stop sign coming out of the compound and turned right, heading toward the highway. Dalton had been sitting in the passenger seat. She'd been tempted to follow, but something, a gut feeling, had her deciding to wait.

Why had Dalton left without Ashley? A couple of times Angel had observed those two, and the affection between them had been obvious. Nobody gazed at a work partner the way they did each other.

He'd be back for her.

While she waited, she read another text from Kyle. He was leaving the country, and if she had a brain cell left, apparently she should do the same. There was a million-dollar price tag on her head. Again, he was trying to scare her. It hadn't worked. She wasn't afraid of death.

Suddenly Dalton's pickup came speeding around the curve. The vehicle swung wide onto the road and then took a sharp dive onto the shoulder. Ashley then burst from the cab. Sobbing, she limped into the shade and placed one hand on a tree trunk. She held her hand over her stomach as if she was about to throw up.

Watching was gut-wrenching. What had happened? Who'd hurt her?

This was the perfect opportunity to get close. Angel drove slowly past the pickup and then pulled off in front of it. She grabbed a couple of tissues from her purse and plastered the most compassionate look on her face she could muster.

"Miss!" she called out. "Are you ill?"

The startled blonde's head whipped around. "What? No. Yes. I'm fine."

Angel's stomach turned over, but she kept moving forward. Slowly getting closer, while holding the tissues out as an offering. "I know I'm a stranger, but you look like you could use a friend right now." She threw on the smile she used while at work. "My name is Angel Honeywell."

"Ashley Hunter," the agent said, taking the Kleenex and wiping her eyes. "Thank you for stopping. Not many people would have been so kind."

At the sight of a bruise forming on Ashley's cheek, Angel's stomach churned, and the taste of bile filled the back of her throat. How had she been so wrong about him? "I know how it feels to have a man hurt you."

"How'd you know it was a man?"

"An educated guess." Angel used her deepest southern drawl, struggling to maintain her caring demeanor. Her fingernails bored into her clenched hands when she noticed the knees of Ashley's slacks were torn. "You're injured."

"Just a few scratches."

"I was just going for a burger. Why don't you join me?"

Ashley wiped a tear from her cheek. Her hand brushed too close to the bruise, and she flinched. "No, thank you, but thanks for asking."

Angel couldn't let her walk away. "I understand you probably have friends who you can talk to, but you look so alone." She wanted to tell her no man had a right to abuse her, but she worried that would be pushing too hard. She put a sad smile on her face instead, dropped her head in a dejected pose, and turned as if to walk away.

"It's my fault. I let myself get hurt."

"You're not responsible. Men are bastards. You can't trust them. If you do, be ready to be beaten and abused."

Of course Ashley had defended him. She probably believed it really was all her fault. She didn't know any better.

"Not all men are that way." Ashley shook her head. "I convinced myself there was more between us than there was. I knew better."

"Your falling in love didn't give him the right to hurt you."

"I hurt myself. He just left for the airport, and it didn't end well." Ashley blew her nose, walked to the pickup, and opened the door. "I'm on my way to get my clothes from his house, or I'd take you up on lunch."

Angel had heard enough. After telling Ashely she hoped she'd be all right, she turned and walked to her rental, climbed in, and drove onto the highway. That bastard Dalton was nothing like she'd thought. His chivalrous acts of helping the old woman with her luggage and then keeping her from a bad fall had been just that, an act.

25

Ashley and Reed paused outside Kyle Beltrane's office. Reed's discovery last night had opened a possibility that had taken her breath away. It was a long shot, but she'd take anything she could get at this point.

He'd met her first thing this morning. Beltrane's credit cards records reflected he'd purchased a clip for a Maxim 9mm pistol, but there was no other proof he'd purchased that particular weapon.

She and Dalton had found a receipt for that same type of gun in Vardon's safe. Ashley had dug through her notes and learned Beltrane's payment of fifteen hundred dollars to Vardon's account was on the same date as the one on the receipt.

Armed with that single anomaly, getting Carl to obtain a search warrant hadn't been easy. She hadn't told him that Dalton was in Houston and not with her. That tidbit of information could wait.

"Are you ready to bluff this guy?" Reed asked.

They were itching to ask Kyle Beltrane questions. She glanced up at him. "This is such a long shot."

"But if it pays off..." Reed winked at her. "If not, we'll both be looking for new jobs."

"Holy shit. You're right." She lifted her eyebrows and waited until he nodded.

"Dalton may kick my ass for this, but I think we go with your gut." Reed opened the door and stepped back, allowing her to enter first.

A young woman looked up and smiled when they entered. "Can I help you?"

Ashley held out her ID and watched as the other woman's eyes widened. "Is he in his office?"

"Yes, but he's leaving for the airport in a few minutes."

Ashley glanced at Reed. Not even a flash of surprise showed on his face. He was the definition of chill. "When will he return?"

"He didn't say. He's closing the office. I've been helping him box up records and shred the rest." She pointed to four cartons labeled and ready to ship.

Reed read one label. "I'll bet his ticket is to the Grand Caymans." He looked at Ashley. "I don't think the U.S. has an extradition agreement with them."

"Look, I'm just a one-day temp." The receptionist stood. "I want to leave if there's going to be trouble."

"Sit tight. If your story checks out, you've got nothing to be afraid of. For now, stay at your desk. Admit no one. Call no one."

Stepping into Beltrane's office, Ashley took in the pale gray walls and plush carpeting. She pointed to a suitcase next to the door. Beltrane, with his back to them, was stuffing papers into a brown leather briefcase.

Reed cleared his throat.

Beltrane whirled around. Fear flashed across his face as he held the briefcase in front of his chest. "Who are you? Billie!" he bellowed, looking past them toward the door. "I told you not to let anyone come into my office."

Ashley identified herself and Reed. "We're here to execute a search warrant." She dropped a copy on the desk for Beltrane to read. "It includes your office and records."

The tension in Beltrane's face vanished. Had he relaxed at the sight of her badge? "What's this about?"

Reed closed the door. "It's about you going to prison for a long time."

Beltrane stood over his desk. He read in silence for a minute before pushing the document away. "Don't think you can threaten me."

"We're not here to threaten you. We're here to find enough evidence to send you to prison." An evil grin crossed Reed's face. "They say federal prisons aren't as harsh as state-run lockup, but that's bullshit." He nodded in Beltrane's direction. "He'll be lucky if he becomes someone's bitch instead of being passed around."

Ashley bit the inside of her cheek to keep from smiling. Reed had read the situation perfectly. Beltrane had already started sweating. "My partner's words may be a little crude, but he's telling you the truth. For now, we're going to chat with you and look through a few records before we have a team come in and scrutinize each one of them." She and Reed had agreed not to tell Beltrane why he was being investigated, but to let him try to figure it out. "First, we'd like to ask you a few questions."

Beltrane blinked a few times. "What happened to your face?"

Reed let out a low growl and took a step forward. "What did you say to her?"

Beltrane's head jerked back, and he waved his hands as if wiping the words from the air. "Sorry, I'm just nervous."

Ashley's hand went to her cheekbone, absently touching the ugly bruise. "It's called bring rude."

Reed strode to one of the plush office chairs, sat, and waited for her to do the same. She liked how straightforward he was with Beltrane. He'd make a great addition to Dalton's Houston team.

"Do you want a lawyer present before we talk?" She held her breath, hoping he'd be so self-confident he would say no. She placed her cell on the desk. Her finger hovered over the record icon. "Do you mind if I record our chat?"

"I am a lawyer, and yes, I do mind." He sat behind his desk, his gaze bouncing from her to Reed.

Beltrane was terrified, and she intended to find out why. "Before we go any further, why don't you tell us why you think we're here."

Beltrane shifted in his luxurious leather chair. His pupils had dilated, and he couldn't keep his hands still. She and Reed waited, both of their gazes locked on him. He picked up the glass on his desk, the water almost sloshing over the edge, and took a sip. "I can't imagine why."

"You make a lot of money for an attorney who doesn't have but one client." Reed leaned forward, placing his elbows on his thighs. He was tall, and that move put him about eye level with Beltrane. "There's no need to respond. We know the answer. Now answer the lady's question. Why do you think we're here?"

Beltrane shrugged his shoulders. "I assure you, as a lobbyist, I follow the law."

"Bullshit. Your next answer needs to be a better one." Reed pointed at Ashley. "She's ready to arrest your ass right now. I'm trying to help you out here."

Ashley put her hand on Reed's arm. "Let Mr. Beltrane tell us why he purchased bullets to a Maxim 9mm when there's no record of him purchasing the gun."

"I didn't," Beltrane stammered. "Don't."

"We find it interesting that a few days after you wired fifteen hundred dollars to Vince Vardon's Grand Cayman account, you bought a spare clip for a Maxim 9mm," Ashley said. "That money arrived in his account the same day he purchased that exact weapon."

Reed leaned forward again. "It's a nice gun. Lightweight, less than ten inches long, pretty damn accurate, and a clip that holds seventeen bullets. You know," he said, scratching his head, "None of this makes sense."

"That means nothing." Beltrane's face turned red. He scrubbed both hands over it. "Doesn't prove anything."

"Then give us a plausible reason why you'd send an illegal weapons broker that small amount of money to an offshore account."

Beltrane shook his head. He'd slumped in his seat and refused to look at them.

Ashley thought he was ready to break. Knowing she was taking a wild guess, she had nothing to lose, so she pushed harder. "A Maxim 9mm was used in two recent murders. Are they connected to you in any way?"

Beltrane's head dropped forward as if his neck could no longer support its weight. "That crazy bitch," he mumbled.

"Crazy bitch?" Reed asked in a low tone. "Say that again." He cast Ashley a glance. His dark eyes sparkled. He'd heard, and so had she.

"Reed, you stay with Mr. Beltrane. I'll contact the federal judge and have a warrant for his arrest here in a few minutes. We'll have all these records sent to the lab." She stood and picked up her cell. Lord, she hoped her nerves didn't give her bluff away. Beltrane was a lawyer, she could only hope he'd be rattled enough to do something to protect himself.

"We already have enough to bury you," she lied, still holding her cell in her hand. Her finger poised, as if to make a call.

"Nobody will bury me. Not with all the information I have."

"What could you possibly have that we want so badly?" she asked. Every synapse in her brain was firing. With no real evidence, they could be on the verge of solving a lot more cases than she'd expected.

"I have plenty, but I demand to speak with a federal prosecutor."

"You demand?" Reed laughed. "You think we're going to disturb one of those guys without knowing exactly what your 'plenty' is? It's not happening."

Ashley took her seat. "Start at the beginning."

"You have to believe me. If she learns I'm talking to you, she'll kill me to shut me up."

"Who is she, and why do you think she's going to kill you?"

"I know who you are. She insisted I get information on you and Dalton Murphy."

"Who insisted?"

"Angel Honeywell."

Ashley felt the room spin. She'd been face-to-face with the serial killer. She'd almost gone to eat with her. What had she wanted?

Reed's hand on her shoulder snapped her back. "What just happened?"

"Nothing." Ashley shook her head. "Go on."

"She was flippant when I told her to make herself scarce. I warned her the people she's been doing hits for are furious with us both. She scoffed. Even offered to locate and kill them. It's like she thinks she's invincible." Beltrane was silent for a few moments. "Maybe I do want an attorney present."

"Too late for that." Reed lifted one shoulder and smiled. "Being an attorney, you know how this goes. We can't make deals or promise you'll get a lighter sentence for talking with us, but our reports will say one of two things. You willingly helped us out, or you steadfastly refused to cooperate. Your call."

"It's never too late to stop talking. If I wasn't scared for my life, I wouldn't have said one word to you."

Damn it. Disappointment washed over Ashley. His request for a lawyer stopped everything. "If you'll excuse me, I'll see about getting an arrest warrant." She stood, knowing they had enough to hold him for questioning, but the arrest was a bluff. She turned to Reed. "Stay with Mr. Beltrane."

He nodded. "We'll be right here when you get back."

"Wait," Beltrane said, just as her hand wrapped around the doorknob. "I walk out of this building unprotected and I'm dead. And maybe you, too."

Reed ran his hands through his hair while shaking his head. "That's not happening. We'll protect you."

Beltrane sneered. "Really?"

"Don't doubt me. You need to be alive to testify."

The room fell quiet for a few heartbeats. Ashley broke the silence. "Well?"

"Ask me whatever you want. Record it. I don't care as long as I get in the witness protection program."

"That's not something I can promise. Shall we proceed?"

"Yeah, whatever."

Ashley's hand shook as she placed her cell in front of him and tapped record. "Please state your name, the date, and the time of day."

Beltrane followed her instructions.

"Are you stating to us, Ashley Hunter and Reed Ballatori, you do not want an attorney present for this conversation?"

Much to her surprise, Beltrane did as he was told. He was sweating profusely now, and mopping his forehead with a tissue. Fear had him in a state of panic, and he wasn't thinking clearly. She planned to take advantage of it, but had to be careful. No way was she jeopardizing this case. "Back to the beginning. Tell us about the gun."

"I am a facilitator, and I do as I'm instructed. The senator specified he wanted someone to shoot his wife. I didn't ask why. I gave the gun to Angel and told her to throw the damn thing in the lake, but lately she does what she damn well pleases."

"You're saying Senator Haley ordered the hit on his wife?" Ashley wanted the name on the recording.

"Yes."

Reed stood and moved next to her. "Why did you buy the extra clip?"

"The stupid bitch emptied the original one at target practice. She had specific instructions to throw the gun into the Gulf, but she kept it."

"Who ordered the hit on Vardon?" Ashley asked.

"I don't have the faintest idea why she killed him. We've done business with him before, and she should have recognized his name."

Ashley fought the excitement racing through her body. "Who ordered the hit on the truck driver?"

"Nobody." A disgusted huff escaped Beltrane's lungs. "I have no idea what the poor bastard did to piss her off."

Ashley's breath caught. "So you're aware the murder of the senator's wife and the truck driver are connected by the weapon?"

When Beltrane nodded, Reed spoke up. "Tell us about Angel Honeywell."

The attorney's head lifted. He looked as if he'd aged ten years in the past few minutes. "She wouldn't tell me why she started leaving cards on her paid hits as well as her personal kills. I warned her we were both going to get killed if she didn't stop with those fucking playing cards."

Adrenaline pumped through Ashley's veins. Could a single credit card purchase for bullets lead to solving even more murders than she'd been investigating? Murders that would lead them to the Queen of Diamonds? "How many hits are we talking about?"

"I'm not sure. They're in the books I was shredding."

Ashley had to know more about this woman. "Less than five percent of serial killers are women, so what makes her part of that number? How did you run across her?"

"I defended a hit man for the mafia years ago. He told me about this young woman he'd met right after she'd hired on as a flight attendant. He saw something in her that led him to teach her everything he knew. She liked watching their eyes as they died. She's also a specialist in different methods of killing."

"Go on," Reed said.

Beltrane walked over to the briefcase leaning against the suitcase by the door. He came back to his desk holding a manilla folder. He dropped it in front of Ashley. "Angel Honeywell. According to my client, she had a horrible childhood. Raped and beaten by her stepfather. Passed around to his friends. I don't know if that's true or not. I never asked. I do know she is fascinated with having you and Dalton Murphy hunting her case. She has a crush on your partner."

"How so?"

"She had me run both your backgrounds. This has turned into some sort of fantasy for her." Beltrane's hands were still trembling as he took a long drink of water. "I tried to convince her not to leave those damn cards. I warned her our clients were furious about how she'd drawn attention to herself. Angel likes being famous."

Beltrane had sweat running down his cheeks. He was getting nervous, and had started rambling. Neither Ashley nor Reed tried to keep him on track. The more he talked, the more they learned.

"Who was this client that taught her how to be a killer?" Reed asked.

"Ever hear of Don Porter?"

"I remember the name," Ashley said. "He spent years on death row. Right before he was executed, his story was all over the news. He never admitted to exactly how many people he murdered."

She opened the file Beltrane had handed her. She wished Dalton was here for this. If the information Beltrane was providing was good, a lot of cold murders could finally be solved.

"I don't suppose you have a picture of Honeywell?" Reed asked. "No? Then describe her."

"Beautiful, but eerie-looking. Ghostlike. Natural silver-blonde hair with pale blue eyes."

The need to bring Dalton into the loop was too much now. Ashley picked up her cell, and without explanation, she stood. "I need a minute."

She walked out to the hallway and leaned against the wall. Her fingers shook so bad she had trouble scrolling through to Dalton's number. She didn't care if he was in a meeting. She had to talk to him.

"Hey." He answered on the second ring.

"I met her. We have her name. You have to be careful." She spit the words out rapid fire and probably not making much sense, but she had to warn him. "She's infatuated with you."

"Slow down. When did you meet her? Where?"

"Outside the compound. We talked, and she gave me her name. Beltrane just gave her up as the killer. He described her perfectly." She couldn't tell Dalton she'd stopped on the road because she'd been crying so hard she couldn't see to drive. She just couldn't. "Beltrane is scared, and he's talking. I've got to call Carl and get a federal prosecutor here, but I wanted you to know."

"Where are you?"

"In the hall outside Beltrane's office. I have to get back."

"I'm on my way. Text me when you and Reed leave the building, and where you're staying."

"That's not necessary. He'll be in custody by the time you get here."

"I'll be there in a few hours."

26

The tension in Dalton's lungs relaxed the second Ashley peeked her head out. He stepped inside, pulled her into his arms, and then kicked the door closed in one move. Her fingers gripped his arms, her nails digging into his skin. He buried his face in her hair, breathing in the clean scent of vanilla. "You solved the case. And who knows how many more. I'm sorry I wasn't there to see it."

She tilted her head back and her eyes warmed his soul. For a split second, he saw sadness in her gaze, but it quickly vanished. She pulled away from him. His blood pressure shot up. She'd tried to cover a bruise with makeup but hadn't succeeded. "What happened to your face?"

"It was me being clumsy." She shrugged and moved to the center of the room.

He wouldn't let her get away without explaining the bruise and exactly how she'd met Angel.

She'd booked rooms for her and Reed in a decent motel, but she deserved much better. The walls were beige, along with the carpet. In fact, the only bright thing in the room was her.

"I should have insisted Nate go alone."

"You did what you had to do." Her tone wasn't harsh, just flat.

"I upset you at the compound. I'm sorry, and I don't know how to fix it. Bring me up to speed on the case and then we're going to figure out this thing between us." He pulled a chair next to the small makeshift work area she'd created and sat, not saying anything else until she joined him.

"We're off the case. All that's left is tracking her down, and we have people who will handle the search. It was much bigger than we anticipated. Kyle Beltrane was put into the WITSEC program. He'll come back to testify. With the information he's providing, many warrants will be issued. Angel Honeywell is wanted for a lot more murders than we thought."

"I'll make sure you get the credit for every single arrest." His fingers itched to touch her, but he could almost see the thick walls she'd erected around her.

"They'll catch her, if the mafia doesn't get there first."

"Mafia?"

"She did work for them, too. But now they want her silenced."

Dalton marveled at how calm Ashley was. He expected her to be pinging-off-the-walls excited. "You know we've both met this Angel Honeywell."

"I didn't at first, but when Beltrane said she was a flight attendant, I remembered her. We've seen her more than once. That's probably when she became interested in you."

"She's crazy," he scoffed.

"That's probably true, but she had a horrible childhood."

"That didn't give her judge-and-jury rights."

"The silver-blonde-headed woman we saw in the video after Vardon's murder wasn't wearing a wig. It was her with her hair down."

Dalton sat back and let her finish bringing him up to speed. She still hadn't mentioned how she'd met the Queen of Diamonds. "You told me you'd met."

"I did. I left for your house right after you and Nate headed to the airport." Ashley's eyes closed and she clasped her hands in front of her with her fingers intertwined.

"Go on," he encouraged her.

When she opened her eyes and looked at him, he almost shivered. He could sense a wall around her growing thicker.

"I left in your pickup to go get my clothes from your house." She paused, and he didn't push. "I was upset and wasn't paying attention. I stumbled and fell in the parking lot, scratching my knees and bumping face-first into the hood. Once I was on the road, I was upset, so I stopped, got out, and tried to catch my breath. Then a woman pulled in front of your pickup. She got out and asked if she could help."

Guilt pulled at his conscience. Dalton tugged Ashley's hands into his, rubbing his thumb against her skin, pushing her for more information. "Go on. What did she say?"

"She assumed a man must have hurt me. I told her I had hurt myself." Ashley blinked and Dalton's heart dropped to the bottom of his stomach. "She invited me to eat with her and I declined. The conversation didn't last ten minutes."

"Remember, this isn't over until she's caught." He'd gone from being elated with the upcoming construction on the Houston compound to facing the realization he wouldn't be seeing Ashley anymore. He held her chin with his thumb and forefinger. "Her name and description are out there, and the world is looking for her. I'll bet Carl was ecstatic."

"He was pleased. He still hasn't mentioned I failed to bring you back into the fold."

"And he shouldn't." Dalton's cell buzzed. "It's Nate. He must've heard from Reed."

"He's headed to Dallas. If you hurry, you might catch up with him at the airport." She walked to the door, stopped, and waited. It gutted him that he saw no excitement, elation, or trace of victory in her expression. All he saw was determination.

"I'm not going anywhere until we clear up our misunderstanding." He didn't want their time together to end this way. Hell, for the first time in years, he cared about somebody else's feelings. He didn't want this to end.

"There is no misunderstanding. We both knew our time together would end with the case."

A low growl rumbled from his chest as he stalked toward her. Wrapping his arms around her, he touched his lips to hers. Again and again, he kissed her gently. Then his kiss grew harder and more demanding. His tongue sought the sweetness of her mouth. Finally, he was granted entrance, allowing him to taste her.

When she relaxed into him, pressing the length of her soft body against his, the outside world with all its problems vanished. The small cinnamon chips in her blue eyes glittered. He slid his hand under her ass and lifted her off the floor. She wrapped her legs around him, aligning herself with his rock-hard erection.

In a few short steps, he tossed her on the bed and followed her down. "Hands up," he commanded. Her top was quickly pulled off, followed by her bra, and tossed to the floor. Working to undress each other turned into a badly choreographed dance, but neither of them laughed. Somehow they managed to strip.

He leaned back on his heels and studied her naked body. "You are so beautiful." He shook his head when she reached for him. "I'm not finished looking."

"Oh." Her cheeks flooded with color.

"Never be embarrassed by me seeing you naked." His hands started at her neck and her traced her body, mapping and committing every inch of skin to memory.

He needed more.

He slid down her body, spread her legs, and then sunk his tongue as deep inside her warm heat as it would reach. One hand slid under her hips, lifting her to a better angle. He'd missed her taste and hearing her soft moans. When he moved his free hand to her clit and rubbed in circles, she shattered, calling out his name.

Bracing himself on one arm, he slid his cock back and forth in her moisture, wetting her clit with each stroke. She ground herself against him until he felt himself notched at her entrance.

"Inside me. I need you inside me."

He smiled down at her, and with one thrust, slid home. This was home. His home. Where he belonged. "You feel incredible wrapped around me."

"More." Her hips moved, sliding him in deeper. "Move. Please, move."

He lifted her legs over his shoulders and pounded their flesh together faster and faster. Something inside him shifted. He wanted to consume her, to take her to a place she'd never been before, to ensure she'd never want another man but him. It took all his concentration to hold on until she came a second time, but he was determined to hear her cry out his name again. Angling his body so his pelvis bone contacted her clit with every stroke, he held her in place and rubbed circles against her.

Ashley's contractions pulled him even deeper, as if her body needed to cling to his. Then she exploded around him. She whispered his name over and over. He surrendered at the same time, filling her with his cum.

They lay in silence until he caught his breath and felt able to speak. He'd just experienced the most powerful orgasm of his life. "I'll be right back."

He returned with a warm wet cloth and cleaned up their mess. Tossing the rag aside, he pulled her head to rest on his chest. "Give me a few minutes and we'll do that again."

"Hmm." With a slight nod, her body relaxed.

Dalton pushed the hair off her face and kissed her forehead. She'd dozed off. He'd let her rest for a while before waking her for round two.

****

Sunlight streaming through a gap in the curtain stirred Dalton awake. Damn. He'd fallen asleep with her in his arms. He rolled over to an empty bed. "Ashley?"

The bathroom counter was free of makeup, there was no toothbrush, and her hairbrush was gone. He quickly slipped on his jeans. A sinking feeling settled in his gut.

She hadn't gone for coffee.

Still refusing to face reality, he reached for his shirt to go looking for her. A note on the table where her laptop had been caught his eye.

He took slow steps, trying to convince himself this wasn't goodbye. He lifted the paper and read.

Thank you for everything.

"Son of a bitch." Crushing the note in his hand, he sunk into a chair. Disbelief morphed into disappointment and quickly segued into anger.

She'd fucking walked away. Walked away without talking to him. Walked away without looking back. Without giving him a chance to make things right. He'd apologized for leaving her to go to Houston. Should he go after her now? Force her to explain why she couldn't forgive him?

Dalton sat staring at his phone for a long time. Last night when they'd made love had been different. It meant something. At least, it had to him. He'd found a woman he could love

forever this time. That she didn't trust him was his fault. After all, he'd been the one to impress on her that he wasn't interested in a relationship.

His cell buzzed and his shoulders drooped when he saw it was Nate texting.

You coming home today?

Dalton finished dressing, flattened the wrinkles out of the note, and stuffed it in his jeans pocket. He slung his bag over his shoulder and typed his response.

On my way.

****

Dalton finished reading the final reports he'd received about the Queen of Diamonds case. His involvement had ended the second the federal prosecutor had become involved, and the information he'd received was limited. He only hoped he'd impressed on Carl that credit for all the forthcoming arrests went to Ashley.

Angel Honeywell still hadn't been found, but every person who'd seen or heard the news over the past few days knew exactly what she looked like. He figured she'd burrowed in somewhere until she felt safe to move around.

Iain's search of the foster care system files had verified the story of a fourteen-year-old girl who'd been found bloody and walking on a major highway. Her stepfather was the first case on record who had been stabbed, his dick cut off, and the playing card left on his body.

Deep down, if he'd admit it, Dalton felt Angel's first kill had been a good one.

He had almost asked Carl about Ashley when he'd spoken with him, but the call was all business.

He'd spent a long time trying to erase his mother's betrayal from his memory. It was time to do what his dad had wanted for a long time. Forgive and forget.

Dalton's interest in one-night dating was gone. He'd finally found the woman he wanted to spend the rest of his life with, raise a family with, and wanted to give his heart and trust to completely. He was going to make this right.

He'd fucked up royally.

He'd made a decision, and now, he had to man up and follow it through.

Kay drew his attention as she walked past Dalton's door for at least the tenth time that day. This time she turned around and walked back to his office, taking a seat.

"Would you like me to start looking into temporary housing near the new compound so you can be on-site quickly if there's a problem?"

"Something I can use as an office and living space would be great. There'd better not be issues with the construction. We're stretched pretty thin right now. If we take the fortune teller case, I'll need at least three or four men to handle it."

"Nate's interviewed a couple of men he thinks will fit in quickly." Kay squirmed in her chair like a kid waiting to be called inside the principal's office for fighting. She had something to say, and looked about ready to explode if she didn't get it said.

Dalton knew all about the interviews, and Kay was aware of that. "You have anything else on your mind?"

"I was just thinking that maybe you should take a few days off before you get bogged down with the new compound and this new case. Maybe take a trip?"

Dalton bit back a grin. "And where would you suggest I go?"

"San Antonio, maybe?" Her gaze was everywhere but on him. "It's a beautiful town. Full of history."

"Kay." He dropped his tone an octave. "Spit it out before you pop a blood vessel."

She glanced over her shoulder. "Nate's going to kill me for this."

"For?"

"Telling you to get off your ass and go after your girl." Kay held her hand out as if to stop him from speaking. "Since the day you got back, you've almost bitten the head off everyone who's tried to talk to you."

"Maybe I didn't want to hear what they had to say."

"Well, you're going to hear me." She stood, went to the door, and closed it. He heard the lock click before she turned back to face him. "Ashley called and asked me about you. I'm breaking her trust by telling you, but she's hurting. You need to make it clear that you don't care about her. Or you could always man up and tell her the truth."

"And what's that?"

"That you're in love with her."

"You don't know that." But he did. He knew life wasn't right without her. It was impossible to sleep without her. Hell, it was hard to breathe without her.

"Then prove me wrong. Settle things with her." The knock on his door had her scooting to the edge of her chair. "That's Nate, isn't it?"

Dalton nodded. "The door is closed, but you do remember the wall is glass?"

Kay's lips formed a perfect O. "Crap. He saw me sitting here."

"Yep." He couldn't hold back a smile as he stood and walked around his desk. He opened the door and Nate stepped inside.

"You two about done in here?" Nate's hand rested on his wife's shoulder. "You don't want to miss your flight to San Antonio."

"Wait." Kay jumped to her feet and whirled to face her husband. "Nate! Why didn't you tell me?"

"Because it isn't any of our business, and for not listening to me, I may turn you over my knee tonight."

Kay huffed out a laugh as she walked past her husband and out of Dalton's office. "In your dreams."

When she was out of sight, Dalton lifted his eyebrows at Nate. "Spanking?"

Nate shook his head. "Not in this lifetime. That woman would smother me in my sleep if I tried to paddle her ass."

Dalton couldn't hold back his chuckle. "You two helped convince me true love exists."

"When it's the right two people, it does." Nate lifted his chin toward the door. "You have her address?"

"Yep."

"Then get out of here."

Dalton pulled his pickup keys from his pocket and twirled them around his finger. "See ya."

27

Angel grabbed her cell, hoping for good news. Hiding out in the woods was driving her insane. She loved her cabin, but the isolation was getting to her. Her mind wandered when she was idle for too long. The nightmares had come rushing back, robbing her of badly needed rest. Leaving the lights on helped, but after she woke up feeling beaten and bruised, there was no getting back to sleep.

She should have killed Kyle the day he yelled at her and said neither of them would live much longer. He was a coward, and she knew he'd turn against her.

Neither the feds, Kyle, nor the mafia would keep her from taking care of this last problem, though. She had to know where Dalton was at all times. She was too recognizable, but Axel and his buddies worked for a price.

Thanks to the internet, she'd bought enough items using one of her aliases that her new disguise would allow her to finish this last job. She was trying on new colored contacts when her disposable cell rang.

"What do you have?"

"Your boy just landed in San Antonio, Texas. I followed him to DFW, got on the shuttle with him, and struck up a conversation. I barely had time to buy a ticket and get on the plane. Told him I was headed there, too."

"What did he say?"

"Not much. He's there straightening out some problem."

"If you lose him, head to the address I gave you. He'll go there first." Angel smiled as she held the Maxim 9 in her hand. "I'll be there in about four hours. I'll check in when I get close."

Angel finished her makeup. She studied the face in the mirror and liked what she saw. The short ash-blonde wig was secured, brown contacts were in place, and the maternity top she slid over her shoulders was perfect. She held a small pillow against her stomach, wrapping it tightly with plastic wrap. She turned to the mirror to judge her disguise. Her fingers splayed over the imaginary baby bump.

Time stopped. She couldn't breathe. She stumbled backward and sat on the bed.

Memories of a doctor standing next to her hospital bed explaining that the damage had been too extensive slammed into her. A fourteen-year-old girl being told her insides were so messed up she'd never have a child.

Angel's hands started tearing at the bundle. As if possessed, she cried out, tearing at the tape, wrenching and ripping it until the pillow was released and fell to the floor at her feet. She didn't cry. Hadn't cried since she walked out of the hospital and into the hands of a social worker.

She opened the bottle of pills Axel had given her for her nerves and swallowed one down without water. Pushing up onto the bed, she stretched out and waited. Thirty minutes later, she'd rewrapped the pillow and was on the road to San Antonio.

Ashley hadn't had any physical contact with Dalton since the day Angel had put Axel on Dalton's tail. If the woman was smart, she wouldn't have anything to do with Dalton when he showed up at her door.

It disgusted Angel that some women forgave their abusers and walked right back into the relationship. That wouldn't happen here. She'd seen the bruise on Ashley's face and the ripped knees of her slacks. But it was her gut-wrenching sobs that Angel couldn't get out of her head.

****

Ashley closed her office door, sat at her new desk, and glanced around at the simple decor. Cream walls and brown leather furniture lent an aura of calm, solidity, and professionalism. A smile tugged at the corners of her mouth. Carl was strutting around like a rooster in a barnyard full of hens. He'd been so pleased with the information Kyle Beltrane had shared he'd forgotten all about her failure to convince Dalton to rejoin the FBI.

He hadn't been far from her mind since she'd returned to her home base. The pride she should have experienced at identifying the Queen of Diamonds paled from the pain she felt that he hadn't reached out to her. How had she let herself fall in love with him? Her finger had hovered over his cell number too many times to count. She especially missed him late at night, when all she had to hold in her arms was a cold pillow.

Was Dalton in Houston pushing the new compound toward completion? Did he know Ash would leave Houston PD and accept a position if offered? Did she ever cross his mind?

Carl knocked on her door, then opened it a crack. "Let's call it a day. Come on, I'll walk you out."

Ashley pushed away from her desk, put a fake smile on her face, and joined him as they made their way to the parking lot.

After stopping by for a carryout order of Chinese food and a couple of bottles of wine, she drove to her townhouse and parked in her assigned slot. She hated leaving her car out in the baking sun. The next available unit with a garage had been promised to her by the complex manager.

This summer was the summer from hell, and had broken records of over a hundred degrees for the past seventeen days, with more to come. She hurried across the parking lot, watching the heat wave roll off the pavement.

Suddenly a tall figure hidden by the shrubs and trees stepped out of the shade into the sunlight. She screamed and dropped both bags. Strong hands gripped her. His scent wrapped around her. "You scared the hell out of me."

"I needed to see you."

She stepped back, stumbling over one of the packages. Dalton grabbed her, steadying her on her feet.

****

The scene played out in front of Angel in slow motion. Dalton had pushed Ashley.

She ran toward the two of them with the Maxim aimed at him.

"Get your hands off her!" she screamed, pulling the trigger.

Ashley jumped in front of him.

Angel screamed as the woman crumpled to the ground. No! He's the one who deserves to die.

Dalton fell to his knees, covering Ashley's body with his. That gave Angel the second chance she needed. This time she steadied her hand and aimed at his back.

****

Dalton ripped off his shirt, using it to stanch the blood flowing from Ashley's chest. He'd lifted his head at the sound of the second shot long enough to see Reed standing over a body.

With his free hand, he dialed 911, succinctly telling them he had an FBI agent down with a bullet wound to the chest. She needed help stat. His mind was whirling. His heart was ready to implode.

He could not, would not, lose Ashley.

"Stay with me, baby." Her lids fluttered but never opened. "Open those beautiful eyes for me."

Her eyes opened to slits. "Hurts."

"That's my girl. Look at me." Dalton pressed harder against her chest. She cried out in pain, and then her eyes drifted closed. "No-no-no. You can't leave me," he begged her. "Stay with me. Please. I can't lose you."

He pressed two fingers against her carotid artery and found a faint pulse. "Don't leave me." Battling tears, he shouted, "Where's the fucking ambulance?"

Time and space disappeared as eternity passed. At last, strong hands caught his forearms.

"You gotta move and let the EMTs help her." Reed's tone got louder with each word. "Dalton! Step back!"

Reed's words finally reached him, and he stumbled over to the side, suddenly aware of the sound of sirens. An ambulance, fire truck, and a couple of police cars filled the parking lot.

The paramedics hovered over her, doing their best to save her life. They moved her to the gurney, strapping her in. He followed. There was no way he was staying behind.

"I'm her husband, and I'm going with her." His body vibrated with fear as he climbed into the ambulance. He'd never felt more helpless. Useless. In the way. The EMTs worked over her while asking him questions about her health. He had no answers except she was on birth control.

The next few minutes were a blur. They were whisked away in the ambulance, and shortly after, through the emergency entrance.

A nurse stopped him at the double doors when he tried to follow the gurney. "I have to go with her," he insisted.

"You can't," she said, pointing to the waiting area. "They'll take care of your wife. I need her information, so have a seat, and I'll be with you in a moment."

He wasn't about to correct the nurse. Let them believe he and Ashley were married. Maybe that way he'd be kept informed. He took a seat facing the area he'd been forbidden to enter so he could see when the doctor came out. There were people he had to call.

Her brother was the hardest. Ash reminded Dalton he was supposed to protect her and keep her safe. It was a promise he'd broken.

A hand gripped his shoulder, and Reed slid into the chair next to him. "Thank you for keeping that bitch from firing again."

"No problem. I'm just glad I was there."

Dalton shook his head, trying to refocus. "Why were you there?"

"Pure dumb luck, and Nate listening to his gut. He was worried Angel Honeywell would come after Ashley since it was her who blew the case open. That, combined with Beltrane's information that she'd had both you and Ashley researched, meant he felt you were safe at the compound, but Ashley was out in the open."

"I thought you were already on a case."

Reed grinned. "I was. Nate sent me to keep an eye on her. I wasn't to contact her. Just observe and protect."

"We're damn lucky you were there."

"I didn't protect her. Nate let me know you were on the way. I was trying to stay out of sight."

"You saved both our lives."

The double doors opened, and Dalton shot to his feet. The nurse walked right past him without so much as a glance.

"They haven't told me a damn thing."

"She'll be OK."

"You saw the amount of blood she lost." He pressed his fingertips into his temple. "I'll never forget the vacant look in her eyes."

"I'll get us some coffee." Reed gripped Dalton's shoulder again and walked away.

Dalton jumped to his feet when the nurse who'd refused him entry walked through the double doors. He met her halfway.

"Mrs. Hunter is still in surgery. I don't have an update, but I can tell you the doctor is concerned with getting the bleeding stopped first." She smiled and nodded. "I'll let you know if I hear anything else."

Reed returned with coffee and some kind of health bar that tasted like cardboard, along with two bottles of water and a couple of sports magazines.

Dalton was grateful because he wasn't budging.

"Mrs. Hunter?" Reed asked, sitting in the chair across from him.

"It's just a little white lie." Dalton took a sip of coffee. "That's better than I remember hospital coffee being. "You square with the police?"

"For now. They'll have questions, but they can wait. The news will be all over them in a heartbeat."

"Angel was good at disguises."

Reed laughed. "You're not wrong. She had a pillow taped to her stomach and was wearing colored contacts and a wig."

"I'm just so fucking glad you were there."

Reed took a sip of his coffee. "Nate and Kay are on the way. They're driving and will leave the SUV with you. You'll need a place to stay, so Kay reserved a room for you at a hotel nearby. I don't know which one, but she'll fill you in."

"I'm not going anywhere."

"We get that, but if Ashley's here for a long time, you may start stinking. Then you'll appreciate having a place to shower and shave."

Dalton scrubbed his hands over his face. "You know, I always wished for siblings. Nate has created an environment where I feel like I have a house full of brothers. You all mean a lot to me."

"We love you too, man. On Ashley's first day at the compound, I warned her you were an enigma around there. Looks like she's loosened you up a little."

"I don't know what she's done to me, but I am a different person when I'm around her."

****

Hours passed, and Dalton paced, jumping up and looking hopeful every damn time those double doors opened.

All the things he should have done, the things he should have said to Ashley, ran through his mind. He'd been so caught up in the Houston meeting about the new compound he hadn't even thought to celebrate her accomplishment. The impact Kyle Beltrane's confession would have on her career was huge.

Hell, the impact she'd had on him was incredible. He'd laughed more, talked more, and had kicked his one-and-done rule to the curb because of her.

Three long hours later, a woman wearing green scrubs walked toward the waiting room, removing her mask.

He rushed to meet her.

"Are you waiting on news about Ashley Hunter?"

"Yes, ma'am."

"She made it through surgery just fine. She lost a lot of blood, though. The bullet entered her left lung, barely missing her heart, and lodged in her back. When I say barely, I mean a hair's breadth from killing her."

"She'll be fine?"

"She should be." The tag on her scrubs read Sadie English.

"Dr. English, what does that mean?"

"I don't make promises. We'll know more when she wakes up."

"May I sit with her?"

"Not yet."

"I'll be quiet as a mouse. She won't know I'm there. Hell, *you* won't know I'm there. I just have to see her."

Dr. English looked him in the eye for a long second. "Walk with me. If I tell you to leave the room, you leave."

"Yes, ma'am." His heart hammered against his rib cage as he followed her through the doors and into ICU. He'd been in these areas before, when coworkers had been hurt in the line of duty. It was a different kind of cold than the rest of the hospital, and so very quiet.

Dr. English stopped by a door and motioned him inside. "I'll be back to get you."

"She's a federal agent. A lot of people will be checking on her. Please, let me stay."

"I don't like making exceptions." She stared at him again for a long minute. "Get out of line once, and you're out."

"Thank you," he whispered.

Dalton stepped into the darkened room and moved slowly toward the sound of a machine beeping. His hands clenched and unclenched rapidly. He'd seen death and near-death more than once, but no experience had ripped his heart out and thrown it to the floor like seeing Ashley under that crisp white sheet.

She looked so tiny, pale, and helpless. Wires and tubes hung from a metal tree supporting three bags that dripped medicine and saline into her body. He moved closer and ran his knuckles down her cheeks. Then he used his fingertips to brush her hair off her forehead. He located a chair, pulled it as close to her bed as possible, sat, and held the hand that didn't have an IV in it.

"You took a bullet for me. I wish you hadn't. If one of us had to suffer, it should never have been you. Hear my voice, Ashley." He swallowed the lump in his throat. There was nothing he could do about the pain in his heart. Only she could fix that. "I need you to come back to me."

He had no idea how long he'd been with her when someone tapped him on the shoulder. "It's time for you to step out."

"She's resting peacefully," he protested. "I'm not trying to make her wake up. I swear."

"Her brother insists he speak with you."

Dalton squeezed Ashley's hand, leaned over, and kissed her forehead. "I'll be back."

He followed Dr. English into the hallway. "No more visits until morning."

His lips pulled into a thin line.

"Mr. Murphy." She'd leaned heavily on the different last name.

"I'm sorry."

He was boiling mad when he stepped through the double doors. Furious that Ash had revealed his lie.

"You son of a bitch. Now I'll have to fight my way back to her room. You won't keep me away from her."

Ash, who was just about the same size as Dalton, moved to stand chest to chest with him. "You get away with calling me a son of a bitch this time. Don't do it again. If you wanted me to back your lie, you should have told me."

All the wind went out of Dalton's sails. "Sorry. I don't normally go off half-cocked, but I'm so worried about her."

"I can tell." Ash sighed. "I gave them her medical history, as much as I could, and was told I couldn't go back because her husband was with her. I'll make sure you're allowed to stay with her."

"Thanks," Dalton said with a nod. "How long have you been here?"

"About an hour." Ash looked at Reed, who was standing to the side. He'd no doubt come forward to separate them if necessary. "Where're Nate and Kay?"

"After they checked in with me, they went to get you something to eat." Reed smiled at a pretty nurse walking by.

"You off duty yet?"

"Let me change clothes, and I'll meet you downstairs in the lobby."

Dalton laughed. "You've been out here hitting on the nurses?"

"Just the one." Reed grinned, flashing his dimples. "I figured now that Ash has arrived, I could take the hardworking girl to dinner. With all these people here, I guess you're in good hands."

"Go." Dalton waved his hand, sending Reed away. "Enjoy."

Ash visited his sister while Dalton counted the minutes until he could return to her side. Nate and Kay arrived with a sub sandwich, chips, and a glass of sweetened iced tea. Grateful for the nourishment, he wolfed it down and waited for those damned double doors to open again.

Nate handed him the keys to the SUV and a parking ticket. "We're flying home. I valeted the SUV so you wouldn't have to search for it. Keep us informed, especially if you need anything."

Dalton shook his head. "Thank you." He jangled the keys in his hand. "For this, and everything."

Ash and a nurse came through the doors together.

Dalton was on his feet and moving forward quickly. "Something happen?"

"The doctor feels she can be moved to a room."

"I can sit with her there?"

"Her doctor said you can. I'll let you know when and where she's settled after the move. It will be a couple of hours. Go get some fresh air."

Dalton stumbled back to his seat. That was the best news he'd ever had. They wouldn't move her unless she was going to be fine.

At Ash's insistence they located the cafeteria and had a hot cup of coffee.

"You're in love with her," Ash said around a bite of food. It wasn't a question.

"Very much so."

"I figured. She wouldn't talk about it when I questioned her. Now, you can."

"I convinced her I would never settle down with one woman. Did a damn fine job. She loves me, Ash, I know she does, but I have to convince her I can be trusted."

"You know the drill. Fuck with my baby sister, and you'll deal with me."

Dalton chuckled. "I'll never hurt her again. You have my word."

They went back to the ICU area, since they had no idea where else they should be, and waited. And waited. At last, the news came that Ashley was settled and he could see her.

Once back with her, the constriction in Dalton's chest eased. He'd been told she'd stay in ICU until she woke, then she'd be moved to a room. But she hadn't, and when questioned, the doctor said Ashley would wake up in her own good time.

So, he waited some more.

With his chair pulled close to her bed, he talked softly to her and shared some of his favorite moments they'd had together.

"Remember the night I quit fighting my attraction to you? I opened my motel door to come to your room and discovered you standing there. That you'd come to me just about knocked me out.

"Remember the drive up the coast of California and the seafood restaurant where you stood on the terrace looking out over the ocean? The wind was blowing those fringes of hair that always escape that tight ponytail you wear.

"Remember the way you insisted we take Lucky with us? She spoke to you with her eyes, and you understood. No more going hungry for that sweet dog.

"I love the way you and my dad bonded.

"Want to know my number one favorite thing about you? It's the expression on your face when you orgasm. Each and every time it happens, I think it's the most beautiful thing I've ever seen."

He rested his head next to her hand. "I'm not leaving until you open your eyes and say my name. Hopefully, you're dreaming about me right now."

28

Ashley listened to the beep of a machine for a few seconds before opening her eyes. Sunlight cast shadows on the dimly lit hospital room walls. Dalton's head was resting on the bed next to her hand. His fingers were wrapped around hers.

Her bed? Why was she in the hospital? She shifted her body to see him better, and pain lanced through her chest. Her gasp had him instantly on his feet.

"Are you in pain?" He headed for the door, then spun and came back. "Want me to get a nurse?"

"Water?"

"Got it." He held a straw to her mouth, and she drank. "Better?" He leaned over and kissed her forehead. His hair was standing every which way, and he looked as if he hadn't shaved in a few days.

"Better." Her chest hurt and her throat felt raw. "I like the wild man look on you, but it makes me wonder how long I've been here?"

"Three days. How much do you remember?"

"Angel tried to kill you." The beeping on the heart monitor sped up. "What happened?"

"You jumped in front of me."

A weak smile touched her lips. "I did?"

A nurse rushed into the room. She checked Ashley's pulse and IV before asking if she was having any pain.

"A little. Only if I move."

Dalton showed her a small button on one of the tubes she was hooked up to. "Push that and it will help."

"Mr. Murphy, if you'll excuse us for a minute." The nurse checked the level of liquids in the bags. "Now that she's awake, the doctor will want to have a look, and she's also due a change of sheets."

He moved silently through the door. "A cup of coffee sounds good."

Once he left, Ashley asked, "He can come back?"

"I don't think you have to worry about that. He hasn't left your side."

A smile bloomed on her face, and warmth circulated deep inside her heart. "Really?"

"Honey, that man talked the most rigid, rule-following doctor in the hospital into letting him stay in ICU with you even after she discovered he'd lied and let everyone believe he was your husband."

Ashley and the nurse laughed when the monitor sped up.

"He's a great guy."

"This monitor and your catheter go away today. Dr. English will decide when the IV can be removed."

After the nurse left, Ashley was determined not to doze off until she saw Dalton again.

A man clearing his throat woke her. She blinked a couple of times, realizing she had fallen asleep despite her resolve not to.

A silver belly Stetson western hat and the person wearing it came into view. "Dad? You're here?"

"Of course. Where else would I be?" He leaned over and kissed her cheek. "As we used to say, you've been kicking ass and taking names. Cracked a major case, and then saved your partner's life. It doesn't get any better than that."

"Thanks." The praise she'd hungered for all her life now wrapped her like a warm blanket. "Where's Dalton?"

"I'm right here, baby."

Her gaze swept the room and found him leaning against the wall just inside the door. He winked at her and sent her that sexy smirk he didn't share often. "How do you feel?"

"Like I want to get out of here."

"We'll let Dr. English make that call." He walked to her, leaned down, and brushed a lock of hair off her forehead. "I'm going to grab a shower. I think Ash needs one, too. You OK with that?" He cut his gaze toward her dad, and then back to her.

"I'm fine. You haven't had much rest the past few days. Get a couple of hours sleep and then come back."

"I'll rest when I take you home." He kissed that spot on her forehead he seemed to favor. "I won't be gone long." With a nod to her dad, he was gone.

"I'm out of here, too. I just wanted to see you were all right with my own eyes."

"Dad." He stopped when she called his name. "Thank you for coming."

"You bet. Listen to the doctors." If she hadn't known better, she'd have suspected that his eyes were wet with tears. It was a shame they didn't know how to connect.

Then a nurse came in, and handed her a juice box. "You know you won't go home until you start eating."

"Yes, ma'am." She stuck the straw into her mouth and pulled in some fruit-flavored liquid. After she swallowed, she teased the young nurse. "You give this stuff to kids?"

"They love it. Drink."

Carl had been by, the police had taken her statement as soon as they'd been cleared by the doctor, and she was pleasantly surprised at the flowers that had been delivered. They had brightened up the nondescript hospital room.

She found the remote for the television and began watching a comedy. She laughed and gasped when the pain in her chest arced through her.

By late afternoon, she was seriously missing Dalton. Dr. English had come and gone, promising the last drip line would be removed tomorrow. And maybe, just maybe, she'd go home in the late afternoon.

She knew he was there before he came into her line of sight. The air around her shifted. Her sense of smell was enhanced. "I was wondering if you'd forgotten me."

"No, you weren't. You knew I'd be back." He chuckled as he crossed the room, then leaned over, and this time, his lips touched down on hers.

"More, please." Her right hand moved to his cheek, rubbing the smoothness that comes after a fresh shave. "Never mind. I have hospital breath."

"I couldn't care less." This time when their lips touched, it wasn't an innocent kiss. This was a mind-searing capture your soul kiss. "Better?"

"Much." She groaned as she moved, but she scooted as far as she could to the right side of the bed. Then she patted the empty spot. "Please. I need you to hold me."

"Whatever you want." He lifted himself up and onto his side. There wasn't much room, but neither of them seemed to mind. He slid one arm under her head and then gently placed his hand over her heart. "Mine."

"What did you say?"

Had she heard what she thought she'd heard?

"Mine."

She couldn't let herself hope too much. "What changed your mind?"

"You did. You made me feel things, want things I've never had. It almost killed me when I woke up and you'd left me behind. Nothing in my life works without you. I don't exist without you."

"I was afraid you wouldn't want me forever."

"Maybe I had to experience the trauma my mom and ex-wife caused, so when life brought us together, I'd better appreciate what I have with you."

Tears welled and slipped from the corner of her eyes. "What do you have?"

He lifted onto his elbow. His dark chocolate eyes were full of love. His thumb wiped the damp trail of wetness off her face. "You. Forever." His lips brushed hers. "I love you."

She pulled him over for a kiss. "I know."

His eyebrows went up. "How did you know?"

"I love you, too. I just wasn't sure when you'd figure it out."

"It was one hell of a surprise to me."

"I wish I'd been there to see it."

"You'll be seeing it for the rest of your life."

Epilogue

Eighteen months later...

Dalton closed the lid on the grill and looked across the compound. Today was the perfect day for beer, wine, and barbecue. The weather wasn't hot and humid in Houston, allowing the team to enjoy being outdoors. He glanced around for his wife, but didn't see her. Wearing the yellow sundress Kay had given her after the engagement was announced, Ashley wouldn't be hard to find.

Reed and Tank were swapping war stories with two new agents fresh out of the military. Ex-Army Ranger Drew Kavanagh and retired Air Force fighter pilot Alex Chandler had been accepted right away. Dalton considered his biggest win was convincing Ash Hunter to leave his position with the police department and join this crew.

Tank had just wrapped up his first assignment, locating and delivering a Texas oil baron's wild and unruly daughter back to her family. Who knew how long she would stay before running away again? It wasn't a big case, but it was an excellent start.

Soft hands slid around his waist from behind. Dalton turned into the arms of his wife, the most beautiful woman on earth. "There you are. You've been fidgeting all day. What are you up to?"

She grinned up at him. "Nothing, and everything."

He snuggled her close against his body, loving how her breasts pushed into him. "You look positively evil. What's up?"

"Ash will man the grill while we talk." She took his hand and led him into the main area of the compound. Like the one in Dallas, their home was the second story of the main building.

"I think I know your secret."

"You do?"

"I noticed you stopped sending candidates to me. You'd like to take the technology position."

She lifted onto her toes and kissed him. "You think you're such a great detective."

Damn, she made him happy. And vice versa. Just looking down at her, he could see she was glowing. The thought hit him like a tidal wave. They'd been talking about having a family.

Was she pregnant?

"You're right. I'm turning in my resignation tomorrow morning."

That doused his theory with ice water. "All I want is for you to be as happy as I am. And I'm fucking thrilled to have you join the team." He took her hand. "Let's go tell the boys."

"You're going to have to clean up your language."

"Why would I do that?" he asked with a chuckle.

"Because I don't want our son or daughter—"

Dalton turned on his heel. They were having a baby. He picked her up and spun her in circles before panicking and carefully putting her feet on the floor. "I didn't hurt you, did I?"

"Am I going to have to put up with that for the next seven and a half months?"

"Whatever you want. You want to be pampered? You got it. You want to not work at all? You got it." He cupped his face in his hands. "I love you so fucking much."

She laughed and smacked his shoulder. "I love you, too. So very much."

He scooped her into his arms and carried her up the stairs to their bedroom. Putting her down, he covered her mouth with his and gathered the bottom of her sundress in his fingers. "Hands up."

"What about the party?" she said with a sexy smile.

"Your brother has us covered." She lifted her arms over her head, smiling as he undressed her. His heart swelled with emotion as he leaned down and kissed her soft stomach. "Mine forever," he whispered.

Ready for a sneak peek at the new series Lost and Found Houston!

Unedited excerpt of

A New Hell

book 1 of the new standalone series,

Lost and Found, Houston

Prologue

Reed Ballatori and Ash Hunter followed Dalton Murphy outside. The humidity was so heavy his clothes immediately started to absorb the dampness. He looked over the completed compound and back to the two men standing next to him. "Are you two ready for this?"

"Damn right we are. I'll sleep better at night if we have to kill every one of the sonofabitches," Ash said as he clapped Reed on his back. "Pretty sure Reed feels the same way."

"Exactly." Reed shifted from one foot to the other. "I don't know how the parents keep their shit together."

"I always sympathized and tried to understand the parents' fear when I was working a case. Now that I have a kid, I don't know that I could hold it together." Dalton's feet itched with the desire to get hip deep in this new case. Lost and Found Houston had been up and running for a few months, but this assignment? It would make or break them.

He glanced around the compound. The office areas and housing for agents who were in town for a few days or training had been completed first. The first of three outbuildings housed a huge gym with state-of-the-art equipment and boxing ring. The Olympic size swimming pool, hot tubs, and steam room sat next to the gym with the firing range a few hundred feet behind them.

Reed Ballatori, Tank Jorgenson, and Xander Trip moving to the Houston division made the transition easier. Keeping with the standards set by the Dallas team, Drew Kavanagh an ex-Army Ranger, and Alex Chandler, better known as Speed, a retired Airforce fighter pilot were two new hires. Convincing Ash Hunter, to give up his job as head of the homicide department with Houston PD and join this team had been easier than expected.

Dalton's proudest moment to date was when his wife, Ashley, delivered their eight-pound, two-ounce baby boy. She'd left the FBI and now managed the financial and technology part of the business, along with their home on the second level plus their two-year-old son, Scotty.

He turned his thoughts back to the challenge ahead. "Reed. Give'em hell."

"Will do."

The three men walked back inside, Reed and Ash headed to their rooms to prepare to leave while Dalton stopped at his admin's desk.

Somewhere in her late fifties, Edie Summers was a found jewel. She was a tiny, anal, organized tornado. She was also smart, disgustingly cheerful, and bossy as hell.

"Is everything ready for Reed and Ash?"

She lifted her right eyebrow, which he'd learned was a bluff. "You've asked me that same question three times."

"I never should've doubted you." He winked at her causing a bright pink flush to hit her cheeks.

"They're on your desk. Reed's new wallet, which looks weather-beaten as hell, a fake ID, credit cards, money, and the paperwork allowing him to carry the Sig Sauer P229 pistol is on your desk. Remind him he'll have to check the gun before boarding the airplane. Ashton stopped by earlier and picked his up. Both of those boys look eminently qualified to pose as a body guard."

"Thank you." Dalton returned to his desk and looked over Reed's new identity. Edie was right, even the wallet appeared to be old and badly worn.

Reed stepped in, a duffle bag over his shoulder. He gathered his new identity and gave him as two finger salute. "Stay in touch. Tell Tank I'm not happy he missed his check in this morning. He's supposed to be the wealthy Texas playboy in the casino but that doesn't mean I don't need to hear his voice."

"Will do." Reed paused at the door, "I'll be in touch."

"I don't need to tell you to be careful. Do I?"

"Nope." Reed gave him a two fingered salute and disappeared out the door. "It's hard to kill a ghost."

Dalton checked the cell that had been set up for updates from the team. Still nothing from Tank.

Ash walked into the office wearing the identical black T-shirt, black slacks, and black books that Reed Had worn. The logo was for a dummy security company that appeared on paper to be well established in the protection of celebrities. "I'll bet you want to go with us."

Dalton chuckled. "Yes and no."

"It's natural to worry."

"It's not that I have doubts about our ability. I don't. We have the right people in place."

"This is a massive op." Ash shuffled through the papers for his new identity.

"The hotel allowed the installation of bugs and cameras in public areas. As long as none were trained on the gaming tables or machines, they agreed to allow an observer to sit with the hotels security who constantly monitored the casino section. It's being so damn far away that bugs me."

"I can imagine." Ash nodded.

"It's the plan that makes me nervous. It's too elaborate. There are too many pieces to the puzzle. One piece, one fucking missing piece, and the whole thing will crumble. We're coming in late to the party and only because the Marchetti's pressured the feds."

"Marcus said they were the animal rescue's largest donor."

"Yeah. The Marchetti's felt the feds weren't moving fast enough. Knowing the sale will be held in Venezuela was the point they insisted we be added to the operation. Their daughter, Mari, is a sharp eighteen-year-old. Stealing a guard's cell and calling her mother took a lot of guts. The last sound her mother heard was a scream."

"Fuck," Ash growled. "I heard the tape. That had to be rough."

"I don't think any of us will forget that sound. You ready to head out?"

"Yeah. I need to be going. We'll take these bastards to the ground. And as long as the feds stay behind the scene, do the recon, and monitor the electronic equipment, we shouldn't stumble all over each other."

Dalton chuckled. "No chance of that happening. Not with one of their own in the spotlight. But you and Reed may be in the position to overhear something valuable."

"We can do this." Ash slid his duffle bag over his shoulder. "Did you do a background check on the Marchetti family?"

"Should I?" Dalton's eyebrows pulled together.

Ash laughed. "Probably not. I just wondered if we had three groups working on this case. Us, the feds, and the Italian mafia."

"Oh, hell no. Marcus has all the big donors to the animal rescue checked out. The last thing they need is dirty money." Dalton stood and followed Ash outside to the parking lot. "You know the plan by heart?"

"This isn't my first rodeo, but I'll humor you."

Dalton didn't respond. He waited, not caring if he'd insulted Ash or not. This was human lives, young human lives, they were dealing with.

"Reed will join the federal agent as her bodyguard tomorrow at the airport. I'm flying out later in today, arriving in Monte Carlo a few couple of hours later. Speed who has just opened a helicopter transport company as a cover will be who we and the agent use for transportation. Do you know this federal agent?" Ask asked. "She'd better be damn good at reading minds and telling fortunes."

"You're right there. She's the only unknown on the team." Dalton studied Ash for a second. "How are you settling in? Miss the homicide division?"

"Not a damn bit. Has Tank checked in?"

Dalton shook his head. Tank had been in the casino a couple of days making himself know as a gambler. "Tank going silent makes me uncomfortable."

Ash shook Dalton's hand. "I'll kick his young ass for making you worry and then make sure he calls."

1

Every red-blooded male on the airplane who could see Valerie Golden openly stared as she made her way to her seat. Not that Reed blamed them. Of the few FBI agents he'd met, none of them dressed like her. She wore black slacks and a form fitting blouse that looked like it was made of spun wheat. Her long dark hair almost matched the color of the pants she wore. She stopped and hit him with a blinding smile full of straight white teeth.

Reed stood and stowed her suitcase. He waved her to the window seat. "Ms. Golden, it's nice to see you again."

"Thanks. The pleasure is mine." Her pale blue eyes sparkled as she flashed a set of white teeth at him with a smile. She glanced around. "Where is Mr. Hunter?"

He took the aisle seat. "Ash? He's on a later flight. He'll be there in time to take over after my shift. We'll be working twelve hours on and twelve off, so one of us will be available to you twenty-four-seven."

She leaned closer. "Are you upset?"

"What? Not at all." He thought that was an odd question coming from an employer to a new employee.

The left bottom corner of her lips pulled between her teeth. "Let me see if I've got this right. You're unhappy with this assignment for some reason. Does working with a woman upset you it? Leave a bad taste in your mouth?"

He settled in the seat next to her. "Are you practicing your physic powers on me?"

Her smile was more of a smirk. "Your body language speaks volumes."

Reed leaned his elbow on the armrest between them, flashing his dimples at her. "Exactly what is my body telling you now?"

She didn't flinch. "You think I'm profiling you, and it pisses you off."

"You might have physic powers after all." Reed laughed at her. She wasn't even marginally correct, but he wasn't going to argue.

"So, I'm right?"

"No. You're wrong." Reed glanced around their seats. The memory of his last assignment and the flight attendant who was a serial killer ran through his mind. "And you ask too many questions."

"Asking questions is how I get to know people." She leaned closer. "I get that we're not supposed to share personal information." She'd lowered her voice to a whisper. "But my life could depend on a man I know nothing about."

Reed settled back in his seat. He didn't know or want to know her real name. She was Valerie Golden, and he was one of her personal bodyguards. She smiled and snapped her seat belt around her hips. His role as her body guard didn't allow friendly conversations. She might as well get used to it. "I'm the guy who's going to make sure you get home alive. The rest isn't important."

"You're not going to tell me anything." Her lips drew into a thin line.

"We've been through this." He leaned close to her ear and spoke softly. "To me and the world you're the famous physic to the stars and rich people. The woman who helped locate a missing kid. Stay in your role, don't ask me personal questions, and I'll do the same."

"I'm also a trained professional," she huffed softly. "Being interested in your background is normal."

"Trained is good. Maybe if the sky falls on us, you'll be more than a pretty face."

Her eyes narrowed and Reed turned away as the flight attendant started issuing safety instructions. The engines powered up and the plane taxied down the runway, picking up speed. The noise put an end to their conversation.

He took out his cell, put in his air pods, pulled up some music, and ignored his new coworker. He'd heard all about the months of work put into building the persona Valerie Golden. She'd spent time in Hollywood, working with the few trusted stars the feds trusted. She'd been flashy and they'd made a point of having her spout accurate tales in front of the paparazzi.

She'd finally made the cover of a couple of popular magazines. The story told was that she'd held a stranger's hand and assured him that the son who'd been kidnapped by his ex-wife was fine. She'd gone on to provide the clues that lead the police to the woman and child. Father and son's reunion had made the ten o'clock news. That brought out the screwballs and she'd been receiving anonymous letters even death threats.

Reed hadn't thought of the story again until Dalton had a request from the other partner in the organization, Nate Wolfe. Marcus Ricci's wife, Chris, ran an animal rescue and one of her largest donors had a missing daughter. The Dallas team was stretched too thin to take on this case.

The FBI had immediately requested a meeting with Dalton. That was the day Reed and the Houston team learned Valerie Golden was a trained operative. She was heading up an elaborate sting to take down the bastards who kidnapped young girls and smuggled them out of the country to be auctioned the off as slaves. The sales were held all over the world and the next one, according to intel, was scheduled to be held on an island off Venezuela.

Dalton had instantly improved on the original plan knowing this could be the case that secured Lost and Found Houston's future.

Reed's role in the operation was to be a bodyguard to the physic, Valerie Golden. The current story on her persona is that she'd had an affair with a client and after the relationship went south, he'd gone to the press claiming she is a fake. He'd witnessed how the rumor mill worked by how quickly her adoring public had turned on her and were currently roasting her on social media. She'd made National news after receiving a number of death threats because they didn't believe in her powers. The story on the news was she'd go into hiding. Resting, relaxing, and meditating was what the doctor had ordered.

Dalton was right. This plan was too elaborate. Too many loose pieces to this puzzle. If this house of cards crumbles, somebody could die.

The plane leveled off and Valerie slipped on a sleeping mask. He leaned his seat back, changed the music to a crime novel, listening until he dozed off. He snapped awake when a hand grabbed his arm. Valerie's fingernails dug into his skin, and her head lashed back and forth. He leaned close to her ear, trying not to startle her too badly. "Valerie. Valerie, wake up."

She released him like he'd burned her and jerked off her mask. Wide eyed, she glanced around. Like she'd thrown a switch, her demeanor went from frightened to icy cold.

"You were dreaming."

"Sorry about that." She pulled the mask back over her eyes.

He wasn't letting her ignore her behavior. "And mumbling."

"Sorry about that," she repeated.

"You had a nightmare."

"I did not. Now, if you'll excuse me, I planned on getting some rest during this flight."

She'd lied and he knew it. "Do you want to talk about the dream?"

"No."

Reed pulled his sleeve a little lower to cover the scratches. The lady had been frightened bad enough she'd scored his skin with her nails. He wouldn't bring up this incident while they were on the plane, but they would be talking about it later. He didn't give a damn if she had skeletons to hide as long as they didn't impact this case.

He rubbed his hand across his stubbled chin. He wasn't too sure how he felt about growing a beard. With his size and new clothes, he would look the part as a bodyguard. He'd laughed when Dalton's wife, Ashley had suggested he stop shaving. She'd said he was too pretty and hair on his face would make him look tougher. He'd laughed, but had considered that a backward compliment. The company had paid for a couple of black suits, a handful of black pullovers, black jeans, and a pair of black work boots.

Their elaborate backgrounds that had been created would hold up to scrutiny. A lot was riding on her to perform. If she pulled it off, they should move through the rich folks in Trinidad with ease.

Reed understood the timeline of the operation had been moved up after the Marchetti's daughter had somehow managed to get her hands on a cell and call home. She'd had just enough time to say she'd overheard her captors say something about an auction in Venezuela. The last thing her mother heard was the scream of her daughter when she'd been discovered on the phone.

Read on for an excerpt from Till the Dead Speak

Preview: Till the Dead Speak

Prologue

Leo Cornetta straightened his five-foot-eight frame to its highest, pushed open the door to his boss's outer office, and then walked inside. He almost ran over the boss's crazy-ass son.

Dylan caught the door, held it open, and then walked into the hall. "Go on back. He's expecting you."

Leo glanced around, discovering that he was alone in the reception area. Fuck. The administrative assistant was never around when an employee was in serious trouble.

"Where's Mary?"

"Running errands." Dylan closed the door.

Leo licked his dry lips, sucked in his gut, and tapped on the door. Without waiting for a response, he entered. The boss seemed to be engrossed in paperwork, ignoring Leo's presence. Finally, he paused, placed his pen just so, straightened it, and then looked up. His expression, a perpetually superior, smug sneer, pissed Leo off, but he was smart enough not to let it show.

"By the look on your face, I'm guessing you haven't sorted out this mess."

"Not yet. I tried to search Charlie's file cabinet, but there's no reason for me to be in there for more than a minute. There would be questions if somebody saw me digging around."

"You getting caught is not my problem. Finding those pictures is more important."

"I'll find 'em, I will. It's just — I have to be careful."

"It was stupid of you to leave both sets of books where someone could find them and take pictures."

"Nobody ever came into my office." Leo struggled not to whine. "And I always worked on the books after the restaurant closed for the night."

"You actually saw these pictures, correct?"

"Damn right I did. Charlie called me in early and waved a stack of them under my nose."

"Then you should have killed him right then instead of giving the old bastard time to hide the evidence."

"The restaurant was full of people. The only thing I could do was promise him that if he'd wait until after closing, I'd tell him the whole story."

The boss waved Leo off. "Your reasons are not important now. Find those pictures."

"That FBI agent is making noises over the coroner's decision."

"Then I suggest you clean up your mess quickly." The boss sighed. The sound of disgust made Leo's balls tighten. "It was your job to make sure no one learned what was going on and you failed. And you failed again when you didn't make sure the evidence was in your possession before you killed him."

"I..." Leo fumbled for a response.

"Stop." Again, the boss held up his hand. "We'll send a couple of guys to rip the old man's house apart. If the pictures are there, they'll find them. Dylan will see to it that the granddaughter gets a proper welcome after she arrives. If she's smart, she'll get the message and get on the next plane to Dallas."

Actually, Leo thought his idea of eliminating Charles Pearson's only relative made better sense.

"Good. Do not let me down." The boss picked up his pen and went back to work. "I will be unhappy if we lose this location."

Leo had been warned and dismissed, but he wasn't finished. "We're going to hold off dropping off the money for a while, aren't we?"

"The schedule hasn't changed. It's your job to ensure things go smoothly." This time the boss leaned back in his chair, folding his arms across his chest.

"Will do." Leo knew when not to argue. He made a quick exit, hurrying through the outer office and into the hall to find Dylan leaning against the wall.

"All done?" Dylan asked.

"Yep. He's all yours," Leo said without breaking stride. "See you later."

Out of the corner of his eye, he saw Dylan's foot swing forward. Leo tripped, failed to regain his balance, and landed face down on the hall carpet face down. The toe of a shoe connected with his ribs, again and again. Pain ricocheted through his body, but he dared not yell or cry out.

Dylan bent over, lifted Leo's head by his hair, and said, "Don't fuck this up."

Leo resisted the urge to speak. He knew to stay quiet. Only Dylan was nuts enough to attack someone where anybody could've seen him. Leo knew that if he let his temper get the best of him, he'd be dead before morning. Hot anger and humiliation boiled through him like lava as he slowly pushed himself to his feet and walked to the elevator.

This whole mess was Charlie's fault. None of this would've happened if he'd stayed at home like most old and dying people. Instead, he'd unexpectedly returned to The Cage right after the money was delivered. Drowning Charlie had been a stroke of genius. His death had been ruled a suicide.

Leo stepped onto the elevator, turned, and smiled back at Dylan. As soon as he got his hands on those pictures, the nut job would join Charlie Pearson in death.

Chapter 1

Samantha Anderson stepped out of the Los Angeles airport car rental office, dragging her suitcase behind her. Before scanning the rows of rental cars, she paused to slip on her sunglasses to lessen the glare of the bright California sunshine. The early March sun warmed her after the chilly ride on the plane from Dallas.

Under different circumstances, she might have stopped to admire the unfamiliar landscape – towering palm trees, brilliant flowers, and flowering shrubs, but she hadn't come to enjoy the scenery. This was a get-in-and-get-out quick trip. With any luck, she'd be back home in Dallas within a couple of days.

Suddenly, a strong arm wrapped around her waist from behind and jerked her backward, seconds before a black SUV brushed past them so close she felt the breeze on her face. Her heart slammed into her chest, escalating her heart rate from normal to supersonic. Her feet tangled with the strangers, and they both tumbled to the pavement, Samantha landing on top of a rock hard chest.

"Oh my God!" Her words whooshed from her lungs. She struggled to extricate herself from the stranger's grip.

"Hang on." The man rolled her off his chest, stood, and then pulled her to her feet in one motion.

"That was close." She took two steps back, trying to catch her breath.

"I'm sorry I startled you, but there wasn't time to introduce myself."

"It's not a problem. Thank you for — wow, I think you just saved my life." Samantha looked up into Texas-sky-blue-eyes. And his voice, deep and rich as warm caramel, didn't do a thing to slow the rapid kathump-kathump-kathump of her heart.

"Welcome to California." He smiled, and the stern expression vanished. "Are you hurt?"

"Other than shattered nerves, I don't think so. Are you okay? You took the brunt of the fall."

"That was nothing. You're Samantha Anderson?"

"That's right." Her knees wobbled slightly as fear circled from her brain to her chest, much like water down the drain. "How do you know my name?" Everything about this trip had her spooked, and this guy wasn't helping matters.

"Easy. I've got you." He caught her by the elbow. "Lincoln Hawkins, but most people call me Linc." He extended his free hand. "Charles Pearson, your grandfather, was my friend."

"That statement isn't exactly endearing." She hesitated, but then shook his hand. "That Charles Pearson is my grandfather is something I still haven't wrapped my mind around."

Her left eyelid twitched. Again. Great. She'd never had a nervous tic of any kind, at least not until she'd heard the name Charles Pearson. Since then, this weird twitching of her left eyelid — a nervous *tic* for heaven's sake — had been rampant.

"It must've been one hell of a shock." He nodded his head as if he understood her situation, which he couldn't possibly.

"That's an understatement." A chill rushed up her arms. "Why are you here? How did you know who I was?"

"I've seen pictures of you. Look, we can get into all that later. Right now, we need to talk about your safety."

"I'll be more careful. Okay?" She pulled her hand from his warm grasp. "I don't usually walk out in front of moving vehicles."

"I don't believe that was an accidental brush-by."

"Excuse me, why would anyone want to run me down?" Samantha's heart started to rumba inside her chest at the seriousness on his face.

"Did the driver stop?" The stranger's eyebrows drew together. "Is he standing here apologizing profusely?"

She held back the sizzle of temper rising in her chest. "Okay. So the driver didn't stop. That doesn't prove it was intentional. Uhm, run your name by me again."

"Linc Hawkins. Look, you've been told Charles Pearson committed suicide, right? Well, I don't buy it. I believe he was murdered, and based on what just happened, you might be next."

The word ludicrous formed on her tongue, but she kept it to herself because no words in Webster's Dictionary could possibly describe the past few days. A surprise phone call from a California attorney, followed by a courier-delivered package containing a last will and testament, then a separate, FedEx envelope carrying a set of first class tickets to Los Angeles and several hundred dollars in cash — with a note: "per diem for your trip" — had knocked her world off center. She smoothed her hands over her hair and straightened her blouse in an effort to gain control of something. Anything.

"The attorney who contacted me said Charles Pearson's cause of death was drowning."

A DNA test had proven the lineage, but Samantha couldn't bring herself to refer Charles Pearson as her grandfather. Not without betraying the memory of the two men she'd grown up calling Papa and Grampy. She only had one living grandmother, and all attempts to reach her had failed. Samantha knew her texts had been read and ignored. Her messages had gone unanswered. Nana wasn't talking.

"I haven't convinced Ham yet, but I will." Linc's gaze swept the rental lot, his eyes constantly moving.

"Ham?"

"Charlie's lawyer, Hamilton Davis. You spoke with him on the phone." Linc held his hand up as if he knew her question. "Look, can we go somewhere and talk? Somewhere not so..." Linc glanced around. "...open."

"Surely you don't expect me to leave my rental here, get in a car with a complete stranger and ride off?" She inched a few feet away from him.

Linc's blue eyes softened as he closed the distance between them, but his walk reminded her of a predator ready to pounce. "I get that you're angry and confused, but you have friends here."

"You're very good at understatements. Look, this morning I took a leave from my job, packed a bag, and then boarded an airplane. Here I stand in the land of movie stars. I'm beginning to think I've fallen down a rabbit hole and landed in Wonderland."

"I'm trying to help. Call Ham. He'll vouch for me."

"Wait here." Pointing to a spot on the pavement, which he moved to, she walked out of hearing distance. She called Mr. Davis's number, waited until he came on the line, and questioned him about Linc Hawkins.

The blonde stranger wasn't exactly Hollywood handsome. He had a look about him, the way he set his jaw, and a glint in his eyes that broadcasted confidence. His clothes were a stark contrast to his behavior. Wearing tan board shorts and a yellow pullover, he looked more like a surfer than a creature of mass destruction. His long, muscular legs, narrow hips, and slim waist reminded her of a marathon runner.

A small ball of heat circulated through her lower stomach and was quickly dismissed. Her life was screwed up enough without adding the problems a man brought. She had danced to that song and failed miserably. She ended the cell phone call and walked back to where he waited.

"Well, did Ham put in a good word for me?"

A smile lifted the corners of his mouth. Two dimples winked at her, changing what she had previously thought an average looking man to outstanding. Goosebumps raced over her skin. Her damned eye twitched again. What was *that* about?

"Mr. Davis vouched for you. He believes that you driving me is a good idea."

"Excellent. Let's cancel your rental and get you out of here."

He followed her inside, waiting while she returned the paperwork and car keys. His hand rested protectively against her back. A sensual, yet masculine, scent drifted from him, imprinting his essence in her subconscious. The aromatic scent would forever remind her of the man who'd pulled her to safety.

The exterior doors swooshed open, and he led her out of the rental office. "I'm parked down here."

He moved gracefully with a rhythm that was almost lethargic, cat-like, stopping next to a shiny red sports car with the top down. He opened the passenger-side door and waited while Samantha managed to fold herself into the vehicle. It wasn't the most graceful entrance, but it seemed to be the best way to get in.

The wind picked up his curly hair and rearranged an already unruly hairdo. A thin red scar ran just in front of his hairline from eye level to his jaw.

He closed her car door, pulling her attention from his face. "I'm sorry for staring. Is it still painful?"

"Only when I smile." His chuckle didn't sound friendly as he placed her suitcase in the trunk and then slid behind the wheel with no effort. He put on dark sunglasses and turned to her. "Now let's see if I can help get your questions answered to your satisfaction."

"Apparently, my grandmother kept this important piece of information from the family for over fifty years. This wasn't a little white lie, and it has me questioning what's real and what's not in my life. So yes, I'm hoping for answers. You knew Charles Pearson, maybe you can help." She wasn't given to rambling but found herself pouring her soul out to this stranger.

"I'll fill in what blanks I can. I'm assuming you asked your grandmother why she kept Charlie a secret."

"She's on a yacht with a friend and won't return my calls. How do you know it's this particular grandmother that knew Charles Pearson?"

"Is her name Ruthie?"

Samantha swallowed hard. "It's Ruth."

"That should tell you something." Linc turned the key and the car's engine roared to life. "Your parents couldn't help?"

"No." Samantha's head ached from being so full of questions. "My mother and father are both gone." She clamped her bottom lip between her teeth to stop it from trembling. This news had been a lot to take in. "If they knew about Mr. Pearson, they never shared it with me."

"I can't imagine how you feel." Linc backed out of the parking spot and sped down the exit ramp.

Samantha tightened her seat buckle. "So tell me why you think Charles was murdered."

"I'm positive Charlie's death wasn't an accident. He bought that café to be near the ocean, but he would never have gone for a midnight swim. In fact, he was scared to death of the water."

"You know that for a fact?"

"Damn right I do. I surf and swim. Back before he got really sick, I tried to get him to join me. He used his most colorful language to tell me there was no way he'd ever stick a toe in the ocean."

"But his death was ruled a suicide."

"That doesn't mean I have to agree."

"Why would anybody kill him?"

"I have no idea, but he'd been acting weird. Distant. At the time, I attributed that to the fact that he was on the losing side of cancer and getting weaker by the day." Linc changed lanes and drove onto the freeway. "But if he really wanted to check out, he'd have chosen a different method."

Her brain was going to explode. She was living in a hailstorm of unanswered questions. "Please go on."

"As far as I can tell, he never tried to keep you or your dad a secret." Linc paused. "He told people he had a son who'd died, your father, and bragged that he was a decorated firefighter. He always followed that up by telling people about his beautiful granddaughter. He spoke about your grandmother, but never shared a lot with the customers."

"So many 'whys' keep rolling through my mind. Why didn't he reach out before he died? Why talk about me but not to me? Why did he leave the property to me? It's just too much."

"Because you were his only living relative? Because he loved you? Because he wanted to atone for not being around? Hell, that last one may be one of those unanswerable questions."

"Please. How do you love a stranger?" She laid her head back, allowing the warm sun and wind to caress her skin. She had to let her brain rest, if just for a minute.

"Sam?" Linc's voice somehow soothed her.

A smile played with her lips. The old nickname, the one she'd shed after high school, sounded appropriate coming from Linc, almost romantic. She opened her eyes and looked down at his hand on her arm.

"Do you want to check into your motel? What would you like to do? We can go straight to The Cage if you want."

"I thought the restaurant's name is The Lobster Cage."

He glanced at her and grinned, showing off his deep dimples. "That's what the sign says, but I've never heard it called anything but The Cage. It's more of a local hangout-bar-enjoy-the-spectacular-view sort of place, with indoor and open-air seating, a full bar, and very good food."

"I'd rather see where he lived if you're not too busy." Her life had turned upside down in the span of a few weeks, and she hated feeling out of control. Maybe Linc could help stabilize it.

"Not too busy at all," Linc said. "You have a key?"

"I do. They were inside the package that Mr. Davis sent me, along with a copy of the will, property deeds, and insurance papers."

"Just know that I'll keep digging into Charlie's death. Something or somebody troubled him, and I want to know who and why."

"Maybe you'll find something at his house. Is it far?"

"It's about a forty-minute drive up the coast road, then east to Thousand Oaks."

As they drove closer to the sea, the breeze whipping around the windshield made tiny prickles on her cheeks, the air cooled and smelled salty. For the first time since leaving the airport, she leaned forward and took in the scenery. A highway sign read Malibu, 27 Miles of Scenic Beauty.

"Oh. My. God." She removed her sunglasses and stared in awe at the most amazing sight she'd ever seen. The Pacific Ocean.

Linc exited the highway, drove closer to the water, and then parked. Colors of every hue in the rainbow skirted a path to the ocean. The waves rolled into different shades of blues and washed onto the sand, followed by another and another. Her heart swelled in her chest at the beauty. Tears filled her eyes.

"You're from Texas and have never seen an ocean?" Linc asked softly.

"I never strayed that far from home, never even went to Galveston. Maybe I should have."

"It's a site worth seeing. Beautiful isn't it? She's powerful and sensuous, dangerous and calming, all at the same time."

Samantha didn't respond. She was too caught up in the site in front of her. No wonder Charles loved living here. She turned and Linc caught her gaze and held it.

"How did you two become friends?"

A smile lifted the corners of his mouth, and his dimples winked. "It happened slowly over the past year. I met him right after I bought my condo and started rehab." He flexed his left hand. "I lost a bit of motor control in my left arm after I had the crap beat out of me."

"You were attacked?"

"Yeah." A cloud formed behind his eyes. "I'm an FBI agent...I was working undercover in your home state when it happened."

"I hope you didn't blame Texas."

"Not at all." He shook his head and waved as if shooing a fly away. "It's old news."

"But you're better?"

"Much." He started the car, turned around, and drove back to the highway, exiting east on to a narrow canyon road that took the pair away from the ocean toward one of California's busiest freeways.

"Okay." She felt a lot better after learning that her new friend was a Fed. "I understand if you don't want to talk about it."

"There's nothing to talk about. Bastard snuck up behind me and hit me. I landed on my belly, and he spent a while pounding on the side of my head. Let's get back to Charlie."

Linc had thrown up a wall around the subject. A tall and wide and deeply impenetrable wall, which she respected. "I will appreciate anything you can tell me about how you knew Charles."

"People called him Charlie." Linc waited until she nodded and then continued. "I discovered The Cage while I was running on the beach. I stopped in for a beer, and he was the first person to greet me and take my order. He didn't have to, but he enjoyed being part of the restaurant team. We started talking, first about nothing in particular, and then we discovered common ground through the Army. He was already fighting cancer, so the next thing I knew, I was helping him out on weekends."

"And he told you about my grandmother?"

"Not in the beginning. I knew you existed because he talked about you a lot. About four months before he died, and after we'd knocked back a few beers, he confided that he'd never met you." Linc blended in with the traffic on the freeway. "After that, he opened up a little on his Ruthie."

Samantha was dumbstruck at the way he referred to her grandmother as Ruthie. It was casual as if he knew her or at least knew a lot about her. Samantha's questions about her own history grew by the minute.

A black SUV cut in front of them, interrupting her thoughts.

Linc slammed his foot on the brakes to avoid impact. The sports car's rear end lost traction and they went into a spin. Life slipped into slow motion. Linc calmly turned the steering wheel into the direction of the slide, and as quickly as it started, the almost accident was over, and he had the car under control.

"Welcome to California." He shoved away a lock of hair that had fallen on his forehead. "You okay?" He glanced at her.

She opened her mouth, but try as she might no words came out. Life had shifted to a new dimension. How else could she explain being in the car with a total stranger who'd just saved her life for the second time today? And he'd been vouched for by another complete stranger. It was so ridiculous, she laughed.

"I could do with less fanfare," she patted her chest. "Y'all drive worse than we do."

"Did you happen to notice the car that cut us off?"

She'd been lost in thought so she closed her eyes and replayed the incident in her head. "It was a black SUV, just like the one at the airport."

Air whooshed from her lungs. Her heart, which had only just now begun to slow down, reacted by pounding against her ribcage. What had Charles Pearson gotten her into?

Exactly what secrets would this trip uncover? And who didn't want her to know those secrets?

Meet Jerrie

A career in logistics offered me the opportunity to travel to many beautiful locations in America, and I revisit them in my romance novels.

I write romantic suspense with alpha males and kick-ass women who weave their way through death and fear to emerge stronger because of, and on occasion, in spite of, their love for each other. I like to put my characters in difficult positions and make them work to survive. If they're strong enough, they live happily ever after.

You'll find four BDSM novellas out there. After losing my husband, my muse fled. My doctor suggested that I pick a genre I would have to dig into and research. In other words, use my brain. ☺ Club Silken is the result. While much racier than my usual work, it's out there, and if you read them, I hope you enjoyed the stories.

If you enjoyed reading my books, please help me spread the word. A couple of sentences on Amazon, Facebook, Instagram, Goodreads, and or a tweet would be greatly appreciated.

I write stand alone stories with no cliffhangers.

One of my favorite things is to hear from readers! You're who I write for!

Social media links:

jerriealexander.com

twitter.com/jerriealexander

facebook.com/pages/Jerrie-Alexander[1]

instagram.com/jerrie_alexander

goodreads.com/jerriealexander

pinterest.com/jerriealexander

---

1.   https://www.facebook.com/pages/Jerrie-Alexander

www.ingramcontent.com/pod-product-compliance
Lightning Source LLC
Chambersburg PA
CBHW060913250626
47159CB00008B/2990